First Edition
First Printing, 2015
ISBN 978-0-9909432-3-5

www.al-barrera.com

All That Remains

And I stood upon the sand of the sea, and saw a beast rise up out of the sea, having seven heads and ten horns, and upon his horns ten crowns, and upon his heads the name of blasphemy.

Revelations- Chapter 13

Chapter 1

Kyle

Lightning lit the world, and Kyle watched through the window. Part of the second floor and a pile of rubble kept them hidden from anything outside. It wasn't much but better than being out in the open. Little remained of the rest of the subdivision, a victim of blight storms and whatever monsters had prowled by in the last thirteen years.

Sara shifted in her sleep, her stomach rumbling as she did.

"At least the storm'll cover the light," Tim said.

"I was with a group a few years back that was spotted by crawlers in a storm like this. The man on watch didn't keep the fire low enough. Only two of us escaped."

Tim stared into the flame. They'd covered it with a tarp to block it from any unfriendly eyes passing by. It provided little warmth, but winter hadn't fully set in yet. What was left of Tennessee wouldn't turn deadly cold for a few more weeks.

Tim shifted, still not making eye contact. "You can get some sleep if ya want. I got guard."

"I can't sleep when I'm being tracked."

"Gotta have nerves of steel for a job like this."

Whether or not this kid had hair on his nuts was up for debate, let alone the composition of his nerves. He couldn't have been older than nineteen. Young men weren't known for having an abundance of courage, and three days in, things were growing grim. "Thanks for the words of wisdom, Tex. I'll make sure and put them on your tombstone."

Times like these scared everyone. Trying to play it tough only led to bad decisions.

"Where's this cache anyway?" Tim never took his gaze off the fire.

If he'd asked once that day, he'd asked a dozen times. What should have been an easy run became tenser by the hour. Supply trips bore less and less fruit every month, and this one had turned into a shit show when the sniffer started tracking them. Doubling back wouldn't help. They had to draw it out and take care of it themselves.

"I told you, we're close. We should get there in the morning."

"This the only one you got 'round here?"

"Maybe so, but you'll never find out."

Tim laughed. "Have it your way. I'm tryin' to be friendly."

"If you want to be friendly, keep your voice down."

He didn't speak for five minutes, a record by Kyle's count. "What's with the two of you anyway?" Tim cocked his head at Sara. "You an item?"

Sara snorted back laughter.

Guess she wasn't asleep. "Something amusing you?"

"He doesn't have the right parts, Tim." She turned over and faced the fire.

It might have been Kyle's imagination, but it looked as though Tim blushed. Hard to tell in the dim light. "I just need a good pack mule. She's got a lower half like a linebacker."

"Or you need someone who can actually read a map."

"That's probably it." He grinned.

A flash of lightning stole night vision for a couple of seconds, more than enough time for something to sneak in closer if they weren't careful. No rain. Nothing to replace the blighted puddles of slop dotting the local landscape with something clean.

"Are we gonna make it back from this?"

There it is.

Kyle had taken a lot of people out on runs. The youngest ones always cracked when the pressure was on. Tough facades became tears; tears became mistakes.

Sara gave him the same look she always did in these situations. The scowl. The furled eyebrows. *These people are expecting things from you, Kyle. They look up to you.* There would be a lecture when they got home.

If they got home. Always if.

3

"We have enough silver to take care of anything that might come at us. Sara and I have been in worse than this before."

But having the artillery didn't mean they'd get away. Shooting guns made noise, and making noise meant a quick death in the ruins that dotted the old world. So they'd draw it out. They'd put out the supply caches for just such an occasion.

"You never can tell." Kyle stood up, brushing the dirt from his knees.

Sara leaned against the decayed remains of a changing table on the rest stop wall. "That's a grim way to look at things."

"It's kept us alive this long."

Someone yelled in the distance, pulling him out of his memories. Sara crept closer to the window, peeking out. "What do you think that was?"

Kyle didn't move. "Betty mentioned there were signs of other people north of the station. Could be bandits."

Tim looked up from the fire. "Bandits? You didn't say anything!"

Kyle clenched his jaw and stared him down. Yelling was never excusable.

He took the hint and continued, quieter, "You didn't mention it."

"There're bandits everywhere, and we went south. Besides, if they want to draw the sniffer on our tail, they can be my guest."

Wishful thinking. Most of the things now roaming the world were animals. Mean animals, sometimes giant animals, but animals nonetheless. Sniffers were different. Sniffers looked for people. They followed you home and brought hell on it. Worse things prowled the night, but sniffers were what kept Kyle awake when he travelled the old roads and highways that had once been the United States.

Sara had picked up on this one pretty quick, but that didn't make it easier to deal with. As long as they stayed ahead of it, they'd be fine. If they gave it a chance to lock on though, if it actually saw them and screamed, it would bring the kind of trouble they wouldn't walk away from.

"You think it'll go after them?" Tim asked.

"I don't know."

"What if it's not bandits? What if it's just folk passing through?"

"I don't know."

Tim pursed his lips and went back to staring at the fire.

"Whoever it was," Sara said, "They're quiet now."

I swear this is the last time I take some greenhorn out with us. It wasn't the first time he'd sworn that and, luck willing, it wouldn't be the last. "If none of us are going to sleep, we should press on. We're only a few hours away. It's out in the woods a bit."

"We should've just gone back." Tim's voice rose as he spoke. "We shouldn't have let it chase us out this far."

Sara stood, dropping the tarp and smothering the fire. "It'll be fine. You'll be telling everyone the story when we get back in a few days. Make yourself sound like a big hero and you'll feel better."

5

If they made it back.

Always if.

They walked through the wreckage of the subdivision, three more ghosts in a sea of them. A reminder of what came before, of a world now gone. Hulking wreckages of cars and houses surrounded them as they made their way down the road. They crept off to one side. Quick, quiet, and small; the only way anyone could get around anymore.

The occasional bolt of lightning streaked overhead. Thunder cracked, but the dry storms that brought this kind of light show seldom came with rain.

They left the subdivision, cutting through a backyard. The orange tinted blight-water that filled the pool they passed rippled in the wind. The woods on the far side of the subdivision were dark, but it didn't take Kyle long to pick up the trail they were looking for.

All three paused at the sound of gunshots behind them. Kyle gestured for everyone to crouch and scanned back the way they'd come. The ground slanted steadily upward, and from where they stood on the trail, he could see the subdivision they'd passed through and the remains of the small town beyond it. More gunshots joined the first. Automatic weapons of some kind.

"Whoever they are, they're well-armed," Sara said behind him.

And they were all going to die. Firing weapons at any time in one of the old population centers was stupid. Doing it at night was suicide.

The *rata-tat-tat* of four weapons firing continued. Two fell silent at the same time, then a third. The fourth kept shooting sporadically. The telltale pause to reload stilled the night for a moment, then firing began again before it cut off suddenly.

None of them moved as Kyle stared into the night. Wherever it came from, he couldn't see it.

"Do you think that sniffer got them?" Kyle glanced at the kid. His eyes were as wide as saucers. "Do you think it'll keep coming after us?"

"There wasn't a screech. Whatever they were shooting at wasn't a sniffer. Even if it was, it'll realize that wasn't what it's looking for." They were bloodhounds, dogs hunting for their masters. Proof positive something with a keen intelligence ran the show. "We need to keep moving."

They pressed on up the trail. The blight that fell in the occasional storms hadn't killed all the plant life. Over the last thirteen years, Mother Nature had adapted in a way humanity hadn't. Some trees thrived in it. They grew huge and gnarly, their bark hard as stone and warm to the touch. The grass grew over Kyle's head. Five-foot-ten if it was an inch. A guy Kyle had wandered with for a few months when it all started called it devil grass. It didn't burn well enough for a decent fire even when dry, and the smoke burned the throat.

Lightning traced a blue finger through the sky. Long stretches of normal trees intersected with blighted ones. Devil grass lined the path, sometimes growing over it. He avoided it when possible. The air around it took his breath away, thick and rotten. Animals grew deformed and rabid.

Whatever the blight was, it did more than bring monsters. It changed everything.

"Why would you hide it this far out in the woods?" Tim whispered.

Stay quiet at night. It was something you learned fast or died. *How did this idiot last this long?* "You'll see when we get there."

"Just seems foolish to put somethin' this far from—"

"You need to be quiet," Sara said. Tim closed his mouth without another word.

With any luck, the gunshots would draw anything that might be living in the woods.

They walked in silence. Branches sometimes broke nearby, and everyone dropped low. Tim reached for the handgun at his hip. A 9mm wouldn't do much but get them all killed. Sara put her hand on the bow hanging on the side of her pack. Kyle grabbed the machete sheathed at his hip. Scars and nicks covered the blade, and old electrical tape wrapped around the handle.

But nothing approached, and they pressed on.

The woods thinned into a clearing. A lone cabin shrouded in darkness loomed out of the night. It might have been a ranger station or a hunting lodge once. Now it was just a reminder of what the world used to be.

Kyle glanced at Sara as they stopped at the edge of the clearing. She shook her head, but he searched the area anyway. When he found nothing, he returned. "I want you two to wait here. I'm going to go make sure it's clear."

Sara fixed him with firm stare. "It's clear."

Tim glanced between them, lost.

"I'd rather be safe than sorry." Kyle stalked across the clearing without incident, moving as quickly as he could while out in the open.

The cabin looked worse for wear. It leaned to one side, standing empty except for cobwebs and broken furniture. He entered the room furthest from the entrance, dropped to his belly, and reached into the hole in the floor where they'd hidden the cache. His hand brushed the knapsack, and he pulled it out. Satisfied the building was empty, he went out to the porch and signaled the others to join him.

"Told ya." Sara walked past him into the cabin.

Kyle didn't rise to the bait. "Tim, you're on watch."

Tim stood near what at one time had been a big window facing the way they'd come; now it was nothing more than shattered glass and a broken frame. From there, they could see out the back of the cabin and to both sides through the windows. Not the best defensive position in the world, but better than being in the woods.

Kyle grabbed the cache. Two MREs, five jars of fruit, and an entire magazine of .45 caliber bullets with silver tips. The water and bullets would be good nearly forever, but the food was hit or miss.

Tim stared at the magazine of silver rounds as if they were gold. They were, in a way. Better. "How'd you find so much of it?"

"We've been doing this a long time." Kyle checked the rounds to make sure they hadn't gotten wet.

"Do ya know how much you could get tradin' that much silver?"

Of course he knew, but people to trade with had become less and less common as the years wore on.

"Man. I've met people who'd kill for that."

"You and me both." Kyle placed the silver rounds into his pack with the ones he already had.

"I thought silver killin' them things was a myth until I saw it. My old man kept a knife coated in it on'im all the time. It didn't slice worth a shit, but I saw him stab an infected guy with it once. Melted him like it weren't nothin'."

"You aren't going to cut me down while I'm sleeping and run off with my stuff are you, Tim?" Kyle gave him a sidelong glance, and Sara rolled her eyes.

Tim's mouth dropped open. "No!" The word dripped with a teenager's righteous indignation.

Sara read the kid clean, and Kyle wouldn't have agreed to take him out and show him the ropes if he thought he'd end up with a knife in his back or a smile on his neck.

"Relax. I'm just busting your balls." Kyle broken open one of the MREs and divvied up the contents. "Make sure you keep watch while you eat." He passed a can of fruit to Tim with his share. The food disappeared as quickly as they could shove it into their mouths.

Kyle scanned the woods as he ate. City centers were dangerous, but the forests held their own perils. "Alright, here's the plan. I want to draw it toward the cabin. We'll leave all our gear in here, douse ourselves with vinegar, and wait for it to follow the smell. Once I can get a shot, I'll go for it. If anything goes wrong, the two of you book it out of here back down the trail." Running wouldn't get them far if the plan failed, but it always paid to have a backup.

Sara nodded. Tim looked at his food without saying a word. Kyle slapped him. Not hard, but not soft either. "And keep your damn eyes up."

A brief flash of defiance flickered across his face, there and gone as quickly as the lightning in the sky.

The next three hours passed quietly, and the sun rose over the ruined world. Light didn't make anything better. All the monsters were out of the closet now.

None of them could sleep, and Kyle preferred it that way. The more eyes out, the better. Sara would let him know when it was getting close, but you never could tell.

After what felt like an eternity, she did. "It's coming. Fast."

Their bags were already stacked in the center of the room. Tim popped the cap off the bottle of vinegar.

Kyle grabbed his arm. "Not in here. If you get it on the gear, it might end up on one of us."

They stepped outside and poured the vinegar on themselves. Kyle took his place near where the trail to the subdivision entered the clearing. Tim's hand shook as he and Sara walked to the back of the cabin.

I'll kill him myself if he fucks this up.

Brush broke a little way down the trail. Kyle unfastened his machete and squeezed the grip so hard it hurt.

Just one swing and it's over.

It strode into sight; tall, and scrawny to the point of emaciation. Its shape was mostly human, but its face was too long, and its nose just two gaping slits. Its black eyes, two orbs set deep into its skull, swept the woods around it. Sickly pale skin hung loose on its body. It wore no clothing and lacked any sort of gender. Only the ridges on its arms and legs adorned it.

Dozens of them picking through what was left of the city, looking for survivors. They had a plan. They weren't animals. The radio was wrong if—

Kyle shook his head, chasing away the ghosts as the thing walked into the clearing the same as every sniffer; head forward, crouching, and moving with a speed that belied its odd shape.

It slowed as it passed him, only ten feet from his hiding spot. Its sniffing deepened. Homing in on them. Knowing they were close.

Now or never, do or die. He wouldn't get another shot.

He dashed without a sound. The thing took another deep whiff of the air, its nostril holes flaring to the size of baseballs. Still three feet away, it turned to look at him so quickly that Kyle tripped in surprise. Its mouth fell open, impossibly huge and full of teeth from back to front.

"I love you."

She looked up at him from the grass, the starlight reflected in her eyes. "I love you too."

The opening notes of the creature's screech, the air raid siren that would deafen him, poured from its mouth.

Sara's arrow pierced its neck before it could finish, and it's cry became a gurgle.

Kyle swung his machete at neck level, and the blade embedded into its neck, black ooze flying in every direction. It tried to scream, its gangly arms reaching to grab Kyle and pull him into its mouth even as the light faded from its eyes.

Not today.

Kyle booted the thing off his machete, sending the creature tumbling to the ground. He closed the distance between them and landed his killing stroke in its face, stilling its struggles as he cleaved the head nearly in half. Thick tar poured from its skull as Sara and Tim moved across the clearing. His hands shook, but he set to work wiping the blade on the grass to hide it.

"What the hell was that?" Tim stood open-mouthed while Sara watched over her bow. Eyes out, searching for more threats. Always looking. Always cautious. Always saving his ass.

Kyle stared at the dark bloodstain on the grass and the pool spreading out from the thing's neck. He'd lost time again. Blacked out. Slower and more broken every day. When he finally looked up, he nodded at Sara, who said nothing as she put the bow away. She knew. She had to know. This wasn't the first time he'd slipped up, but it could have been the worst.

Tim dropped the question, but he never missed an opportunity to grate on Kyle's nerves. "Why couldn't we have done that two days ago?"

Kyle walked back toward the cabin without a word.

"It could draw something smart enough to go looking for North Fifteen if it sees we're runners," Sara said as they followed behind.

"Oh." Tim looked at his feet.

"Yeah. Oh." Kyle knelt in front of the bags inside. "If you don't think, you get people killed. And keep your damn eyes up."

"So what now?" Tim asked, unfazed by the reprimand. "Do we head back?"

"We double back and pick up supplies on the way." North Fifteen wasn't in any real danger of starving, but their caution and persistence had gone a long way to make sure that was the case.

When he turned around, Tim searched the wood line, sweating despite the chill in the air. *This kid is gonna lose it.* But hadn't he just lost it too? "Pack all of this up for me, will you? I'm going to check the area and make sure nothing followed it."

Tim set to work putting everything into their packs. Kyle gestured Sara over with a nod and stepped out onto the porch. "Keep an eye on him."

"He's fine, Kyle. He's just nervous. Are you okay?"

"I'm fine. Just keep an eye on him." He walked toward the trail they'd come up. His hands shook, and his stomach jittered. Just nerves. Always nerves after a kill. Getting away from the others was a good way to calm himself. People relied on him. He had to stay cool, especially if the kid was losing it. When you lost your cool, bad things happened.

The building crashed down as the behemoth slid into it. A rain of concrete and rebar surrounded it. The little girl in the window vanished in a cloud of dirt and debris the size of a sandstorm as the building lurched and crumbled. He couldn't look away from where she'd been seconds before. The dust washed over him and stung his eyes, blocking out what little light was left behind the red clouds. The emergency sirens kept wailing.

He shook his head to clear the image. *Keep cool.*

He took a few deep breaths and ran his hands through his hair, tangled and ratty after months without a good wash. The edge of the forest held no threats. He did a few laps around the clearing anyway. Eyes out, senses keen. Things had a way of popping up when you let your guard down. He wasn't going to die today.

As he focused his attention outward, his inner calm returned. He walked up to the porch, stopping when he heard Sara and Tim talking inside.

"Well I found y'all," Tim said.

"I just don't think you should get your hopes up. Too many people always draws them. There are no more cities."

"Yeah, but I heard there was one here. People saw it, people been there."

"It's bullshit, Tim." Kyle leaned against the door, arms crossed. "There are no more cities. North Fifteen is the biggest I've seen."

"You been out to Atlanta?" Tim's voice took on a note of defiance, but his eyes held a look of defeat.

He couldn't blame the kid. He couldn't have been much older than five when everything went to shit. *Does he even remember what cities look like anymore?* It didn't matter; ideas like that got people killed. "You go to a place like Atlanta, you die."

"But the guy said—"

"But nothing. Those streets are filled with infected. You keep moving, or you stay way out of the cities." Kyle sat next to Tim on the floor. Sara stared daggers at him. To hell with her. He might not want to hear it, but it would keep him alive. "I'm telling you the truth. I've—"

"We shouldn't have come back here. This is place is full of ghosts." Not one of them was going to get out alive. He knew it.

"I've seen it."

"So you been there?" Tim's eyes sparkled like a goddamn child's. Only rumors of people going to the big cities ever reached into the country. Anyone who said they'd been was usually lying or drunk. Probably both.

"Not Atlanta, no. But I've been to other cities. It's always the same. Dead. Trust me. North Fifteen is the best we've got."

Tim sighed and rubbed his face, running his hands through his hair much the same way Kyle had. "I heard it was better here."

"It is, even if that's not saying much."

By the time they returned to the subdivision, the clouds had broken and the lightning had stopped. Pieces of blue sky peeked through on a cold November morning the same way it always had. Daylight did nothing to relieve the oppression of the destruction around them. Red vines and burnt orange grass, signs of the blight moving in, covered the remains of what had once belonged to humanity. Marking it. Making it theirs.

"Should we check 'round here?" Tim stepped over pieces of a garden shed collapsed in the street. "Might be somethin' left."

"It would take too long. We'll head back toward North Fifteen and hit the exits along the way."

Sara kept her nose buried in the map. "There might be a pharmacy if we go a few hours out of our way at the first exit. If that's a bust, we can check the one further down."

"Agreed." Most of those dot-on-the-map towns had been picked over by monsters, runners, and bandits, but you never knew what might turn up.

"Do you think anythin' would be left in a pharmacy? Don't people check all those?"

"Only one way to find out. We need more antibiotics." He and Sara hadn't explored thoroughly when they came out this far. The highway they had walked to get out here stretched further south, branching off into a few small towns and connecting roads that might lead to undiscovered treasures.

More likely, they led to a quick death. Kyle knew the area around North Fifteen, every hiding spot and overlook for twenty miles around it. Anywhere this far out might as well have been the moon. It was the whole reason they'd dropped supplies here.

"Well, we'll just head back and branch off. Couldn't hurt to look out around here and get a lay of the land." Sara folded the map and put it back in her bag.

They left the subdivision, finding the highway that led back north. It had been an interstate once, now just an empty road with abandoned cars slowly surrendering to rust. They stayed off it as much as possible. Being in the open made them too easy a target. Instead, they kept to the side in the high brush and trees.

Thirty minutes out of the subdivision, Sara gestured for them to get down. Tim opened his mouth to ask something, but she silenced him with an upraised finger. Kyle lifted his eyebrows as he unhitched his machete and did as she bade.

"People. On the road further up."

"How can you tell?" Tim asked.

She ignored him.

"How many?" Kyle asked.

"I don't know." Sara grabbed her bow and one of the arrows from the quiver attached to her bag. Tim pulled out his 9mm. Kyle didn't like guns. They drew too much attention, and made every idiot feel as though they were invincible.

Still, creatures didn't use weapons, people did.

"How far?"

"Not very."

"Alright. Let's keep moving. We'll avoid them if we can."

"What if they're just runners like us?" Tim asked.

Could be, but after the gunshots from last night, Kyle wasn't keen to find out. "We keep moving." He waved for them to follow, placing his machete back into its strap and pulling out the .45 on his hip. They crept along the side of the road, keeping quiet and low. Monsters might rule the world, but humans were still the cruelest things that walked it.

"Give us your supplies or your life."

All the guns pointed at them. One itchy finger, and everyone Kyle knew was dead. He moved slowly to unstrap his bag. They might get out of this alive if everyone kept cool.

Richard went for his piece. The first shots rang out, and Kyle hit the floor. He fumbled for his .45 as the hard impact of metal on meat thudded all around him. Richard fell, blood pouring from his mouth, his eyes wide.

"Kyle," Sara said. "Do you hear that?"

Lost in his own world, Kyle hadn't heard the child's cries from the road. He knew what Sara would say before she said it.

"Let's take a look."

It could be a trap. Some people used kids to draw other groups. Sometimes teenagers *were* the bandits. The few times Kyle had seen them, most had less hair on their face than Tim.

"He's just a boy," Karen said. "You can't."

19

"He's going to die slower if I don't." Kyle leveled his gun at the kid screaming on the ground. He had to do it. If he didn't, the kid wouldn't just suffer, he'd draw everything for a mile.

"I've got to. Look away."

"We should keep moving," Kyle said.

"Are you kidding me?"

"It's a trick. You heard those shots last night. There could be people up there waiting for you to poke your head up so they can pop it off."

"Or it could be a little girl. What's wrong with you?"

Sara had been around since the world went to shit. She'd seen a lot, and she had a good head on her shoulders. That was half the reason Kyle stuck with her. She knew better. She knew what people were capable of.

"We keep moving."

Tim crept out of the brush and toward the road. Kyle tried to grab him by his bag, but realized what was happening a moment too late. Lack of sleep made him slow, and his fingers only brushed the straps as Tim walked into the open.

"Get your ass back here."

Tim was already halfway to the road. Without a word, Sara joined him.

This is it. This is how you get everyone killed. One sloppy move, and poof, there goes everything you've known.

He crouched in the brush and watched them move up the incline toward the road. He almost kept going.

Leave them here. Let them get themselves killed.

Too familiar. He couldn't watch it happen again.

He willed his feet to carry him on, but they wouldn't. Instead, he joined Sara and Tim. They reached the edge of the road fifteen feet before him and leaned against the hill, peeking over to see what was going on.

"It's just a little girl," Sara said.

He peeked over the incline. The highway held few cars in either direction. Nowhere for people to hide. A child sat by herself at the center of the highway, her face buried in her hands, gently rocking back and forth. He could see blood on one hand and a thick stain of it coating her golden hair. She couldn't have been older than ten.

His heart tore apart looking at—

The girl in the window, looking down as the thing in the streets crushed the cars and came straight toward the building where she stood. Even that far away, he could see she was crying, one hand pressed against the glass.

He shook his head clear of the image. The road was be empty of vehicles, but the tree line on the far side could be hiding anything. The hills of Tennessee made the perfect spot for an ambush.

Tim didn't wait. He walked to the girl. Kyle didn't try to stop him this time.

"Hey." Tim put his gun away. "Hey, little lady."

There was a sharp intake of breath as she pulled her hands away from her face. She didn't move, just stared, teary-eyed.

21

He opened his hands in front of him, showing her they were empty. "It's okay."

The girl sobbed harder.

Sara stepped over the incline, putting her weapon away. Kyle squeezed his .45 tighter.

"It's alright." Tim's smile looked as scared as the little girl. "We aren't going to hurt you."

The little girl looked up at Sara. Her lips quivered as if she was trying to speak.

"It's okay." Sara approached, all pretense of caution gone. She knelt next to the girl, Tim joining her. "It's okay, sweetheart." She wrapped her arms around the girl, who cried harder. "It's okay."

They're going to bring hell on us. "Bring her over here, Sara. Sara!"

Sara picked her up and returned to Kyle, Tim just behind. She reached the edge of the road, the girl sobbing in her arms. He moved back toward the woods and gestured for them to follow. A few feet behind concealment, he stopped and turned around. The child grew hysterical as they surrounded her.

"Put your weapon away," Sara said.

He didn't, and he wouldn't. She gave him a final, fatal glance and returned her attention to the little girl. "Shh. It's going to be fine." Sara held her tight. "What's your name?"

She didn't respond. Kyle looked around them. Daylight didn't mean safe, and this kind of noise was trouble. Nobody had eyes out.

"Tim, keep watch."

Tim tore his gaze from the girl.

"Sara has it under control. Keep watch."

Sara wiped blood away from the girl's face with her shirt. "My name's Sara." She held the girl's face in her hands and stared into her eyes.

The girl slowly focused her attention on Sara.

"Sara," she said again.

The tears stopped. A full minute passed. Her eyes dulled, and her face slackened. She couldn't look away.

"Sara." Her voice was silk and roses. Hypnotic.

The light of terror on her face went out. Tim stopped keeping watch as it unfolded.

"Now. Tell me your name." It was a command, not a question.

"Kaylee."

"How old are you, Kaylee?"

"I'm seven and a half."

Born into a world that already ended. Tough break.

"Good." Sara let go and blinked a few times. "Now Kaylee, how did you get out here all by yourself?"

Tears welled up again.

"We have to be very quiet, okay? It's not safe here."

Her eyes glistened, but she didn't cry. "I was with my mommy. The monsters came out."

Sara glanced at Kyle. That look shared everything they might have said. *Her family is dead.*

"They found my mommy and her friends."

"Was that the shooting last night?"

Kaylee wiped her eyes and nodded.

"Do you know where it happened?" Kyle asked.

She pointed back the way they'd come, toward the subdivision.

"On the road?"

Kaylee nodded.

"Tim and I will go check it out. You stay here with her."

"There's monsters." Kaylee wiped away more tears.

Kyle unhitched his bag and dropped it on the ground. "We know."

The site of the massacre wasn't hard to find. Blood smeared the highway fifteen feet in every direction. They'd backtracked along the road and kept a closer eye on the pavement. Only ten minutes outside the subdivision, they spotted the first body parts.

There wasn't enough left to tell for sure, but it appeared as though three adults had been torn apart. Pieces of them remained, hunks of flesh in rags. What few parts of the group were left lay inside a ring of dilapidated cars.

They tried to make a last stand.

He expected Tim to say something naïve like, "*My god, how could this happen?*" But he didn't. Kyle had to give the kid credit.

A machine gun poked out from under the wreckage of one of the cars. Kyle picked it up. Broken and gnawed on.

"Look for anything left."

They fanned out and searched the site. All the weapons were destroyed. Whatever found them had shredded apart most of the food remaining in their packs too. Kyle examined the guns. Military grade. Good condition, aside from the bent barrels and chew marks.

"Look at this."

Kyle approached the remains of a torso wearing military body armor. Tim stared down at it, that dumb as a puppy expression plastered across his face. "What is it?"

"Gear the army used to wear."

"Where do you think they got it?"

"I don't know." He hadn't seen armor like that since the early days, when the government still had control.

From his apartment window, he watched them drive by in Humvees. Young men and women, scared to death by the look of them. The last radio broadcast had said everything was under control. If that was the case, why was the National Guard here? More red clouds dotted the horizon as a voice blared from a speaker on the front Humvee. "Stay indoors. Keep your doors locked."

"I thought they all got killed?" Tim asked, pulling Kyle out of his thoughts.

"Me too. They might have just found an old armory." A trail of blood led onto the side of the road. "Come with me."

They followed it to the trees, the trail widening. They didn't have to go far to find the last body. They could still recognize it as a person. A woman in her forties with graying blond hair. Kaylee's mother, if Kyle had to guess. More of her remained than the others, but her torso was a bloody cavity, ripped out and eaten. A handgun lay near her, the barrel twisted beyond use.

A silver chain dangled from her clenched fist. Kyle knelt, careful to avoid the blood, and opened the hand. Inside was a USB drive on a necklace, *Property of the United States Government (PABT)* stamped across the front in big, black letters

"Haven't seen one of those in a while."

He handed it to Tim, who mouthed the words to himself. "What is it?"

Hard to believe everything's changed that much. "People used to keep computer information on these. Back when people had computers."

"Why would she have one?"

Kyle shrugged. He took it back and put it in his pocket. They searched what was left but found nothing worthwhile. "I heard four guns shooting last night, and I count five people plus the little girl. I don't think anyone else got away."

"You sure? We should look more."

Kyle respected that the kid wanted to find survivors, but the world didn't work like that anymore. "We need to be as far away as we can before nightfall. Whatever did this is going to come back." He hadn't seen them leave pieces behind before, but the whole thing was upsetting enough without mentioning that to Tim.

Kid probably noticed anyway.

They started back down the highway, hidden from view amongst the trees, leery of any prying eyes.

After a few minutes, Tim spoke up. "She's a scanner, ain't she?"

Kyle didn't respond.

"I ain't gonna tell anybody."

Kyle grabbed Tim's arm. "No, you're going to forget you ever saw anything. Do you understand?" He squeezed harder than he meant to.

Rumors were all it took to get someone kicked out or killed. He wanted to believe North Fifteen was different, that the people were better. Runners Kyle and Sara had gone out with had figured it out, but nobody had spoken up yet. Most of them were dead or moved on by now. *Another time bomb waiting to explode.*

"I didn't mean nothin' by it." Tim frowned and pulled his arm away. "I've never seen one before is all."

"If people found out, they might do stupid things. Maybe they wouldn't, but Sara doesn't want to find out, and neither do I."

Tim furrowed his brow. Angry or upset, Kyle couldn't say. "I wouldn't do nothin' to get Sara hurt."

Kyle recognized the sincerity there. "I'm sorry."

"S'all right." He spit, his eyes focused only on the road. "But she is, huh?"

"Yes, she is, and it's saved our lives more than a few times."

They returned to the hiding place among the trees where the others waited. Sara watched them approach, a look of expectant dismay on her face. Kyle shook his head.

"Did you find my mommy?"

Sara had gotten some of the blood off her, but red still smeared her hair.

How did this little girl get away? Now wasn't the time for questions, and he didn't know how to respond to hers. His silence was apparently enough. Kaylee buried her face in Sara's hip.

"I'm sorry." Kyle knelt next to her, his big, dark hand engulfing her pale fingers. "I really am."

They passed several exits before night showed in the sky. More of the blight covered the land here. In the woods on the hills around them, jet-black trees towered above the oak and pine. Gnarled, leafless branches reached toward the sky. Fingers painting dire warnings and profane pictures in the clouds.

They left the highway, looking for a gas station Sara recalled seeing. Most of the building lay open to the elements when they found it, but a bathroom in the back still had a door and a roof over it. Kyle didn't like boxing himself in, but being in a closed space was the best way to make sure nothing saw them. Every move rolled the dice, and every decision was a gamble. Exhaustion wouldn't let them go any further. Running for supplies without sleep led to mistakes, and there was no room for error anymore.

Kaylee curled up with Sara as the blue sky turned orange and then red, finally descending into black. She hadn't said a word since the news of her mother's death, and Kyle wasn't eager to push it. The last thing they needed was a crying kid.

He watched them sleep on first guard. The howl of something huge in the distance tore through the stillness of the night. The new gods of the Earth, roaring their foul decrees onto the hills and mountains.

Chapter 2

Sara

"Mommy." Kaylee grabbed the edge of her mother's jacket.

"Honey. We aren't in the bunker anymore. You need to hush." Miriam looked into the darkness. They should have hired the guide that had offered to take them to Oak Ridge. Wandering around in the wild was stupid. But how could you trust strangers out here? Who knew if they were telling the truth, or if they wouldn't make off with your guns in the night? Maybe leave your corpse for good measure.

Something moved in the brush to the right. More than one something.

"Oh god." Miriam fumbled with the pistol on her belt.

"Just stay behind us, Professor Stern." Mike cocked his MP5 and scanned the woods. *"If anything attacks, Randy and Paul will keep moving with you. Steve and I will stay behind and cover. Just like we planned."*

Nothing appeared, but something watched them. She could feel it in her bones. Not for the first time in the last thirteen years, she wished the sky were still alive with planes and helicopters. The flimsy protection of the cars around them was little better than being in the open. The rusted metal under her hands was another reminder of what the world had lost.

The woods on the side of the highway came alive with growls. The first crawler poked its head through the brush. It walked into the open, revealing a scaly dog's body that ended in a long reptilian tail.

She fired two rounds without thinking. The sound of the gun startled her, as if she hadn't expected it. Kaylee screamed and backed away, tripping over herself and falling.

"Don't!" Mike screamed.

The things had heard them now, even if they hadn't seen them. It was fight or die.

They rushed forward without missing a beat. Six more burst through the brush, barreling toward the group.

Mike aimed his weapon at the creatures closing on them. He shot straighter than Miriam and took one down with the first burst. Steven shot into the pack without aiming, spraying bullets.

"Professor Stern, let's go!" Paul grabbed her hand.

It wouldn't work. They wouldn't get away.

"Now!"

A crawler jumped on his back as he turned to flee. It bit into the base of his neck, a flood of crimson washing down his chest as his eyes widened and his mouth moved without words. Randy dropped his gun and tried to pull it off.

"Where's Kaylee!"

Two of the things broke past the cars.

Kyle woke her as two crawlers collided with Mike and brought him down.

"It's your turn for watch."

She rubbed her eyes. *Just a dream.* But it was more. Sometimes only pictures or sounds came through. Not this time. This time she'd seen everything Kaylee had when her mother was killed. She looked at the sleeping girl huddled on the mat and blanket. *That poor child. She saw the whole thing.* She'd hid under a car and watched as a parade of monsters violated her family, devouring the remains and searching the bodies.

Searching the bodies…

They didn't do that. Something stank about the whole situation, but Sara didn't know what.

She brushed hair away from Kaylee's face, wondering if she was dreaming about the attack right now. How she could ever sleep again after seeing what she'd see was beyond Sara.

"You all right?" Kyle asked.

She nodded. He wouldn't understand if she tried to explain it. He couldn't know what it was like to feel what someone else felt, to see what someone else saw.

Kyle rolled over on his makeshift bed and closed his eyes. She settled in and passed her watch thinking about Kaylee. When the time came, she woke Tim up and laid down next to the girl.

They left as the sun came up.

"We should look around the area before we go. There may be a pharmacy nearby," Kyle said.

They made their way farther down the road, but only deserted farmland sickened by blight marked the way, the devil grass slowly creeping out to overtake the pavement. After an hour, they doubled back to the highway and continued on toward North Fifteen.

Travel took longer than in the old world. Staying off the roads, keeping quiet, and avoiding attention required more care than walking once had. By the time afternoon rolled around, they'd only just reached the exit Sara suspected might hold the pharmacy. They turned down it and continued their search.

Kaylee wore a distant expression, looking inward to whatever memories would undoubtedly haunt her for the rest of her life. Sara held her hand, letting her deal with her issues in her own way.

After a morning of silence, Kaylee finally spoke. "Where are we going?"

"Back to our home." Sara squeezed her hand as they turned off of the highway and followed the exit.

"What's there?"

"Well… some people. Food. Shelter. It's safe there. There's even a little boy about your age."

"Is it under the ground?"

Sara furrowed her brow. "It isn't underground, but it's safe."

"Momma says nothing's safe anymore unless it's underground."

Kyle looked over his shoulder at them, but Sara shrugged. Neither of them had ever heard of underground communities.

"Where did you and your momma come from, Kaylee?"

She turned away. When no answer came, Sara tried something else.

"Did you go far to get here?"

"We walked for a really long time. Momma said we were still far away too."

Something from her dream tickled the edges of Sara's mind. "Were you and your momma going to Oak Ridge?"

This time, Tim glanced back at her.

He knows I'm a scanner. He didn't feel like the kind of guy who would hate someone for something they couldn't control, but it was so hard to tell.

"How did you know?" Kaylee asked, snapping Sara back to their conversation.

"I'm a good guesser. Kyle says I'm the best guesser he's ever met."

Tim stared as she spoke. She raised her eyebrows questioningly at him. He blushed and smiled, returning his gaze forward.

"Yeah. Momma said there were people there that could help."

The excited expression on Tim's face cut short with two shakes of Kyle's head. He wanted it to be true so badly, but the cities weren't safe anymore. "Did she say who these friends were?"

"No. She just said we had to get there quick. The monsters were coming to get us. Momma didn't… Momma." Her voice caught.

Sara wanted to know more about the well-armed group travelling in the middle of nowhere, but there was a time and place for it, and it was neither here nor now. She tried to change the topic, anything to keep the girl from crying again. "If your feet are tired, I can carry you for a little bit."

"I don't need to be carried," Kaylee said in a very adult way.

"I don't mind."

"No, thank you." She dried her eyes on the sleeve of her jacket.

Sara smiled, but her heart hung heavier. *I guess you've got to grow up quick nowadays.*

The road stretched on, and the cover of trees thinned out. A gas station standing largely intact hid from view around the curve of a hill.. "With me, Tim. Sara, watch her."

They weren't gone long. "Nothin' in there but spiders."

The trees vanished altogether a little farther up the road, giving way to a pile of rubble that might have been a strip mall. A red and white sign hung from the side of a half-collapsed building a little farther down the road. Only the *P* and *H* that had once spelled pharmacy were still visible.

"Let's take a look," Kyle said.

They crossed a section of road where some unimaginable force had pulled up the pavement, the ground churned and sprayed in every direction. A path of destruction led into the distance on either side of the road. Something had torn through this small town, knocking down buildings and laughing in the face of human ingenuity. Probably one of the many tornados that had come with the storms when it all started.

Red clouds in the sky and a twister as wide as a barn screaming through this place. The winds moved so fast a signpost shot through a car someone had abandoned on the side of the road.

A flash and it was gone. No twister, and the abandoned car was just a hulk of ruined metal turned on its side. She could have figured it out even without the visual. She'd seen enough of them when the blight came and they'd formed three or four times a week. She let go of Kaylee's hand and rubbed her temples.

They left the torn street behind. The back half of the building sloped into broken bricks and steel girders. The front doors sat twisted on their sides, ripped from the frame. Nature had started to reclaim it, and here the blight was nowhere to be seen. Just sprouts of trees and tall grass growing where a parking lot had once been.

"Think there's anythin' left?" Tim asked as they approached.

"Only one way to find out." Kyle hitched his bag a little higher on his shoulders.

Sara rolled her eyes behind his back. Everything he said came out like something from a bad adventure movie.

He gestured for the rest of them to hold back as he approached the doors, loosening his machete and pulling it out. He stepped through the broken portal and vanished.

Sara looked around at the corpse of the town, taking it all in while watching for anything that might be watching them. Only thirteen years later, and it was already hard to picture this little strip filled with people on a Saturday afternoon. Cars driving by on the highway stopping for gas. Kids riding bikes to grab a magazine from the pharmacy. All gone, and probably never coming back. She'd watched TV shows about how quickly signs of humanity would vanish if anything ever happened to mankind, but she'd never believed it. Now she couldn't see anything else. One day, nobody would know it had ever been there.

"Looks empty." Kyle poked his head out the door. "But there might be something in a back room I can't get to." He went back inside, and the group followed.

Light found its way into the pharmacy from holes in what remained of the roof and huge gaps in the walls. Shafts of sunshine pierced the dusty gloom, casting the room in a dull glow. All the shelves lay toppled over, victims of looting and whatever other disasters had struck. The back half of the building disappeared into a mess of crumbled stone.

"There's a door in the back. It looks like it might lead to a storeroom, but it's blocked." Kyle led the way. "We might be able to get through."

They passed piles of debris and cobwebs. A single door stood on part of the collapsed wall, the roof still jutting behind it and covering whatever might be back there. Two huge pieces of concrete blocked the door. Fallen rubble. They set to work clearing it.

After a while, Sara looked at Kaylee, who gazed around the store with dismay.

"What's wrong?"

Kaylee took a moment to respond. "I don't like it here."

Sara stepped away as Tim and Kyle moved the first slab or broken roof from in front of the door. She knelt down to meet Kaylee's eyes, but the girl looked away.

"It feels like there's ghosts."

Sara moved a strand of hair from her face. "I've been walking around for a long time, and I've never seen a ghost." She smiled. It wasn't exactly true, but the girl didn't need to hear that. "You probably don't have to worry about any showing up now."

Her words had little effect. Kaylee kept searching as if something might appear. "I still don't like it. We aren't going to stay here, are we?"

Sara glanced back at Tim and Kyle. "No. We'll find another place." They wouldn't be able to get far at this time of day, but they'd find something before the sun set.

Tears glistened in Kaylee's eyes.

I have no idea how to deal with this. In her mind, she was as far away from the mothering type as a person could be. *What am I supposed to say to a girl who saw her family killed?* That word stuck in her head: Family. The woman, Miriam, had been Kaylee's mother, but the other four felt like soldiers. That was impossible. All the soldiers, and the country they'd protected, were gone. Nothing left but survival.

"Got it," Kyle said behind her as they moved the last piece of concrete aside. He grabbed the edge of the door and pulled.

It collapsed toward him with a loud screech, spilling him on his ass. Kaylee wrapped her arms around Sara's waist.

"Woo!" Tim said. "Nice."

"Shut up," Kyle whispered from the floor. He listened as the crash echoed around the building.

Sara listened too, but not in the same way. She relaxed everything she could without falling over, moving inward; like breathing, only deeper. Her eyes closed, and she reached with her mind, imagining herself spreading out in every direction as far as she could.

Old cars, tornado, pavement, a baby bird, and an old walking cane split in two, held by old lovers watching the world die. Trees, woods, and grass. She reached out a little farther, looking for anything that might have heard them, but nothing came back to her.

She exhaled and fell back into her own body, untangling herself from the world around her. "It's safe."

He shook his head and cocked it to the side like a stupid dog. After a moment, he relaxed, and Tim offered him a hand to help him up. "Let's take a look."

The condition of the back was worse than the front. The collapsed roof and wall filled most of the space, and what few shelves remained were twisted and fallen. Piles of garbage and junk littered the floor, the remnants of cardboard boxes that had dissolved over the last thirteen years.

They sifted through the refuse, Kaylee sticking close to Sara. Most of it was food, but it was broken open and decayed. The few unbroken items were long past their expiration date.

"Well, fuck." Tim picked up a glass can of spaghetti sauce at least twelve years past edible. "This was a waste a' time."

"Most of the pharmacies kept their medicine locked up," Kyle said. "I didn't expect we'd find it in the back room."

"So what do we do now?" Tim sat on the floor. "It's gettin' dark."

Kyle took his bag off his shoulders and set it down. "We camp here."

"What about that gas station up the road?" Sara asked. "The one we stopped in?"

He paused to consider it a moment. "Not a bad idea. We'll be closer to the road in the morning." He grabbed his bag and made his way out of the storeroom and into the dwindling daylight outside.

No door blocked the light, so they kept the fire low and covered. No one spoke. Not finding antibiotics would be bad news to go back with. More exits down the road might hold what they sought, but Sara wasn't optimistic. After sharing a meal, she drew last for guard, lay down, and slept. Kaylee curled up in front of her.

Something shifted on the edge of sense. A moving bubble. Like her, but not like her. Closer now. Coming down the highway toward them, but not looking for them. Looking for something else. It knew, but it couldn't let them know. Get back out into the darkness and touch the other places. Its presence shook her. A tumor walking the Earth. A walking cancer.

Sara backed away, drawing herself in as tightly as she could. A dog curling up in a storm to hide from the thunder. More creatures walked with it. Crawlers probably. Maybe infected. So hard to tell when you were being quiet. She couldn't let it see her. She couldn't let it touch her. If she did, they would all die.

Sara sat up in her bedroll. "Put out the fire."

Kyle didn't ask, just dropped the tarp, smothering the flames in an instant.

"What's—"

Sara put a hand over Kaylee's mouth. "I need you to be quiet like a mouse. Can you do that?"

Kaylee nodded. Tim sat up as well, and Sara thanked whatever deities might be watching that he kept silent for once.

The seconds stretched into minutes. She waited, prepared to feel that cancerous thing so alien to her mind. Nobody moved. Nobody spoke. No sound came from outside.

She chalked it up as a bad dream just as it approached from down the highway. Her vision blurred, and everything spun. A soft moan escaped her lips. It rattled and shook her, tore and broke her.

Don't see us, don't see us, don't see us, she chanted again and again in her head. For it to see them meant a quick and violent end.

Kyle, quiet as a shadow, grabbed her with Kaylee between them. "What is it, Sara? What's wrong?" His concern washed over her as a wave.

She stomped it out as best she could, hoping whatever was out there wouldn't notice. "Be still, Kyle, and be very quiet."

Whatever it might be, it passed them on the road. A dozen little black specks crawled across her mind with it. Mental cockroaches. Monsters. It wanted something. It searched as she did. Its mind went over the gas station. A sonar looking for a submarine. It didn't ping off them.

Don't see us, don't see us, don't see us.

Her fists balled so tightly that her knuckles popped. A vein in the side of her neck throbbed dangerously.

Don't see us, don't see us.

A trickle of blood ran from her nose onto her lips.

When it continued farther down the road and out of reach, she took in a deep gulp of air, a psychic swimmer coming up from a dive. She unclenched her fists and panted, blinking back the dark spots in her vision.

"Water."

Kyle grabbed the canteen from next to her bedroll. She drank it fast, much of it spilling down her face.

"What in the hell was that?" Tim asked, his eyes wide. "Was that a seizure?"

Sara sat up and looked around at them as her pulse returned to normal. Kaylee crawled away and huddled in a corner, staring over her knees at Sara. Such a small thing in such a big, bad world. Kyle held Sara by either shoulder, the only thing keeping her from falling over.

"No. Something was out there. Something really bad."

"Is it close?" Kyle didn't let go.

She shook her head. "No. I don't think so. It moved past us."

"Well that's great. That's fuckin' great." Tim stood up. "You expect me to believe that shit?"

"I don't give a damn what you believe," Kyle said. "But if you don't sit and be quiet, you'll believe it on the side of the road."

The defiance on the boy's face vanished, and he sat back down.

"It's fine, Kyle." Sara put her hand over his.

He pulled out the last of the two MREs they'd split, handing it to Sara. She didn't feel much like eating, but she needed to; it always helped after scanning.

"I've never seen that happen before." Kyle sat back down on his makeshift bed.

"Me either." She shoved more ten-year-old government bread into her mouth. "Something was looking out there."

"Looking for what?"

She stared into the middle distance. "I don't know."

The next day took them farther down the road. Six more exits, six more disappointments. They walked in line, Kyle in the front, Kaylee and Sara in the back holding hands. The blighted landscape hunched over the side of the road, menacing and ugly. Black limbs from gnarled trees reached at them, watching as they passed. The air here hung heavier, making it harder to breathe. It choked the life from the world as surely as the monsters themselves. Or maybe that wasn't right. Maybe it didn't kill life, just changed it. Turned it into something horrible and alien like that thing from the night before.

"Is it always like this?" Tim asked as they turned down the highway from the latest failed exit.

Kyle moved around a flipped car without looking back. "It happens."

"You think you got everything 'round here already?"

"I doubt it."

"What'll you do when it's all gone?"

Sara smiled. His questions didn't bother her, but a sigh from Kyle said his patience was thinning rapidly. "We'll have to move on," she said behind him. "The vegetables we grow don't provide enough protein, and we can't farm animals."

"How do you know—"

"So you just run from monsters and look for food?" Kaylee asked.

"We do what we have to do." She squeezed Kaylee's hand. Any sweetness the truth once held was gone. "It'll be all right."

"It's sad."

The girl was too smart for her own good.

"Just keep your eyes out. Getting closer to home doesn't mean we're safe." They wouldn't reach North Fifteen until late evening. It was Kyle's way of tabling that kind of talk. The blighted growth and abandoned cars clogging this part of the road were a mute testament to everything gone by. Dwelling on the state of the world led into a downward spiral that had ended more than one life. Better to focus on the present.

They walked on in silence. Sara looked over her shoulder time and again, expecting whatever it was to creep up on them. *Thirteen years of living in a nightmare come true, and there are still surprises.*

They checked one last exit before calling the trip a bust. Everything closer to North Fifteen had been picked clean over the last few years. Neither Sara nor Kyle was keen on traveling with a child any further than they had to.

By the time evening settled over the world, they were approaching the turn off that led to North Fifteen.

"Almost back now." Tim rubbed his hands.

North Fifteen didn't come closer than a two-hour walk to any other buildings in the area. An old, broken-down lumber mill and a warehouse wouldn't have looked like much to Sara thirteen years ago, but today it would be a sight for sore eyes and a respite for sore limbs.

"Yes, we are, so just keep your eyes up."

Something tickled the edge of Sara's senses. "Kyle?"

He turned to her, raising an eyebrow. They'd missed something. Failed to notice something important. She shook her head. "It's nothing. Let's keep going."

They reached the dirt road that turned off the highway. In the days of cars and GPS, nobody would have given it a second look. Just an old country road in an old country part of the state. They followed the hills into the woods. Weeds and plants crept onto the path as Mother Nature slowly reclaimed the world from the people who'd lost it.

A buzz in her ears brought Sara to a stop. Something still wasn't right. Kyle stopped too, but not because of her.

"Where's the guard?"

Nothing moved in the woods.

"We should have seen one by now."

"Maybe they're further down." Tim dropped his hand to the gun on his hip.

"Sara," Kaylee said. "What's wrong?"

"Nothing, sweetheart. Just stay close, okay?" Sara fell into herself, taking the deep breath that let her mind out of her body. Her stomach turned as the world shifted outward, accompanied by a feeling like diving into a cold pool. No people anywhere near them. She gasped as she came back into herself. "Something's wrong, Kyle."

"Yeah."

An icy stone dropped into her stomach.

"We'll keep going." He pulled out his gun.

Staying off the road would have been better, but the brush was too thick even at this time of year. They would have made twice as much noise trying. The lump in her stomach grew, the certainty that something had gone wrong in their absence. Kaylee squeezed her hand harder, picking up on the tension without knowing why.

They walked for another ten minutes. "We should have seen somebody by now." Tim fingered his trigger. "Where is everyone?"

"Be quiet," Kyle whispered.

Sara wanted to reach out again, but the dawning realization of what they were about to find made it unnecessary. They turned the last bend in the road to see the old timber mill only a few hundred yards in front of them, the dilapidated warehouse they called home a little farther behind it. No signs of life.

"I want you three to stay here. I'm going to go have a look."

"No, Kyle." Sara let go of Kaylee and grabbed his shoulder. "Let's just go."

"Go?" Tim said. "Go fuckin' where?" He shook his head and stepped back. "They're probably just changin' guard."

Sara had lived with these people for years. They weren't changing guard. If nobody was on the road, that meant one thing. "Come on, Kyle. Don't." She wanted to tell him he knew what he'd find already. He didn't need to see it. "It's gonna be dark soon."

"What the fuck are you talkin' 'bout?" Sweat beaded on Tim's forehead. His voice rose. "We gotta go let them know we didn't find anythin'."

Kaylee ran up to Sara and grabbed her free hand.

"Shut up," Kyle said. "Just shut the hell up, Tim."

"Fuck you! There's nothin' wrong here." He looked past Kyle and shouted, "Hey! We're back!"

Sara tried to stop him, but it was too late. Kyle holstered his gun and brushed past her. Tim backed away, but not fast enough. Kyle slugged him once, twice in the mouth before he could get a hand up. His gun flew into the brush as he fell to the ground. Kyle jumped down and straddled him before he had a chance to recover, one hand over his mouth and the other pinned to his neck.

"If you ever yell like that again, anywhere, I'll kill you."

"Get off me you—"

Kyle squeezed his throat, cutting off whatever Tim had started to say. He outweighed Kyle by at least twenty pounds, but it didn't help him.

Kaylee hid behind Sara, who watched the whole thing unfazed.

"I'll cut your fucking head off and leave it for something to eat." He squeezed a little harder. "Be calm. Keep your head."

He let go. Tim sucked in a gulp of fresh air and coughed. Kyle didn't move off him, just gave the boy a chance to get his bearings.

"I need you to be cool. Be cool, and nobody gets killed. Get hot, and everyone dies." Kyle stood "Do you get me?" He extended a hand.

Tim nodded, Kyle helping him to his feet.

Kyle walked to where the gun had fallen into the brush and picked it up, handing it back to Tim grip-first. "Be cool."

He took the gun without a word.

Sara wouldn't have handed a gun to somebody she'd punched in the face, but they had bigger issues. "Nobody answered."

"What?" Kyle turned toward her.

"Nobody answered when he yelled." She looked down the road at the closest thing to a home she'd had for thirteen years. "Please, Kyle. Let's go."

"Wait here. Keep an eye on them." He pulled out his gun. "I want you all to stay in the brush. Keep out of sight. If I'm not back in fifteen minutes, leave."

"Kyle." She didn't like the desperation in her voice, or the way her throat caught. It reminded her too much of when all of this started. "Please. Please, let's just go."

"I need to know, Sara."

He walked down the road.

Chapter 3

Kyle

The sweat on his palms made the gun slick. *Keep it cool. Just like you told the kid, keep it cool.*

He tried to stay out of sight as he approached the mill, but it was impossible. The old road made a corridor straight to the loading door. A perfect place to keep a watch for any bandits or monsters. Part of him hoped Tim was right, but he wouldn't let that hope sink in. Thirteen years of running and fighting had made Kyle hard, and being hard meant looking at the things nobody else wanted to see. But on that off chance, he had to check. He owed it to these people.

The trees on either side held unknown terrors in the diminishing sunlight. Sara was right; things like this got people killed. He shook the feeling off as he broke past the line of trees and into the clearing.

The first bloodstain pooled on the ground outside the door. He stared at it, keeping to one side of the entrance. The crimson gore had crusted on the ground, and a trail led back into the mill.

Kyle took a deep breath. *They're dead. Everyone here is dead.*

Something moved inside, a scrape of a foot against the ground. Kyle squeezed his gun tighter and peered around the corner.

The nearly spent daylight spilled into the building from the open entryway. Inside, makeshift walls and sheets for curtains created a hallway leading to the front of the building. The roof reached for the ground in spots, and rust dominated the walls. Still, it had always looked like home. Now, lifeless forms littered the ground stained dark with blood. Some were intact. Most were torn to pieces.

Another scrape echoed from deeper in the mill. A thousand thoughts ran through his head. It could be a survivor. Or one of those things had stuck around to eat. *It could be one of my friends turned into an infected monster.*

He crouched low and stepped over the red stain into what was left of North Fifteen.

The smell of blood filled the air in the darkness. He blew out a silent breath. Chunks of what might have once been a woman covered the floor in front of him. The sheet that at one point had blocked off a bunk lay in red tatters.

Melissa.

That bunk belonged to her. He stared at the pieces of a woman he'd once made love to, unable to tear his gaze away. All of this, all over again.

Another scrape emanated from the shadows in front of him.

Karen choked on her own blood. He held her in his arms, ignoring the pain from the bullet in his leg.

"It's going to be okay." He rocked her gently. "Everything is going to be fine."

The look of terror in her eyes didn't fade, but life did. Slowly at first as she tried to gurgle out some final words to him, then all at once.

"I promise, it's going to be okay."

His heartbeat sped up, and suddenly the large room was too small to move in.

I need to get out of here. I shouldn't have come here.

He backed away, no longer caring what might be left. This place was dead now, like the rest of the world.

Feet shuffling in the darkness shattered what was left of Kyle the Runner. He was Kyle the Sociology Professor again, scared and fleeing.

He slipped on the puddles of half-hardened gore, falling feet over head onto the floor. The world exploded into colors as his skull struck the ground.

Little girl in the window—

Richard dead on the ground, the gun still in his hand—

Karen choking on her blood—

"I don't have anywhere to be." Sara said. "Might as well come with you for a while."

A thousand pictures flew through his mind as something moved toward him. The pain and the stink of blood twisted his stomach into knots. Distant humming in his ears blocked everything else out. He gasped, trying to suck in air as he spun over, slicking the front of his clothes in cruor and pieces of people. The thing closed on him, only ten feet away now.

Its teeth chomped together. The thing he'd once called Betty shambled toward him, closing the gap with every second.

His gun wasn't in his hand anymore. He searched the ground around him. Too late. She—*it*—was too close now. He pushed off the ground, trying to get to his feet. The puddle under him shifted the world and landed him on his back.

It was only five feet away.

He reached for his machete.

Two feet away.

It caught in its sheath.

The Betty-thing tumbled onto him, reaching for his face with her teeth. Blood seeped from the hole in her neck as she snapped at his eyes again and again. He pushed as hard as he could, desperate to keep her from biting him, but her legs were sprawled, and he couldn't get free.

He tried to scoot out from under her without being bitten. One of his legs came free, and he kicked her in the stomach. More scraping in the darkness as she launched backward through the air. He squirmed father away and touched something cold and metal behind his back.

His gun.

He grabbed it and aimed as she crawled toward him. The .45 roared in the darkness, deafening him to the other infected closing in. The Betty-thing's head burst as the round passed through it.

The sheet to his left pressed toward him. The line holding it in place stopped the infected long enough for Kyle to get to his feet. He aimed at the outline in the linen and squeezed the trigger, blowing whatever it was backward. He sprinted to the door as screeching and moaning advanced from all around, the noise dulled by the ringing in his ears.

He fled into the sun's last light. "Run! We need to get the hell out of here!"

Sara and Tim stood, weapons ready, down the road. Something howled in the distance, an unnatural, guttural screech. Tim said something to Sara. She shook her head, picked up Kaylee, and turned down the road the way they'd come.

A loud moan rose behind him as seven walking corpses, infected people he'd once known, shambled out of North Fifteen.

"Hurry!" Tim yelled.

Kyle looked back for the last time at what had been his home. Another howl drifted toward them. A second answered it, then another, then another. The twilight came alive with horrors closing in as they fled.

"Give her to me," Tim said as they caught up with Sara. She handed over a silent Kaylee. "Where do we go? What are we supposed to do?"

More howls echoed in the woods, closer than before.

"I don't know," Kyle said.

"You don't know?" Tim brushed back his hair with his free hand. "Well fuck, man—"

"We need to get away from here before we think about anything else." Kyle holstered his gun. "Everyone's dead." Control slowly started to reassert itself. They needed him. He had to stay cool. "We can worry about everything else if we don't—" He was going to say, "*If we don't get eaten.*" "We'll worry about it later."

Kaylee buried her face in Tim's neck.

"The semi?" Sara asked.

"Yes. Let's move."

The cacophony of the damned surrounded them as they hurried down the path to the highway. Kyle huffed, his head pounding with every step. The trip that took ten minutes in took a third as long going out, and soon they were on the pavement again, short of breath and out of time. They stopped as more cries rose from the trees across the road. Whatever they were, they were getting close.

"Just a little ways up the road, Tim. Let's move." Kyle started jogging north. Each step sent a wave of pain through his head. Black spots wriggled before his eyes, and more than once he almost veered off into the woods without knowing why. *Just keep it cool a little longer. Almost there.*

They arrived quickly. A semi-truck turned over on the side of the road, long forgotten by the world. The hatch into the back of the cab was just above ground level.

"Get her in there."

Tim set Kaylee down and jerked open the small door. She crawled in without being asked, Tim and Sara behind her. Kyle shut them into pitch blackness. The old truck's living space smelled like ten years of rot and animal droppings. The sounds outside became distant points of noise. They caught their breath while Kyle pulled off his bag and dug out the bottle of vinegar.

"What happened to North Fifteen?" Tim asked.

A thousand tons of sand split open Kyle's head and poured itself inside with every heartbeat. "I don't know." He splashed the vinegar around the trailer, covering everything in its stench. "Whoever was left became infected. They're all gone now."

"Everyone?"

"I don't know. I assume so." Kyle put down the bottle and rubbed the sides of his head in vain.

"We gotta go back and make sure, man. They might be in trouble."

"They're dead. They're all dead," Sara said. "If we'd been there, we'd be dead too."

"You can't know that." Tim's voice rose. Angry. Indignant. Scared.

Kyle began to respond, but everything turned sideways. The howls became the distant shriek of wind, and the sun smiled at him. He fell backward, and though he thought he would hit the floor of the cab, he never did. He kept falling, past the ground and into the Earth. The world above him drifted away, leaving him to float farther and farther into nothing. The blight covered everything. The face of his dead friends looked at him, taking pity on his plight.

"Come join us, Kyle. Don't suffer anymore. There's nothing to suffer for now."

Richard and Karen smiled and reached for him. Melissa and Zac, Betty and Lucas. All of them beckoned to him, begging him not to torture himself anymore.

Tim and Sara stood over him while a little girl he thought he knew cried silently in a corner of a dark room.

The little girl in the window maybe? Who could say?

"Do you think he got bit? What if he's infected?"

"Then we'll kill him when he turns. Not before."

They needed him. They relied on him just as everyone at North Fifteen had, just like everyone he'd met before.

"They don't need you, bud. They'll be fine," Richard said behind his shoulder. "You do too much. Let go."

It wasn't true, and Richard would never have said something like that, stupid as he might have been sometimes.

"I'm not ready yet. They still need me. Stay away."

The pain returned, but not as bad as before. He wasn't falling, he was lying down. He dimly recalled getting into the truck with Tim and Sara. He tried to call out to them, but sleep pulled him back into its loving embrace.

The mattress under him stank. When he opened his eyes, the darkness was the same as when they were closed. "Where are we?"

Someone had put a blanket over him while he slept, but the cold still seeped in. He would have seen his breath if there were any light.

"Still in the trailer," Sara whispered. "It's been about seven hours."

Kyle let that sink in for a moment. "What happened?" He tried to sit up, but a dull throb in his head cautioned him to reconsider.

"You passed out."

"Is there anything outside?"

"The howling stopped an hour or two ago. We haven't opened the door."

"Good. Don't."

Someone rolled over. "Did you get bit?" Tim asked.

"No."

"You sure?"

"I think I'd remember that."

"We checked you for bites but couldn't find any." Tim was quiet for a few seconds. "We don't have any antibiotics. Any food. Any anythin'."

Quiet settled over the trailer. One ten-minute walk into a building had cut short all their careful illusions of home and safety. Little food, little water, and no hope of getting more the next day, possibly ever.

Kyle took a deep breath and released it slowly. He'd been here before. Anyone who'd survived this long had. Without provocation, the opening speech he'd given on the first day of his freshman classes back in Memphis came to mind.

Don't be afraid to ask questions. Trust your gut. Your first answer is usually the right one... Unless you're stupid, then you should study more.

He and Sara weren't stupid. "You come up with a plan yet?"

"Well." Sara took a deep breath. "We think we should get as far away from here as possible first. Then we need to find some supplies."

"Solid. We can work with that." He blew into his hands and rubbed them together.

"Are you all right? What happened in there? I thought you were dead when you passed out."

"I hit my head when…" *Betty's teeth gnashing inches from his eyes.* "I hit my head. I'm fine."

Tim cleared his throat. "Look, I know nobody wants to hear it," he said in the best impression of an adult Kyle had heard from him thus far. "But we don't have to wander around lookin' for supplies if we head to a city."

Kyle sighed, but said nothing.

"Look, I'm just sayin', Kaylee's mom had friends they were looking for in Oak Ridge, right? Might mean there's more people there."

"Or there might be a hundred thousand infected that'll kill us."

The streets of Memphis were filled with them. Thousands of bodies moving around, looking for anything that wasn't infected and devouring it. Richard's house was only a few blocks away. If they could stay out of sight, they might get out alive.

"Momma talked to them."

"What?" Sara asked. "What do you mean? She saw them?"

"No. She had a radio at the place we lived that she talked to them on."

Quiet followed her statement. It was ludicrous. The imaginings of a child.

"That stuff hasn't worked in a long time. Did your mommy tell you about it?"

"No," Kaylee said in the defiant way only a child could. "Mommy had radios and computers she talked to them on. I saw it a lot. She said we had to go because we had something they needed and it wasn't safe anymore."

"See?" Time laughed. "What did I say? There are people out there."

Kyle could imagine the smug look on the Tim's face. "When was this?" Kyle asked. "I haven't heard of anyone using a phone or the internet in ten years." This little girl couldn't be much older than she'd said she was. No way they still had wireless communications when she was born.

"We left a while ago. Maybe a few months? It was right after my last birthday, and I was born on September second."

She was wrong or she was lying. There was no way. The blight storms knocked out anything that used delicate electronics. "You're mistaken." EMP or something like it, Kyle never knew which. Mysteries remained mysteries in a world gone mad.

"Am not! And I don't lie." Tears thickened her voice.

"Kyle, enough," Sara said. "Kaylee, do you know where your mommy and you came from, or where those friends are?"

"I'm not supposed to talk about it with people outside. Momma made me promise."

Sara scooted over to the girl. "This is really important. Don't you think your mom would want you to be safe with her friends?"

"Yeah." But she didn't sound certain.

She was just a kid, and kids misremembered things. Still, here they sat, grilling her. "We want to take you to them, but we need to know where they are," Kyle said.

She fidgeted. "I don't know where they are. Momma just said we were going to Oak Ridge."

"She had to tell you more than that," Sara said. "Didn't she tell you what to do if you got lost? Did she tell you what her friend's names are?"

Kaylee sniffled. "She said I would die if we got separated. Monsters or bad people would get me."

At least her mom was honest.

She didn't have to open up all at once. It would take time to get to Oak Ridge if they decided they had a death wish.

Tim scoffed. "You ain't gonna die, Kaylee. I promise I'll look after you." He pulled her close, the noise echoing around the dark trailer.

"We need to know everything you can remember. What did your mommy say about her friends?" Sara asked.

"I don't know. Just that they were in Oak Ridge."

Kyle scoffed at their ludicrous optimism. "This is ridiculous, Sara. Do you really want to go into a high population center looking for a few family friends who might not be there?"

"Well where the hell else are we going to go? We can't go back to North Fifteen if it's infected. Who knows what else might be around there? We were lucky to get away once. Do you want to wander around for a few years like we did before? Almost die a hundred times and nearly starve to death every week?" Her voice rose with every word. "You want to wander out east or down south and hope we find enough food and water to stay alive? Say our prayers every night and hope we find antibiotics if one of us gets bit again?"

"I get it. Calm down."

"No, goddammit. Everyone's dead but us, Kyle. We need a plan. We've got a kid with us, for Christ's sake."

Bad things happened. You died or you moved on, end of story. He thought of all his friends who'd said at one time or another there was a safe place somewhere, pushing away the flashbacks that threatened to wash over him. Richard thought Atlanta was safe, Karen thought it was that little town on the ocean, Tim thought it was Oak Ridge; it was all the same. A dead world didn't cater to the wishes of the living.

"You got a better plan, Slick?"

Kyle didn't like Tim's kid's tone, but he made a persuasive point.

Chapter 4

Sara

Kyle had run with large groups before, and it had always ended badly. Two or three might survive scavenging, but more than that was asking for trouble, especially when one was a child. They needed to go to ground, to find somewhere safe and make a real plan.

That brought Sara back to North Fifteen. A few flashes of a violent end had drifted through the ether to her, slow and dreamlike, but she pushed them away. Thinking about it put a lump in her throat that threatened to turn into sobs. All of those people, all the lives they'd made together surviving in a world where that was a feat in itself, all gone. You always knew it could happen when you left the wire, but that never made it easier. She hoped a few of them escaped to somewhere they could find food or water, but she was a pragmatist above all else. Anyone who got away wasn't likely to survive on their own for long.

"How long do we wait before we check outside?" Tim asked. Three hours had passed since Kyle decided to help find the girl's family friends.

"We could peek out," Sara said. "Should be mid-morning. We can start heading north along the highway then east. We'll have to either cut across a lot of open terrain or go way out of our way to stay in cover. We can decide that when we get moving. I need to pee, and I'm sure Kaylee does too."

"I'll do it." Tim moved toward the door.

"The hell you will." Kyle grabbed the hatch before Tim could get there.

A brief flash of red (*ANGER*), gone as quickly as it appeared, pulsed out of Tim. She'd have to talk with Kyle about the way he was treating the guy. They might be the only four people left on the planet, and she wasn't going to have them kill each other. Where all the hostility was coming from was beyond her. Kyle wasn't known for his gentle touch, but he wasn't usually punching people either.

Kyle turned the latch and swung the door out an inch. The daylight on the other side was blinding. The smell of sweet air swept in. She'd forgotten how badly the trailer stank. She couldn't be out fast enough.

She shielded her eyes and let them adjust. Countless bugs skittered on the rotten mattress under them. Kaylee noticed too, letting out a small groan.

Kyle glanced back. "What are you moaning at? That might be lunch soon."

"No way!" Kaylee smiled, the first one Sara had seen since they found her. She was a pretty girl. She would be a lot prettier if she wasn't covered in three months of dirt and dried blood.

Kyle poked his head out. "Looks clear." He stepped outside.

She grabbed Kaylee's hand as they got out. "Come on, let's go use the ladies' room." She led her around to the far side of the truck, keeping her eyes out in case anything still lurked nearby, before taking her pants down and doing her business. Kaylee followed suit, Sara watching the woods only a few feet away.

"Sara," Kaylee said when she'd finished, not meeting her eyes. "I'm sorry about your friends."

The lump in her throat returned. "Me too."

The guys were done too by the time Sara and Kaylee walked back around the truck. She caught a good look at Kyle in the full light of day. He wiped some of the crusted blood on the side of his face. The rest of his skin was pale and sickly. He'd always been skinny, but now he looked emaciated. The bags under his eyes stood out against his black skin, making him look sixty, not forty nine. "You feeling okay?"

"I'm fine."

Tim interrupted before she could follow up. "So do we go back and check for supplies? You said yourself you cleared this whole area out."

"No." Kyle finished cleaning himself. "There were infected around, and god knows how many more crawlers might be lurking."

He hefted his bag onto his shoulders and cinched the straps. "We'll head north. We've got another bug-out bag two days that direction."

"Is it as big as the last one? It might be a while before we find anythin' else."

"I don't remember. I guess we'll find out."

They started quibbling about making the food last and the best places to search, but Sara had bigger concerns. She reached out to the world around her, trying to find anything. She told herself she was looking for creatures, but she knew what she really wanted. One last look, one small glimmer of hope that somebody, anybody, was still alive at North Fifteen.

The world around her drew in, and small points of information spoke to her from the ether.

A rabbit here, a bird there, and a dozen infected milling about her home. Black specks of nothing touching her mind.

She pulled back into herself as the first tears ran down her face. Kyle caught her gaze for a moment before turning away.

Sara started walking north, Kaylee in hand.

A few hours into their trek went a long way to clear Sara's mind, but it didn't make things easier. They stayed on the side of the highway. The trees occasionally vanished, leaving them exposed in fields overgrown with grass long wilted by the November cold. Moving kept the chill at bay, but it would be an uncomfortable few weeks on the road.

Kyle, ever stoic, was dealing. Tim seemed less affected by the events at North Fifteen. He'd come there a few weeks ago after hearing about it from one of the other runners. All the way from Texas, if he could be believed.

"Tennessee is still inhabited. People been tellin' me that the whole way up."

"Yeah? Then why weren't they living there?" Kyle asked.

That little comment was the seed of animosity between them. Kyle was an alpha dog, no doubt about that. But sooner or later, that kid would bite back. He'd supposedly lived with his family on a ranch. It wasn't difficult to imagine what had happened to leave him alone on the road, and nobody was quick to ask. That kind of thing left scars, and scars were liable to make someone think they were tough. And even if he hadn't come all the way from Texas, he was by himself when he'd found North Fifteen. It took more than big talk to stay alive by yourself in a world like this.

A sign before a stream of rusted cars said Shelbyville was only fifteen miles. "Might be somethin' to be had there," Tim said as they passed.

Kyle stared at the sign, the wheels turning. He took off his pack and set it on the ground, sitting on top of it. "The place is a wasteland. Lots of things waiting in the buildings for people to come poking around. Same as every city I've seen so far. The cache is past it."

Tim followed Kyle's lead and sat on his pack. "You been here?"

"Yeah. It's only half a day's walk from—" He almost said home. "From North Fifteen. Of course I've been here." Kyle pulled out the last of the MRE they'd been sharing and a can of fruit.

Sara shook her canteen and listened to the half-empty swishing sound. They still had a few bottles, but those wouldn't last long. Boiling worked well to remove bacteria from uninfected water if it came to it. The orange blighted stuff was no good no matter what you did to it.

"So have either of you ever been to Knoxville?" Tim asked.

"A long time ago," Kyle said. "Before all of this. I would go there every few years for a conference and hit the town."

"What about since then?"

"That supply cache is as far north as I've been. I tried going to Florida when this all started. It gets worse if you go south along the East Coast." Kyle stared at his bread as he spread government cheese across it. "I'd heard Canada wasn't hit as bad, so we tried to make it up there. North Fifteen is as far as I got."

"It was bad between here and Texas too." Tim kicked a rock, and it rolled down the bank of the highway and into the tall grass. "Hard to say what's worse. At least there's places to hide in all the woods here."

An ex-Army guy Sara had met in Kentucky had called everything south of Tennessee the Dead Lands. She never had any desire to find out why, but she guessed Tim would know well enough. She eyed him up and down. Skinny, awkward, and not prone to eye contact. *How did he make it when everyone at North*

Fifteen didn't? "I haven't been to Knoxville, but I was near there. I heard it was bad."

"How bad?"

Teenagers, ever the uncouth ones. "Bad enough that before all the news stopped, the government refused to allow anyone to report on it. Don't get your hopes up."

"But that was a long time ago, right? It might be better now."

She didn't respond. Everyone in Lexington thought they'd be safe there too. They were wrong. Sara, her little sister, and her mother packed up and made south at the first sign of trouble, all the way to Tennessee where her uncle lived. Only Sara made it out alive.

"We should keep going." Kyle strapped on his pack. "Dwelling on the past never helped anyone."

The highway passed the edge town, and the abandoned buildings were visible from the road. Looking over the wreckage of humanity, it was easy to feel as though the world had become host to an invasion. Not people from Mars, but something more sinister. The news had never said what actually happened. Maybe nobody had figured it out. The cities and towns were hit first, the military was totally ineffective, and now people crawled and hid amongst the debris of their old life, caked in dirt and searching for scraps.

Maybe Tim was right. Maybe somewhere out there, Detroit or Mexico City, there were people still living something of a normal life. Maybe the East Coast and the South were the only two places hit. No evidence was forthcoming, and it was impossible to tell in a world without phones or internet. She could only go off what they knew, and that was precious little.

Thinking like that always hit her nicotine spot. "I'd kill for a cigarette," she whispered to nobody in particular.

"Maybe we'll luck out and find some," Kyle said.

She could only hope. Thirteen years out of date might not taste great, but it would get the job done. She could have quit a dozen times in the decade and change since she last paid for a pack, but every time the craving started to go, she'd find another one. Keeping in shape in a world where you might be eaten any day was pointless.

Something in Shelbyville twinged at the edge of her senses like the buzz of electric lines. No way of knowing what would pop up when that happened. Sometimes it was the pain of people who'd died when the world fell apart. Other times she'd see things before they saw her.

Something in the town slept. Its mind hibernated, but it still reached outward, outward, outward. It looked for people. Not like a sniffer looked. It wanted something besides food.

"What's wrong?" Kaylee pulled her hand away. Sara had clamped on her when the vision hit.

"Nothing. We just need to keep going."

It might have been the thing that passed the gas station a few nights ago.

Or the thing that wiped out North Fifteen.

Anger and sadness bubbled up in her, but there was no place for it. She pushed it down.

Kyle stopped and looked at her. She gave him a nod and kept walking. They still had a few hours of daylight left.

They needed to use it.

Twilight fell on a long stretch of road with no exit close in either direction. Kyle led them a few hundred yards off the pavement and into a field overgrown with tall grass. He and Sara dug out a fire pit and put a tent around it with their shelter halves. Blankets covered the open ends, with a small hole left to drain the little smoke the wood produced. The space closed in tight around four people, but they fit.

"I don't like being in the open. Makes me feel like an animal." Tim stared into the fire as he ate.

"We're all just animals." Kyle poked the wood to keep the flame low.

Tim didn't respond, instead closing his eyes and trying to sleep.

"You've got last watch. I'll wake you when it's time." Kyle rolled over and went to sleep as well.

Sara was left to keep an ear out as best she could. Posting a guard outside would draw attention, so they stayed in the tent and listened for trouble. Vulnerability was a fact she'd learned to accept, and camps like this hammered the point home. She looked at Kaylee, already fast asleep, and brushed the hair from her eyes.

"Pacific Applied Biology Technology." Momma said. *"The cutting edge in biological research. All those taxpayer dollars and we can't get one damned thing to work."*

"Alchemists tried for a thousand years to turn lead to gold." Heather leaned back in her chair. *"They never succeeded either, but they advanced science anyway."*

"You think we'd have better odds with that?

Kaylee slipped deeper into her dream, and Sara followed.

"We'll be okay," Momma said. "We're safe in here."

Kaylee wouldn't look her mother in the eyes. That was her lying voice. She could always tell when Momma was lying.

"I promise, sweetheart. We're going to make everything better."

The world around them glowed with a million lights, but darkness waited at the edges. Kaylee looked away as something moved out of the corner of her vision. When she turned back, her momma was gone.

Sara took her hand off Kaylee as she shifted in her sleep. She might be a child, but spying was spying, and nothing was more private than a dream. It put a few more puzzle pieces together though. Kaylee and her mother had apparently lived in a bunker. Sara got that much from the brief glimpse into the girl's subconscious. She wondered if there were a lot of those scattered around the old United States. Important men and women going on as if nothing had changed inside their holes. That would explain how her mother and the family friends still had the use of modern technology.

And if those family friends in Oak Ridge had a bunker too, that might mean they were really safe. Kyle was right of course; nothing could live on a city's surface unless a lot had changed over the last decade. That begged the question of how they'd find anyone if they were buried underground.

"Pacific Applied Biology Technology," Sara said to herself. Maybe that was the key. She could try reading more from Kaylee, but her abilities didn't work like that. The other person had to let her in, and the girl was still traumatized.

"You seein' somethin' right now?"

She jumped when Tim spoke, unaware that he was watching.

"Just little pictures here and there. Nothing big."

He looked past her, into that middle distance reserved for thought. "What's it like?" He blushed a little, as if he'd asked her what kind of underwear she preferred. "I never met someone who could do it before."

"It's like catching a peek of a movie. You get just a little bit, and then it's gone."

"How'd you figure out you could do it?"

Thirteen years ago, when a car accident killed her mother and sister, her abilities had been born. She hadn't been nearby, but she felt it as if she'd been in the Jeep with them. The snap as her mother's neck broke. The thud as her sister flew through the windshield when the Humvee hit them from behind. The first time she'd scanned, it hurt. Birth was always painful.

She hadn't shared that with Kyle, and she wasn't going to share it with Tim. "It just happened one day."

He didn't seem happy with the answer, but he didn't push her the way he did Kyle. *Guy has a knack for hitting the right buttons.* "You should get some sleep. I imagine Kyle's gonna want to push most of the way to our bag tomorrow."

His thoughts drifted to her: *Who put him in charge?* But Tim never asked it.

She needed to talk to both of them before their tension spilled over and put everyone in danger.

Men. Ever wagging their dicks around.

The supply cache collected dust in the rest stop where Kyle and Sara had left it. It contained enough food and water to last nearly a week between four of them, but none of the ammo they'd kept in the last one.

"So what now?" Tim slumped the wall. "We got enough shit to last us a bit. Do we just strike it east?"

Sara poured over the map. "We can try to avoid Murfreesboro or go right by it." She put the map down and rubbed her face. "So we either break brush or risk going by population centers. Starve or get eaten."

Kyle drew in a deep breath and let it out slowly. "Alright. I say we cut north on the highways. It's faster, and these supplies won't last us forever."

"You changed your mind 'bout the cities pretty quick."

Sara expected Kyle to say something snarky, but he didn't.

"I don't see what choice we have. Crawlers and worse things spend the days in the woods or old buildings. We'd have to hunt for food, and for that I'd need to use my gun. You're a runner, right? We'll scavenge for supplies around Murfreesboro."

Tim puffed up when Kyle called him a runner. She'd figured that punch in the face outside North Fifteen would have bruised his ego. Things were stressful. Maybe she wasn't giving him as much credit as he deserved.

"Sounds like we have a plan," she said.

They divided the supplies between their packs. It wasn't much, and it wouldn't last long. Once they had spread the gear around, they took the highway north toward Murfreesboro.

The Tennessee landscape belied the danger the world possessed. Tree covered hills rolled as far as the eye could see. The sun shone in the sky, but they ducked for cover at the howls of unnatural things; a poignant reminder that even daylight wasn't safe. When pileups of cars blocked the way, they picked their way down the center of the broken road.

Tim clambered over an old Jeep, and Kyle handed Kaylee to him.

"How old are you?" she asked.

Tim helped her to the other side as Sara climbed over. "Why do ya wanna know?"

Sara pretended not to listen, but she'd been rather curious herself.

"I just want to know."

"Old enough to know you should be quiet."

Kaylee looked away. Sara didn't think he'd meant to be mean. When she'd been his age, people hadn't respected her much either. Everything was different now.

Sara wiped a strand of hair from in front of her eyes. "I don't think she's trying to card you for booze."

"What?"

The comment had gone over his head. Kyle laughed, and Tim blushed.

"I miss somethin'?"

Sara shook her head and smiled. "Never mind."

Kaylee looked confused as well but kept quiet.

Sara's smile faded. Betty had been in charge of the recreational supplies at North Fifteen. Hooch and smokes, the occasional bag of pot or bottle of pills. People's attitudes about those things relaxed once the world ended. Betty wouldn't be handing out booze anymore, and she wouldn't be hearing jokes either.

I wonder if she was turned into one of those things?

She drew in a deep breath through her nose, determined not to tear up. People died, and as sad as that might be, it was something you had to accept. Accept, but never get used to.

Tim grabbed her Kaylee's as they squeezed between an old Buick and a pickup. "Sorry, Kaylee. I wasn't tryin' to be mean."

She didn't respond, but she didn't let go of his hand either.

That night, they found an old shed behind a farmhouse that hadn't been destroyed. Sara sat up long after Tim and Kaylee had

76

fallen asleep and watched the night sky through a broken window. Her thoughts were raw. She hadn't been able to shake the images North Fifteen, and she hadn't spoken since the afternoon.

If Kaylee can hold it together, so can I.

The girl had seen her mother killed. Everything she'd known her entire life had been ripped away from her, forcing her into a cruel world populated by monsters.

"You okay?" Kyle whispered from his bedroll.

That question always struck her as ridiculous. "I'm fine."

"You're full of shit."

Says the guy who passes out when he bumps his head. "I've just been thinking about Betty all day."

He furrowed his brow. "You can't do that. You know better."

He said it so goddamn matter-of-factly. She wondered if it was that easy for him. Just push it aside. Never think about it. Compartmentalize life so much that nothing hurt anymore. He had told her about his past, about the people he'd run with before and the bad ends they all came to. He never talked about it though. He never said he missed them. Her closest friend in the whole dead world was an emotional cripple.

"Thanks, Kyle. That's helpful."

"Hey now." He grabbed her hand. "You know it isn't like that. We've got people to look after right here. If you spend too much time looking back, you don't see what's right in front of you."

"How can you say that?" Tears welled in her eyes. "How can you just forget them?" Every time she lost someone, it hit her. A stronger person might have grown accustomed to tragedy.

"I'll never forget them. Never." He squeezed her hand. "I'll tell you what. If we find these friends of hers, and they've got somewhere safe to hide for a while, we'll build a memorial for North Fifteen."

She gave him a frank look.

"I'm serious. Nothing fancy, just something so that other people who pass it by will know they're there. You've got my word."

Kyle wasn't a man to break a promise, and his sudden sentimentality touched her. "Okay."

"Good. We've got to hold it together for these two. It's not just the two of us this time."

She looked over at Tim and Kaylee, curled up and sleeping against one another. The girl had taken a liking to him. "I can't believe how well she's holding up." Sara wiped the tears from her eyes.

Kyle let go of her hand and rolled over, his yearly supply of kindness spent. "Storm's still coming on that one."

The road stretched on, and it appeared Kyle was right. Kaylee spoke, but seldom. Tim could occasionally drag her out of her melancholy, but his attempts became rare by the end of the day.

The farmhouses they passed were mostly destroyed. The few remaining held nothing but the crumbling remnants of shattered lives. Mom-and-pop gas stations on the lonely highway were little more than ruins. Nothing presented itself for scavenging as their stock of supplies dwindled, and the rusted hulks of old cars slowed their going both on and off the road.

"So if this is a bust, what do we do next?" Sara asked when Tim and Kaylee were a little way in front of them.

"We could continue out east, hit the coastline. We might beat winter if we go south."

That meant a lot of walking over or around mountains. "There'd be plenty of water, but food would be a problem."

Kyle didn't respond. There was nothing to say. Hard times were never further than a day away.

"Look." Tim pointed at a building on the farm side of a field. From the road, it looked to be an intact two-story farmhouse. A dirt road, mostly overgrown with weeds, led off the highway and toward it. "Think there's anything there?"

Kyle shielded his eyes and peeked at the sun. "It'll be getting dark soon anyway. We'll check it out."

They approached the building with caution, sticking to the tall grass as they followed the path. Few buildings remained undamaged anymore, and both people and things used them for hiding. Caution was always the rule of the day.

They drew closer. The windows and doors were gone. A tire swing, frayed and ready to fall, hung from the only tree in the yard.

The children loved the tire swing. They played in it for hours.

Sara willed the phantom memories away. This wasn't the time. Still, the mirage of two little girls playing by the tree took a moment to fade.

"You okay?" Tim asked.

She put a finger to her lips. If Kyle heard him, he ignored it. "I'm going in first. If you hear anything, you know what to do, right?" He stared at Sara as he spoke, not even acknowledging Tim.

She nodded. Without another word, Kyle crept across the lawn and toward the dilapidated front porch, pulling out his machete. He vanished inside.

"Momma made pie!" Lisa ran to the porch and slipped inside, Jenny just behind.

"Don't eat it all! Save me some!"

Sara tried to push the memories down, but they were powerful. She reached up—

"I couldn't eat the whole pie if I wanted." Lisa sat at the kitchen table. Momma had already laid a piece out for both of them.

"No fighting, you two, or you won't get any after supper."

"We weren't fightin', Momma," Jenny said as she sat at the table. "We was just playin.'"

"Sara." Tim shook her. Kaylee hid behind him. "Jesus, what the hell is wrong with you two?"

She couldn't always hold the memories back, and they didn't always ask for permission. "I'm fine." She could taste the blueberry pie. It made her stomach growl and her heart ache. "Just keep it down."

"Is that how scannin' works?" Tim asked. His accent could have come right out of Jenny or Lisa's mouth.

"Sometimes."

"What's scannin'?" Kaylee asked. Neither of them had a great sense of timing when it came to questions.

"Scanning', and I'll tell you later. Just keep very quiet for me, okay?" She didn't want to give the memories any more attention. They'd come back if she did, and when she was in them, she couldn't see anything else, couldn't do anything if Kyle yelled inside the building.

Miraculously, they fell silence. Ten minutes passed before Kyle poked his head out and waved them over. They moved out of the high grass and up the steps, the porch creaking under their weight. The smell of blueberry pies wafted out as Sara walked through the door.

The farmhouse would have never been called pretty, but it was classic Americana. Little of that character remained, just a relic's bared bones. The floral wallpaper had faded until only one in a hundred red roses were visible. Any finish the floors once had was gone. Wind and cold found their way in through the countless cracks in the walls.

"Nothing here?"

Kyle pulled the vinegar out of his bag, dousing the doorway. "Nothing I saw." He circled around the nearby living room then the kitchen, sprinkling. "There's a basement I didn't check, but it was quiet. You should look upstairs." He stared into her eyes and nodded. A signal.

She cocked her head, but he said nothing further. Kaylee and Tim sat on a nearby couch that had seen better days. "I'll do that." She took the stairs inside the entrance. From the landing on the second floor, three doors led into separate bedrooms, all of them open. She entered the closest one.

An old pink bedframe stood against the wall, the mattress long gone. Most of the furniture was either broken or beat up, but on top of a nearby shelf sat a line of surprisingly well-preserved dolls. She ran her hands over them. Some of them were porcelain. One though…

Jenny grabbed her ragged cloth doll when Momma called her downstairs. Three tornados had run through in the last week. Three. The town was gone. Not broken or in a bad way, just gone. The neighbors were sleeping in the living room.

Sara grabbed it. It couldn't hurt to give Kaylee something. The owner wouldn't be back anytime soon. Everything else was weather-beaten beyond use. She returned to the living room.

Kyle sat on the floor. "We're running low on vinegar."

Tim scoffed. "We're runnin' low on everything."

Kyle gave him a sharp look. "Then why don't you check the basement and see if you can find anything. Be careful."

Tim walked into the kitchen and vanished down the stairs.

"Kaylee, I have something for you." Sara handed the doll to her. Kyle gave her a subtle nod. Hard he might be, and heartless sometimes, but softer inside than out.

Kaylee looked at it for a moment. "Momma made me one like this when I was little. I lost it." She stared at the thing as if it would speak.

"It's okay." Sara squeezed Kaylee's leg. "I know it's hard, but it's going to be okay." Raiders or rapists could have found the little girl. Roving gangs would have done terrible things to her. In desperate times, people were known to eat strangers. She hadn't met any cannibals, but she'd heard the stories, and after the things she'd seen, they were easy to believe.

And yet she couldn't call this girl lucky either. Nobody was lucky anymore. "I promise." The kind of lies children expected to hear.

Kyle rubbed his temples.

"You okay?"

"I'm fine."

"I think I might'a found somethin'," Tim said as he returned to the living room. "There's an old pantry in the basement. Still some stuff left."

Kyle and Sara followed him down the stairs, Kaylee in tow. The temperature rose a few degrees; cold, but more bearable. In the summer, the dirt floor might have stunk, but in the November chill, it only smelled of dirt. The big room held mostly furniture and rusted tools. Tim shone his flashlight into a small root cellar tucked into a corner. Jars of pickled products lined the shelves.

"Looks like our food troubles are over." A huge grin spread across his face.

Sara grabbed her light from her pocket and turned it on. A mattress sat in a corner of the cellar with several empty jars around it. Nobody had been there in a long time. She took one of the jars off the shelf. The vegetables inside had turned brown.

"These have gone bad. Pickled beets don't stay good more than a few years."

Tim's face fell. "What? But it looks fine."

She cracked open the jar, and a rancid smell filled the room. "They're not."

"It can't be all of them." He opened another jar, shying away as he took a whiff. He set it back, top still off, and checked another. All reeked of rot.

"Fuck!" He threw the jar onto the ground. Glass flew across the dirt, turning it dark where the liquid fell. Kaylee hid behind Sara.

"Keep it the fuck down." Kyle took a step toward Tim.

"Why? What the fuck does it matter? We're going to starve, and we've got no place to go." He shook his head and stared at the floor.

"If you don't keep it down, I'll tie you up outside and let you see what bad really looks like."

A flash of (*ANGER*) coursed through the air.

"Guys, this isn't helping."

"Is that what you're gonna do, old man?" Tim stepped up to Kyle, who was already dropping his pack.

Sara stood between them and slapped Tim in the face. He stared back at her, the hurt plain in his eyes. "Get a grip." She turned on Kyle. "And you. How old are you, Kyle? Huh? Aren't you closing in on fifty?" She walked back toward the steps. Everyone got scared. Everyone worried. Taking it out on one another wasn't going to help. *Did they both forget we have a little girl with us that just lost her mother?* "Honestly. Why don't both of you go feed yourselves to something ugly?"

Kaylee's lower lip quivered as they climbed the stairs to the kitchen, then up to the second floor. Her eyes misting over with tears.

"It's okay. They're just worried."

Kaylee didn't reply. They walked into the little girl's room. (*Lisa*) Sara sat against the wall opposite the window, watching the burnt sky darken into night. They should have gone back to North Fifteen. The stores had been enough to last everyone for weeks even without regular runs. Boxes full of food sitting in a locked room. Rotting away with the rest of the world. Turning to dust as the human population dwindled to nothing.

"Those are pretty." Kaylee stared at the porcelain dolls on the shelf.

"They're nice. But the one you've got there was her favorite."

Kaylee looked at the one in her hands. "How can you tell?"

Sara patted the ground next to her. Kaylee sat. Some of her hair was still darker than the rest from the blood. Sara ran her hand through it, untangling small knots as she did.

"Well, I see things when I touch something, or when I go somewhere where something important happened."

"Like what?"

"When we came here, I saw two little girls. And when I met you, I saw your mom loved you very much."

Kaylee didn't speak right away. "You saw my momma?"

"I did."

"Did she say anything?" Her voice caught. She held the tears held back with a stoic look as she gazed into the golden glow outside.

The kind of lies children expected to hear. "She said she loved you very much and that you were going to be okay."

Kaylee tried to cover her sob by taking a deep breath. She hiccupped, and when she spoke again, her voice held a hoarseness that hadn't been there before. "She said the monsters would get me if I got lost."

"I won't let the monsters get you."

She sniffled. "Do you promise?"

Sara pulled her close, leaning Kaylee's head against her chest. "I promise."

"Well where are we gonna go to?" They talked quietly so the children wouldn't hear. Everyone'd had enough scares in the last few days. The rumors of all the things in the woods were too much.

"We'll pack up and leave. We can stay with my uncle in the city."

"What if it's worse there?"

"We can't stay on the farm. Too many things in the woods. Too many monsters."

"Get up." Kyle shook Sara awake. The sun outside had vanished, replaced by an overcast night sky. "Get up, we need to move."

Something stirred on the edge of the woods only a few hundred yards from the back of the house. Low, four-legged shapes moved in the darkness, several hulking shadows among them. The bigger ones, the skinless apes.

Tim grabbed Kaylee, putting a finger over his lips as she stirred. They vanished into the hallway.

"How long?" Sara asked.

Kyle dumped the last of his vinegar onto the spot where she'd been sleeping. "Just noticed them a moment ago. They're coming this way."

Her mental radar picked them up as sleep dropped away. The black spots floating across her mind. Dozens were out there, a horde of them. Most were moving past, but some were approaching the house. Too many.

Kyle motioned with his head, and Sara followed him into the hallway. Someone had pulled down a drop staircase into the attic. Kaylee and Tim were halfway up, Kaylee frantically pointing to something on the stairs. Not a monster of any kind though, and Sara had no time to look. She climbed as Tim and Kaylee vanished into the attic. The ladder squeaked under her weight. It wasn't loud, but it didn't need to be for it to be heard.

Kyle was behind her when he stepped off.

One of the hulking shapes appeared in the doorframe below, and a grunt echoed through the empty house. Sara crawled into the attic, her heart hammering in her chest. Kyle had gone for the doll.

He grabbed it and crept back to the ladder, taking it slowly, moving as quietly as he could. The thing grunted again, louder this time. It moved into the house, several crawlers trailing it, taking huge whiffs of air.

He made it up. He pulled the lever as the first crawler put its foot on the steps. Sara prayed silently to any passing gods that the ladder wouldn't make noise as Kyle closed it. It didn't, and only the softest click sounded as it locked back into place.

The crawler bounded up the stairs as the portal closed. Everyone froze. Moonlight flooded in from a nearby hole in the roof and a broken window at the far end.

"Momma! Momma!" Jenny yelled as she ran through the door. "I got a B on my math!" She bolted down the hallway to the kitchen where her mother cooked dinner. The smell of chicken filled the

*house. Jenny jumped up and down as Momma wiped her hands on
her apron.*

*"Let me see, sweetie." She looked over the paper. "I told you'd
do good if you studied."*

"I did good 'cause you helped!"

If it heard them, it would have howled. Screamed. Something to
ensure their swift demise. Below them, furniture broke and monsters
moaned. Outside, crawlers' cries pierced the stillness, and the
hairless apes called out to their brethren.

Kaylee shifted in the moonlight, and Tim put his arms around
her, a finger over his mouth. Her face scrunched up and her lower lip
trembled, but she held the tears. She clasped the doll to her chest,
holding it for dear life.

Sara wanted to explain everything to her, make her understand,
but this wasn't the time. So they stayed that way, huddled,
frightened, and cold, until long after the sun rose.

.

Chapter 5

Kyle

He eased the attic ladder down. It made an outrageous amount of noise in the quiet. He waited for the sound of creatures below, but nothing came. He glanced at Sara, who looked worse for wear after a night without sleep. "If they were still here, they'd have heard that."

They couldn't stay in the attic forever. They needed to get as far as they could while daylight lasted. They'd already wasted two hours making sure the things had gone. He dropped the ladder the rest of the way, and it slammed against the floor with a bang. He went first, expecting the worst. He always did.

"Alright. Five minutes and we're out of here."

The grim events of the night before had taken the fight out of Tim, and Kyle too for that matter. *A whole pack. Jesus, if they'd smelled us, we'd all be dead.*

Kaylee nearly tripped going down the ladder. She rubbed the sleep from her eyes when she reached the floor.

"Want me to carry you for a little while when we go?" Tim asked.

Clutching her doll, she nodded without a word.

Almost killed for a toy. Kyle didn't know had what had possessed him to go back for that. It probably would have been there if they survived the night.

"He's just a boy, Kyle." Karen said. "You can't."

"I've got to. Look away." He pointed his gun at the kid.

He shook his head until the voices went away. The flashes always worsened when he was tired. The headaches too. Something was wrong with him. In the old world, he'd go to a doctor and get an MRI. Make sure everything in his noggin was connected like it should be. Not anymore. The days of CT scans and doctors were gone. Nothing worked like it should. Why would his head be any different?

Sara and Kaylee descended the stairs to the first floor. Tim stared out the window in the little girl's room.

Kyle watched him for a moment. "You okay?"

"I'm fine. I just wanna say I'm sorry."

"Where's that coming from?"

Tim tilted his head and furrowed his eyebrows. The weighty bags under his eyes lent seriousness to his words. "I don't know. If those things got us, I don't..." He looked up but didn't reach Kyle's gaze. "I just don't want to die with something like that on my chest."

That look in Karen's eyes broke through two years of fighting, two years of survival. "I'd rather not die with any regrets."

91

"You can't think like that." Kyle put his hand on Tim's shoulder. The kid didn't look at him, but he didn't pull away either. "People get edgy sometimes." He wanted to apologize too, but the words wouldn't come out.

They left the farmhouse and headed toward Murfreesboro as fast as they could. The land had been torn up badly, and the blight had hit it particularly hard. Black devil grass rose from the pavement, and the thick orange slop that came with it filled the holes in the highway. Even in the cold, the air was hot and moist. They detoured a few hundred yards out of their way to avoid wreckage and giant craters in the landscape, sometimes venturing into the woods. Never for long though, lest some creature still lurking nearby see them.

Once the things had left the house, Kyle had snuck over to the attic window and watched some of them wander into the forest behind the house. Others had gone down the road, away from Murfreesboro. It wasn't unheard of for them to double back though, and the ones in the forest could be anywhere. They weren't safe.

There were a lot of them out there. Thousands. Millions. The creatures had overrun the cities. Rumors from New York had said the things were being held off street by street, but rumors had stopped coming out of New York years ago. People became less and less common. Infected became the norm; doing their part to ensure the human species wouldn't last another few decades. Over the last two years, bumping into other runners and travelers had all but stopped. Nobody knew what the situation was overseas.

After the tornados ceased and the electronics died, there were enough creatures to mop up the survivors. Time didn't diminish their numbers. Coming close to them was a matter of when, not if.

But they didn't see any as they travelled. Tim watched the trees though, as alert as he should be given the state of the world. "How much further we gonna go?" They'd been walking for eight hours, taking turns carrying Kaylee. The sun wouldn't last much longer.

Kyle shifted the girl to his other shoulder, wishing she'd show more of the big girl attitude she had when she'd insisted she could walk only a few days before.

"As far as we can. If those things come roaming this way in the night, there might not be an attic to hide in." More than that, a bigger town might have supplies.

"It ain't going to matter if we all pass out from being tired."

"Alright." Kyle stopped. "You awake?"

Kaylee nodded against his neck, and he set her down. The farm fields on their right were nothing but a blighted mess. The devil grass had taken over everything. Across the road, a half-collapsed church stood in an open area of unblighted wilderness. The stark contrast between the highway's two sides was jarring.

"We'll stay there then." Kyle pointed toward the church.

Sara clucked her tongue but said nothing.

"Maybe we'll luck out and they'll be some left over communion wine."

She rolled her eyes. She seldom thought he was funny.

They walked across the road and picked their way through the field. The left side of the building had collapsed into a path ripped out by a tornado. The Spanish moss had moved in, and grass sprang up among the remaining pews. The right side still stood intact, but for how much longer was anyone's guess. Shadows hid a few doors.

Looking at shelter made him tired. He might have been more cautious if he didn't feel he would pass out soon.

They stepped over the threshold and into the ruins, checking corners and behind pews. A giant wooden cross leaned against the remains of an altar, half exposed to the elements. The doors in the back were sealed from the other side or led out into the open, the rooms long since destroyed.

None of the sanctity remained here. Any holiness that might have once suffused the land, if there were such a thing, had long since vanished. God had called in sick thirteen years and running. Maybe longer, depending on who you asked.

Kyle didn't dwell on it for long. "We can post camp in the corner and set up shelter halves. We'll dig a pit and light a fire tonight." Staying too long in the cold meant getting sick. Not only would that slow everything down, but it could also be a death sentence. He set to work digging with the little shovel in his pack.

Sara looked at the cross, Tim following her gaze. "Don't think I ever saw a cross that big," he said. "Daddy used to say they were everywhere."

Sara wrapped her arms around herself. "They were. You couldn't get away from it. When things started to go bad, people flocked to places like these."

"Churches?"

"Anything they thought would save them." She walked over to Kyle, setting her pack down. "It didn't get them very far."

Kyle had heard all her stories. The church she'd grown up in. The pastor that tried to pray away the gay. Her mother leaving after her father died, taking the kids and getting out of that toxic place. Kyle had written endless papers and books on religion and sociology. Those places did the kind of harm that didn't go away.

"Can you give me a hand setting up the shelter halves, Tim?"

Tim helped but kept talking. "Couldn't all a been that bad."

"All the ones I ever saw." Sara sat in a pew, still staring at the cross.

Tim strung a length of wire from a door handle onto a plank of wood and draped his shelter half over the corner. Sara handed hers to him. "My daddy told me churches did a lot of good for people."

"Churches did a lot of good for churches."

Richard had been the same way. After the world ended, religion became a hot topic for conversation. Inevitably, someone would bring up God's wrath, and Richard would shoot them down. Sam Harris couldn't have done it better himself.

"Does this seem like a good time for this conversation?" Kyle asked. The last thing they needed after the last few days was another blowup.

"I'm just sayin' what my daddy said."

"I know, but everyone's tired, and not everyone likes talking about it."

Tim looked at Sara and seemed to notice her discomfort for the first time. The way she held herself as she stared at the cross, the way she sneered. "Oh. I'm sorry, Sara. I didn't mean nothin' by it."

The guy's apologized twice in a day. Growing up right before my eyes.

"It's fine." Sara brushed a loose strand of hair behind her ear. "Different life, right?"

It couldn't have been that different if it still hurt her so much.

He divvied food and handed it out as they broke camp the next morning. Another day's worth, day and a half max, was all that remained.

Stores, houses, and barns had dotted the way so far, but as they drew closer to the city, the sprawl became denser and, by proxy, more dangerous. Kyle's headaches worsened as the day wore on. Sara's warnings as she felt things became more frequent.

"Another one somewhere," she whispered.

"Coming for us?" Kyle had asked Richard that question in Memphis, but he couldn't remember why.

"I don't think so."

Kaylee eyed everything as if it had all grown teeth. In many ways, it had.

Kyle noticed. "You okay, kiddo?" The pressure behind his right eye blazed on and off, making it twitch.

She nodded and squeezed Tim's hand.

They moved on. The wrecks of cars grew more frequent, and much worse. At some point someone had cleared a path, but it was in the middle of the road where they dared not travel. Instead, they stuck to the trees when there were any, and low in the ditch on the side of the highway when there weren't.

The day drew on, tension simmering below the surface. Kyle handed out the last of the day's food, making sure Tim and Sara received more than he did. They needed to find shelter soon. Something to hide them when night came. He already felt naked without any vinegar. Anything that caught their scent and was smart enough to follow it could trace them.

Kyle tripped, and the sudden jolt sent searing pain through his head.

"Great minds think alike," Richard said. He might be right, but so did morons. The food stores on this farm wouldn't last forever.

"What are we going to do when this runs out?" Kyle asked. Karen looked up when he said it. Her eyes were puffy from crying.

"We'll go back to the city. My neighbor kept tons of food in the house. Seventh Day Adventist. I'll bet there's enough crap in his basement to keep us fed for half a decade."

Going back into Memphis would be suicide. Kyle told him so.

"Kyle." Sara's whisper was hard. It wasn't the first time she'd said his name.

He looked around, trying to get his bearings. "Yeah. Yeah, I'm fine."

Tim shook his head. "Bullshit. We need to find a place to stop for a while."

He wanted to argue but couldn't. His heart beat a cadence in his head, pulsing painfully with every drum. "You might be right."

Piles of rubble that had once been a city littered the landscape, but many buildings still stood. The country highway vibe had given way to the country city. Nothing tall remained, just one story structures on hills around them. The big creatures, or tornados, had torn apart overpasses. A car stuck out from the side of a nearby building, tossed through the wall by some tremendous force. All around were signs of strength so ferocious it was nearly incomprehensible.

"We'll move a little ways to the next exit and see what we find."

The road held more cars and more signs of civilization. Here, Mother Nature was slower moving in, but the effects were starker. Weeds grew over half-destroyed buildings. Trees had sprouted in the middle of the road, already impressive in some places. Cars had begun to break down from rusted frames into piles of scrap.

They turned down the next exit into civilization's ruins. Sara put a hand up. She cocked her head, listening to things no one else could hear. She pointed down the street ahead. Kyle strained to see through the shadows of the buildings and wrecks.

A dozen infected swayed in the shade of a half-collapsed motel.

She pulled the bow off of her bag. "We move past. Stick to the right side of the street, and do exactly as I do."

A less experienced runner might try to take them out, come up quietly and stab them in the head before they knew what hit them. But thirty more could be waiting in the wings, drawn by the sounds of a scuffle. Crawlers could be nesting in that building.

The thing that scared the piss out of Sara a few nights ago could be around. The hair on his arms rose at the thought.

She crept into the ditch, the others behind her. They passed businesses and occasionally climbed out to cross a driveway. Kyle peeked over the edge of the ditch at one such crossing. They were far enough past the motel, and on the far side of the road. But where there was one infected, there were always more.

Nothing showed itself. He climbed onto the grass and crossed the driveway leading to a dilapidated burger joint, staying low to avoid being seen until he reached the drop on the far side. Tim came after, Kaylee holding his hand.

Something grabbed his ankle and moaned. He spun around, nearly tripping over himself. He hadn't seen the infected man's upper half in the tall grass. It pulled itself closer, trying to get ahold of Kyle with its teeth. He didn't give it the chance. He pointed his machete downward, the tip aimed at the top of its head, and thrust it through.

He hadn't seen the rock on the far side of the thing's skull either.

The blade struck it, ringing out as Kaylee and Tim joined him. Inside of the building, one of the infected wailed. Sara jumped out of the other side of the driveway and ran across. Kyle waved for them to follow and took off along the ditch.

Glass broke above them. Something made its way out of the restaurant. Kyle snuck a glance behind but couldn't see anything outside the ditch.

More cries answered the first from the ruins of the street above. Rusted metal moved, and feet shuffled. The only saving grace was how slow those things were. With any luck, they could find a place to hide before the infected wandered over.

Unfortunately, the only exits were going up, or the storm drain that ran underneath the next driveway. Not a hard choice. Kyle dropped to his knees and started pulling out the debris that blocked the drain. Tim set Kaylee down and joined him.

"Just keep it cool," Kyle whispered. "They haven't seen us yet."

Tim kept pulling out branches and putrid bits of filth. If the drain was blocked all the way through, they'd have to go over top, and they'd certainly be seen.

The small tunnel was clear on the far side. He grabbed Tim as the last of the debris came away and threw him into the sludge-filled drain. The stink of rotted vegetation was overwhelming. He took Kaylee by the shoulder and guided her in as a moan called out above them only a few feet away.

Sara gestured for him to go first, but he shook his head. She climbed in.

A pebble tumbled down the side of the ditch, and a shadow crept over the edge of the embankment. He pressed against the driveway as the shadow grew larger.

"There were a million of those things, Richard." Kyle said. *"We can't go back to the city again. It's suicide."*

If it saw him, he'd run the other way and draw them from the others. All the noise they'd make would attract something else—a crawler or, one of the ape things—but at least the others would get away.

A broken car shifted on the pavement above. Kyle risked a glance. The infected was staring back the way it had come. He didn't miss his opportunity. He dove into the drain.

Something hit the ground behind him.

Shit. He might have led it to everyone else.

There wasn't much room to maneuver, but he turned to look behind him. It had slid down the embankment but was trying to climb back up. It hadn't seen him.

He faced forward and crawled silently through the cold sludge. Tim's face appeared, blocking the daylight. Kyle emerged from the pipe, covered in filth. The ditch curved off to the right and disappeared behind a bend. Sara and Kaylee were already out of sight as Kyle and Tim dashed after them.

The crashing and moaning faded behind them. *If we get out of this, I'm never coming into a city again.*

They rounded the corner as Sara shot an infected with an arrow. It flew true, taking the thing between the eyes. She slung the bow back over her bag as Kyle and Tim caught up. "There's a gas station across the street," Sara whispered, out of breath. "We can get across and go in one of the broken windows. I didn't see anything up there."

He didn't like crossing out in the open, but they couldn't hunker in a ditch all day either. Things would only get worse come nightfall. "Alright." He climbed up the side and peeked over. Old cars and garbage littered the road. A gas station stood intact across the street, an older one with a small shop in the front and a connected garage. The windows were busted out, but the doors were still attached. He crawled back down.

"I love you, Kyle," Karen said.

"You're just drunk."

"Tim, you go first. Sara, you take Kaylee and go second. I'll go last."

Concern painted her face. He'd blacked out again.

Back around the bend, something tumbled into the ditch.

"Did you get all that, Kaylee?" Sara asked. The girl nodded.

Tim climbed the ditch, vanishing from sight. Sara did the same, Kyle handing Kaylee to her. They disappeared over the edge, and Kyle pressed his back against the hill, counting to five before he poked his head up.

They made it across the street without incident, and he moved to follow.

"It's been four years. Maybe they rot like normal dead bodies?" Richard said.

"I don't think so, man. We've seen them everywhere. They get dried out, but they don't die. They're filled with that black shit and fungus. I think that's what keeps them going."

The others murmured their agreement one way or the other. It didn't matter to Kyle; he wasn't going back. If Richard insisted, then he'd leave. The thought of abandoning him after all these years didn't sit right, but he'd been getting more and more unhinged as time went on. He took stupid risks and put everyone in danger. Kyle didn't want to die, and he didn't want to see Karen die either.

He grabbed her hand.

"We can't last taking what's left on the side of the highways forever," Richard said.

He wasn't wrong. They'd picked up too many people. They were up to unlucky thirteen. It wouldn't be long before someone made a mistake. That many people couldn't hide as well as they could when it was just four of them.

Sara was already halfway back across the street when Kyle snapped out of it. He blinked twice. Her hand was around his arm before his senses caught up, pulling him onto the road.

Everything came back. They needed to get somewhere safe. The gas station. The things behind them.

"I'm alright." But she didn't let go until they crossed the street.

The sun had already started to set. Kyle climbed into the display window in the front. Tim and Kaylee sat behind the counter near a door to the garage. Most of the shelves had been knocked over, but the few that remained hid them from view outside.

"Fuck, man. What the hell was that?"

Kaylee shook, holding her knees to her chest, wide.

"I'm fine."

"Staring off into space with your head poked out like a rabbit? That ain't fine. That ain't fine at all."

"Nothing in here?" Kyle asked. Nobody responded. They kept staring at him. He didn't want to talk about it. Acknowledging his illness wouldn't make it any easier to deal with. Things were bad enough without him slowing them down. "I'll check."

Tim put a hand up and pulled out his pistol. "Let me do it. You rest for a second."

Kyle wanted to argue, but his head pulsed to the beat of his heart, a ten-ton hammer slamming his brains. He slid down the wall next to Kaylee, covering his face with his hands, as Tim vanished into the garage.

"He's going to get us killed with that gun."

Sara stared at him. "It's getting worse."

Neither of them had talked about it before. What started as occasional headaches had become momentary lapses in memory and moved on to blackouts. Both knew the truth of it; if something really was wrong with him, it didn't matter. Nothing could be done.

"I'm fine dammit."

"Are you sick?" Kaylee asked.

"I'm still well enough to take care of you."

Tim walked back into the room. "Nothin' in there. But you gotta see what I found."

"Bad?" Kyle asked.

Tim looked between him and Sara. "Better just come look."

He got up and followed. A big hole in the far side of the ceiling let some light in, but otherwise the dwindling sun didn't pierce the gloom. The two big rolling doors still stood, preventing anything from seeing in. Shelves covered the back wall, and auto parts littered the floor.

"What is it?"

Tim gestured him to the back corner where a door was hidden from view. He flipped on his flashlight and stepped inside. A room filled with dust. More shelves, all bare. A few canned goods and old food wrappers remained, but otherwise the room had been stripped.

"The cans ain't good, but I found somethin' else." He shone the light on one of the shelves.

"What am I supposed to be looking at?"

Tim pointed with his free hand. "The dust, man."

A thick layer of dust had settled across the shelves, but not everywhere. There were lines where boxes had been moved. Recently. No new dust had settled there. It had to have happened within the last week.

"Good eye." Kyle wouldn't have noticed that himself.

"Means other people been through here. Not too long ago either."

"Yeah, it does."

"Means we might want to be more careful too."

As time went on, more and more of the people on the road were as likely to rob someone as look at them. Kyle had some experience in that department.

"That it does." He walked back into the garage. "Looks like there might be other people around."

Sara nodded. She blanked out, staring into nothing as she scanned. He wondered if that wasn't what he looked like when he had those flashbacks. A few seconds later, she returned.

"If they were here, they're gone now."

"Good. The last thing we need today is more company."

"What's wrong with other people?" asked Kaylee.

Sara stroked the girl's hair. The red stain still streaked through the blond. "Not everyone out there is nice, sweetheart."

Kaylee thought about it. "That's stupid. Why wouldn't everyone work together when things are bad?"

The question struck Sara silent.

Tim spoke up first. "People don't always do what they should."

"But that's stupid."

Kyle smiled. "You aren't wrong there, little lady. Not one bit."

Chapter 6

Sara

Tim sat with Kaylee in the garage while Sara and Kyle kept a quiet watch near the front of the store. Night cast the outside in threatening moonlight, and the infected were restless.

Sara hoped they would settle by morning. With their food supplies dwindling, they couldn't afford to be stuck in one place for long.

"We still don't know where we're going. You're going to have to scan Kaylee sooner or later."

Sara rubbed her forehead, brushing a lock of hair from her eyes. "The girl's been through a lot. I keep wondering what we're going to do if she doesn't know anything. We can't wander around a city blind."

"Not much we can do about that now."

"I'll do it in the morning." Her stomach lurched when she thought about it. She could read Kaylee and see nothing. No memories of a bunker. No safety. No chances.

Kyle nodded and stared out into the night. The occasional moan rose in the distance. The infected weren't smart creatures. They stayed in the spot where they'd died and come back, devouring anything that drew close. That was what made cities so dangerous. In places where people had died by the millions, there was no room for the living. The dead and the damned ruled the world, leaving the survivors to struggle in its shadow.

"Does your head hurt?"

When she'd first seen him blank out, she thought he might be turning into a scanner. That didn't make sense though. When those things had showed up, people could scan. It wasn't something that happened eventually, or you grew into; you could scan or you couldn't. His gradual change was something else.

Kyle shrugged. "Not like we have any aspirin."

She grabbed his hand. "The way you just stood there today scared me. What if one of the infected had seen you?"

He spit on the floor. "Then I'd be dead."

She'd gotten by fine on her own, and she'd had other friends before him, but she couldn't entertain the thought of losing him. Death from some monster or thief was expected. It was easy to forget that *anything* could put you in the grave, even if it didn't have claws and teeth. She'd lost too much in the last week.

"Don't talk like that. Not after everything—" That hard lump formed in her throat again, the one that told her tears weren't far behind.

Kyle looked over at her but said nothing. He let go of her hand. "It's okay, Songbird."

She hated that nickname, and he knew it. But it made her smile, and the tears retreated. "Don't leave me with these damn kids, Kyle."

He laughed quietly.

"Is it going to hurt?"

Sara had been explaining the process to her since they woke up. "You won't feel anything. It'll be like you're asleep."

Tim sat nearby on a tool bench, watching. He'd had more questions about the whole thing than Kaylee.

"Will I see anything?" Kaylee squeezed her doll close to her chest.

"You'll see whatever I see." Sara suspected she didn't want to remember anything, afraid of what might bubble to the surface. The idea of this fragile girl being so terrified of the past at such a young age broke her heart.

"Okay. What do I have to do?"

"Just lay back and close your eyes. I'm going to touch your head, okay?"

Kaylee did as she was told, lying on Sara's blanket. Sara put her palms over the girl's temples. Getting inside someone's consciousness wasn't as easy as touching the echoes of the world. The mind of another human twisted and turned, breathed and moved.

You could only come along for the ride if they wanted you there. Sara focused inward and grazed the edges of Kaylee's thoughts.

The girl tensed under her, and the connection fell apart.

"It's okay. That's just me."

"That felt funny."

"I know, but don't let it scare you or it won't work."

Kaylee settled back down and Sara tried again, easing herself away from the physical world and drifting into the hidden one, the deeper one. Kaylee jumped again, but only a little. The tiniest of connections appeared between them. Sara—

She poured herself into the hole in Kaylee's defenses. Slowly at first, the barest trickle going in. Kaylee relaxed, and already Sara could feel the girl's mind falling away into the same inside place through which all scanners travelled. The breach in the walls around Kaylee's thoughts widened, and more of Sara fell in.

She could sense Kaylee all around her. This wasn't just her world, it was her everything. All the things that made the girl surrounded them. She'd tread carefully. An intrusion here would be the worst kind a person could make.

The world shifted. She saw it the same way she would inside her own head. Pictures of people flew by. Kyle, Sara, her mother, and the people she'd traveled with. The doll that Sara had given her hung over everything as a chandelier. Attached to it was the promise she'd made; she'd keep Kaylee safe.

She willed herself forward, drifting through the fog of the soul. Kaylee's voice touched her from somewhere inside. "What is this?"

"This is you. Isn't it pretty?"

It was, and Kaylee agreed. The prism of colors and pictures wove a tapestry of life. Sara kept moving, walking through the mist and heading toward the place where the memories lived.

"Don't forget, Kaylee, nothing in here can hurt you."

A flash of memory appeared.

"I won't let anything hurt you," Kaylee's mother said in the distance.

"That's right. I'll look out for you too."

She passed by the memory, searching deeper. Kaylee might not have known everything about her mother's plan, but she must have overheard something.

"We did it," Miriam said into a phone. The office wouldn't have looked out of place on a military base. Cold brick and tile, no windows, and neatly kept paperwork.

"The compound has a ninety-eight-point-seven percent similarity to silver."

The world changed again, and Kaylee watched her mother work in a lab from a nearby window. A man gently bumped her elbow and smiled. Kaylee's father.

The power flashed, and a glass beaker fell from his hand, shattering on the floor. Alarms went off. He stepped back, and a piece of glass broke through the bottom of his shoe. He groaned.

"What, Ryan?" The fear in Miriam's eyes broke Sara's heart. "What happened?" She saw the pool of blood under his foot. "Oh my God."

Ryan said something, but his voice was garbled.

Everything spun fast. Too fast. Kaylee grew upset. Sara stood in a bedroom, a cheerless brick thing, watching Miriam speak to Kaylee. "Where's Daddy?"

Kaylee started to panic, and the dream world reacted. The fog swirled. "There was an accident." A tear ran down Miriam's face. "Daddy's gone."

Kaylee shook her head as the fog changed color from black to red and back again. "When is he coming back?"

Sara backed out of the memory and into the formless void of Kaylee's mind. "Just be calm. It's okay."

"I don't want to do this anymore. Can we stop?"

Sara didn't want to hurt the girl, but if they didn't find what they needed, none of them was going to survive. "Can you go a little further?"

Great wracking sobs shook the world. Everything turned blue around them, and the doll hanging over Sara's head rocked back and forth.

"I don't want to do this anymore. I don't want to see anymore. Please don't make me! Please!"

Sara took herself out of Kaylee's mind. The girl hung on for a moment before letting go. She could have held Sara in there as long as she wanted, but the grip loosened and then vanished.

Sara opened her eyes. Back in her body, drenched in sweat, the world spun. Kaylee stared up at her, crying. She threw her arms around Sara, quietly sobbing into her shoulder.

"It's okay." She stroked Kaylee's hair. "Everything is going to be okay."

It took hours to calm the girl. Sara didn't want to pressure her into revisiting her past horrors, but they'd be out of options soon. Kyle wanted her to press in for another round, but Sara refused. Doing something like that again too soon could shut Kaylee down, and if she wouldn't let Sara in, they'd never get the answers.

"We're going to be out of food by the end of the day, Sara. We could use a win."

They stood in the front of the garage while Tim packed the last of the gear and Kaylee sat quietly in the corner. She hadn't spoken since she stopped crying.

"She isn't going to find us food."

Kyle ran his hand through his hair. "This isn't the time to be soft."

She couldn't do it. Not after what she'd seen in Kaylee's head. She didn't understand it all, but it seemed her father had died in a lab accident. The poor kid didn't even remember his voice. Going in now would put them right back in the same place. Kaylee needed distance. She needed time.

Two things they didn't have.

The infected had quieted at some point in the night, and there were no signs of anything else nearby. It was past time they left.

"You sure you don't wanna look 'round here for food?" Tim asked Kyle.

"Too risky. I'd rather get out of town and look around the outskirts."

Tim glanced between them. "We're gonna starve if we don't do something."

"We'll tighten our belts. Something'll show up." Kyle hiked his bag up on his back. "It always does."

They left the gas station, staying as far from the wreckage that lined the way as possible. The trees along the side of the road were blighted and ugly, and Kyle wouldn't let the group walk in them. Superstitious or no, it was better to be safe than sorry.

The sound of infected sent them hiding behind the remains of buildings or under cars. It happened frequently enough that Sara was glad they weren't going into the city proper. It'd been a long time since she'd been in any of the places where people used to gather. Lexington had scared her more than anything she'd seen since. The tornados came, followed by the endless lightning storms. Mother Nature wreaked havoc upon the world, and the churches that weren't blown down filled with terrified people begging for God's mercy.

They never got it.

The night went on for weeks, and in the night, those things came. The big ones trampled cars underfoot, and the smaller ones picked people apart as they ran. The creatures washed through the city like a wave of the damned, and nothing was the same after. The dawn finally came when the storms stopped, but the world it revealed was changed. The things the monsters left, those infected, were worse. That mockery of life. She would eat a bullet before she became one of them.

Skirting the edge of the city meant avoiding the worst of it. Within an hour, the road gave way to highway again, freeing them from the moans of the dead. The urban sprawl became endless lines of cars, abandoned by people trying to flee. Here, the tornados had been particularly bad, and huge swathes of the road were gone.

In the middle of the half-destroyed highway, among several lanes of wrecked cars, they found an old camper. Kyle waved them away and inched toward it, pulling his machete out. They needed a place to lay low while they scavenged. They could go no farther without supplies. The risk of being stuck on a highway in the middle of nowhere with no food or clean water was too great.

Kyle ripped the door open and stepped inside. A moan came from within, followed by a meaty thwack. Tim began to move in, but Sara placed a hand on his shoulder.

He needn't have worried. Kyle stepped outside, dragging the remains of an infected, and waved them over. "It'll keep the wind off us, but there are too many holes in it to make a fire. There are a of couple blankets in the back. They smell like shit, but they're in one piece."

"Any food?" Tim asked.

Kyle threw the infected into the ditch on the side of the road. "Don't you think I might have mentioned that?"

(*ANGER*) pulsed off Tim, but he held it in check. If things ever started to look up again, she might mention to Kyle that a teenage boy who could barely read held his temper better than a grown man with a doctorate.

The old motorhome's interior was more weatherworn than the outside. The wallpaper had peeled away to nothing, and most of the windows were gone. The damp had turned everything yellow, and it reeked of rot and mold.

Kaylee covered her nose. "It stinks in here."

"The smell will cover our scent. You two will be safe in here while Tim and I go out scavenging." He set his bag down. "You know the drill."

If he wasn't back in two days, don't wait up. She could take care of Kaylee where Tim might not be able. Kyle could look after her too, but given how frequently he'd been blacking out, it was the only smart way to split up.

"Alright. Let's head out now, Tim. I don't want to lose any daylight." The sun had already ridden past the noon mark, and a cold day slowly descended into a colder night.

"You look out for, Sara, okay?" Tim smiled at Kaylee. She nodded back, serious as a statue.

They left without saying anything more.

The mattress in the back squished when she stepped on it, and vermin had gnawed it half to pieces. No good for sleeping. She dragged it to the front and blocked the space where the windshield had once been. It didn't cover the whole thing, but it was close enough. She tied the door shut with a piece of electric cord before sitting in the back room with Kaylee, stroking the girl's hair in a way that comforted one as much as the other.

After a long while, Kaylee spoke. "What was it like before?"

"What was what like?"

Kaylee looked over her shoulder at Sara. "Everything. Before all the bad stuff happened."

Sara stared at the ceiling while she thought of the right way to put it. "Well, things weren't always perfect, but they were good. There used to be cities where you could go and see thousands of people walking around at the same time—"

"Momma showed me pictures of them."

"And those cities were everywhere. People could spend a lot of time doing the things they liked to do, like playing sports and reading. Do you know how to read?"

"Yeah. I liked to read a lot, but we didn't have a lot of books where we were at."

Sara took her opportunity. "Where was that?"

Kaylee hesitated.

"I promised"

Sara pushed it aside, not wanting to intrude on the girl's thoughts any more than she already had. "I don't think your momma would mind if you told me. We're trying to help you find her friends, remember?"

Kaylee picked at the dirt on her fingers, keeping her head down. "We were under the ground. It was really far away though, and we had to walk a long way to get... to get where we were."

Sara knew that much already. "Do you know what your momma did there?"

Kaylee squirmed a little. "She worked for the people who were going to fix everything. She said they used to run the country."

Unless they had an army hidden away in the bunker with them, it seemed unlikely they were going to fix much of anything. "Sounds like she was very important. Do you know how they were going to fix it?"

Kaylee shook her head. "No. I just know they were."

"Are your momma's friends underground too?"

Kaylee played with a frayed string on her doll. "I think so."

That explained a lot. If there were still groups of people in the cities, they would have to be underground. It raised questions as well.

"How many people are underground?"

"I don't know. Momma told me important people had plans in case bad things happened."

Kaylee had given her a lot to think about, and she let the conversation drop. Underground. That would mean safety. Food. Water. Everything they lacked. Sara had seen Miriam talking on a phone when she scanned Kaylee. She'd seen the lab for herself. The girl hadn't been lying. For the first time in a long time, Sara was excited about the future.

That excitement didn't last long. They still had no food, and they were a long way from Oak Ridge. Even once they got there, they had no idea how to find these people. Miriam might have had a radio or a phone to contact them. They were flying blind. She'd have to scan Kaylee again and hope something came up.

If the last decade had taught her anything, it was how to keep her head clear. "Were you the only little girl underground?"

"Yeah. Everyone else was old."

Sara smiled. "What's old to you?"

"Sixteen."

She laughed. "Oh really? So Tim's old?"

"Yeah."

"And I'm old?"

Kaylee smiled as the sun drifted slowly behind the clouds.

"Sara, wake up. Sara."

Night had already fallen. "What's wrong?"

"Someone's outside."

Sara perked up and reached for the knife on her belt. "What did you hear?"

"Someone talked."

Sara stepped outside of herself and scanned the area.

Three men standing in the ditch nearby, talking. Hard men. They looked at the infected corpse.

The infected man. A butcher. Get the camper, get to Grandma, get to the farm. Had to find Grandma.

She focused on the living men. "Fresh kill," the big one said. "Check around."

They felt dirty, but that wasn't new. Nobody in the new world survived without scars. But something else about them pinged alarms inside her. These weren't nice men.

Sara snapped back into herself. "I need you to be extra quiet, okay?"

Running into other people would have been tense with all four of them. With only two, one of whom was just a little girl, Sara's heart raced.

They sat in silence. She could hear low whispers. They knew something was amiss.

Please, just keep walking. Don't look for anything.

A whisper outside the back of the motorhome dashed any hopes Sara had. "Check the RV."

Her mind went blank. "Don't come in here!"

Someone outside gasped.

"I'm armed."

Quiet for a moment. "No need for threats, lady," said a deep voice from outside. "Is anyone in there with you?" The question was innocent enough, but fraught with implication.

"Yeah, there's a few of us, all armed." She put her finger to her lips and pointed at a cabinet under a nearby sink. "Hide," she whispered. Kaylee eased the door open. By some miracle, the cabinet was empty. She crawled inside.

"If anyone else is in there, speak up. We're just scavengers." They were probing. Friendly people didn't probe.

"Tim, train your gun on the door, shoot anyone that comes in. Did you hear that? We don't want any trouble. Just move along."

Nighttime. Things could be out there, moving closer with every shouted word. Inside, her heart beat faster with each passing second. Not nice men. Not nice men at all.

Nobody spoke. She hoped they wouldn't be stupid enough to shoot a gun through the RV's walls. Not only would that be the end of her and possibly Kaylee, but it would also draw anything nearby.

"Get lost before you bring trouble." She closed the cabinet where Kaylee hid and placed a few things in front of it, just enough so it wouldn't be obvious. She didn't know what their game was, but they weren't getting Kaylee.

She positioned herself to the side of the door. Nobody responded outside for a full minute, then two. Even in the cold, sweat beaded on her forehead. Her hands shook. She took a few deep breaths to calm herself. She hadn't been scared as a child when things were bad and people were threatening; she wouldn't be scared here.

Maybe they moved on. Just friendly runners like they said. Not knowing what else to do, she closed her eyes to scan the area.

"It's just her in there." A man peeked through the space in the windshield between the mattress and the wall. "She's got a knife." It wasn't the man with the deep voice.

"If you come in here, I'm going to use it. I don't want any trouble, just get lost."

"That's twice now you've threatened us," said the deep voice from outside the door. "We aren't bad guys. Why don't you come out?"

"I said get lost. I've got nothing for you." She wracked her brain. Every alarm in her head was going off. "I'm infected. If you touch me, I'll bite you, and you'll be infected too."

Everything outside went quiet. She crept silently to her bag and grabbed her bow off the back. She took an arrow and put her back to the mattress at the front. First one through the door would get an arrow in the eye. They weren't going to touch her or the girl. She'd kill herself before she let that happen again. She'd take Kaylee with her if she had to.

A third voice spoke up, this one younger and unsure. "Let's just leave her alone, man."

Harsh whispers came from outside. Anxiety started to give away to fear, but Sara wouldn't let it take hold. She'd survived in hell for thirteen years; a bunch of assholes weren't going to bully her now. She sucked in a great breath and blew it out slowly. If they didn't leave, she'd take at least one of them down before they got her.

Someone pulled on the door, but the tie held. "Do that again and I'm cutting off a finger. Get lost."

She could hear her heart beating over the wind. Then pavement being hit hard.

Someone was charging the door. She readied herself.

The door busted in on its hinges with a bang, but didn't fall off.

"You're going to draw every monster for miles, and they're going to eat you alive."

"Just open the door, bitch. Last warning," said the deep voice.

"Let's just go, man." The younger man's voice shook as he spoke.

Someone was pushed onto the ground. "Shut the fuck up, Pete. You ain't had pussy since pussy had you."

There it was, all laid out. The big guy ran the show, and he wanted her. He'd be the one killed if that door broke. The fear soured, turning to disgust, then anger. *Goddamn savages.* She worked herself up. Better mad than scared.

He pounded his fist on the door, and Sara's pulse beat in time with it. She wished she'd kept her mouth shut. They might not have checked the RV if she had.

The door slammed in as someone kicked it. A giant slab of a man stepped through half a second later, his gun raised.

He didn't see Sara or the arrow she loosed.

It didn't reach maximum velocity in the small space, but it flew fast enough to pierce his neck. The shock on his face barely registered before she threw her bow aside and jumped to her feet, grabbing the knife. She charged across the short space, blade poised to sink into his goddamned eye.

The blood pouring from between his fingers as he grasped at the shaft spilled onto the floor. She raised the knife over her head as she closed the last few feet. She stabbed hard, but he had the presence of mind to move. The blade dug into his arm and pulled from her grip as he gurgled a scream.

A gun bashed the side of her head. She stood there stupidly for a moment, looking at the man bleeding to death against the door before it hit her again, knocking her to the ground.

"Holy fuck, Gary." The window peeker. She hadn't seen him step up.

Gary mumbled something through a mouthful of blood. He stumbled past the window peeker and outside, falling to his knees.

"Holy fuck, Gary," he said again.

"Don't just fucking stand there, Jerry," said Pete. "Help him!"

Jerry and Gary? The thought might have made her laugh, but they were shouting. They were going to draw something. She struggled to her knees. Hot and sticky blood ran down the side of her head. She moved for the knife a few feet away.

"No you don't, you fucking cunt!" Jerry strode over and grabbed Sara by the hair, pulling her out of the RV. She latched onto his hands, clawing at the wrist, the sudden pain in her scalp bringing her around.

"You fuckin' bitch! We weren't going to hurt you!" He slapped her hard enough to make her ears ring, and she fell onto the pavement.

A few feet away, Gary struggled to breathe. His color had gone. That gave her a perverse pleasure. She might die, but Kaylee would live, and that fucker would die with her. Pete's hands were around the arrow, but the look of terror on his face said he didn't know what to do.

I never got to say goodbye to Momma.

She pulled herself away from Gary's mind, not wanting to touch it. She couldn't feel sympathy for a creature like him. His kind was worse than the things that ate people. She opened her mouth to say as much when a boot caught her in the face.

"You fuckin' bitch!" Jerry's chest heaved with every breath. She looked up. The rage in his face made his thoughts clear.

She wasn't going to survive this.

Another boot stomped on her nose, and when it went away, she'd lost vision in her left eye. She faced the RV's door so she could see the cabinet where Kaylee hid. She hoped the girl would be safe until Kyle came back. There was no chance of her surviving on her own.

Another kick dug into her back.

"Stop! Come help me with Gary!"

Jerry walked over to his fallen friend, and Sara rolled over to watch. He wasn't moving anymore. Pete's hands still covered the wound, but Gary was no longer one to be counted among the living.

"We gotta do something, man," Pete said.

"Ain't nothin' to do. He's dead. That bitch killed him."

"No, man. No way! He ain't dead!" Pete shook Gary's body. "Wake up, man, you gotta stay awake."

125

Sara leaned up on her elbows. The knife sat in the RV's doorway. If she could crawl over and grab it, she might be able to get out of this.

Jerry pulled a gun out from behind his back before she had the chance.

"That bitch killed him. Now I'm gonna kill her."

Pete jumped to his feet. "Wait, man, wait!" He put his bloody hand on the man's jacket, leaving a stain. "Don't."

Jerry pushed Pete away. "You on this cunt's side?"

"No, but Mark's gonna wanna know what happened."

Just a scared child, no older than Tim, who didn't want someone else to die.

Jerry stared at him for a long moment. "Yeah. Yeah." He looked at Sara. "He's gonna wanna know what happened to his brother." He stomped toward her. "He's gonna wanna do this himself."

Hate emanated from him in waves. Sara thought of Kaylee hidden away in the RV, and of never seeing Kyle's face again. She thought of her mother and sister dying, and of the monsters overrunning Lexington.

Everything came out in a burst of power she never knew she had.

Kyle, I need you!

The thought blasted from her mind with such power that her ears rang.

Jerry took a step back and looked around, suddenly unsure. Pete reached for his gun in the holster on his hip, smearing Gary's blood everywhere. They'd heard it. Whatever she'd done, they'd heard it.

"What the fuck was that?" Pete asked.

"I got no fucking idea." Jerry raised the gun over his head.

"No, don't!" Pete tried to stop him but too late.

He's trying to protect me, was her last thought before the gun struck her between the eyes, knocking her out cold.

Somewhere back in the city, Kyle heard her scream.

Something else did too, only a little further away.

Chapter 7

Kyle

Kyle, I need you!

The noise blasted into his skull like the sound in an IMAX theater. He remembered hearing somewhere that those things had been capable of deafening an audience. The thought occurred slowly, as if someone had said it underwater. Everything went sideways, and he fell to the ground.

"Holy shit." Tim knelt down and shook him. "Kyle? Kyle!"

"I'm alright." He came around as quickly as he'd fainted. It was like being caught inside a wind tunnel; after everything turned off, the world became oddly still. "I thought I heard…" He stared off into the distance.

"What?" He stood over Kyle. "You ain't goin' all loopy, are ya? 'Cause if you are, I'm not draggin' your ass back to the RV."

Kyle furrowed his brow, pausing to stare at Tim.

"I'm just sayin', we'd have to tough it out here is all." Tim offered Kyle his hand.

Kyle took it and stood before dusting himself off. A useless gesture in filthy clothes. "I heard Sara scream. Something's wrong."

"I didn't hear nothin', man."

They weren't far into the city. They'd been checking every building that looked like it might have food on the way back. The best way to avoid starving to death was to be thorough.

"I'm telling you, they're in trouble. We're going back." He returned to the window they'd climbed in through at the back of the building.

"Woah, man." Tim put his hand on Kyle's shoulder. "You sure you didn't have another one of your weird spells?"

"If I'm wrong, we wasted a few hours. If not…" He let the implication hang in the air. Kyle crawled through the broken window and into the woods behind the property. The scream of a sniffer drifted on the wind. There was no mistaking that sound. It started as strong as a sonic boom and tampered off into a high-pitched air raid siren.

"Fuck," Tim said under his breath. "You think it got them?"

Kyle listened for a few seconds. A second sniffer joined the noise, then another. "It's coming from a different direction. Whatever that's about isn't good though. Let's get moving."

They traced their steps back to the RV. Night had fallen. They'd intended to keep searching as long as they could. Kyle hadn't told Tim or Sara that he'd left the last of the food for her and Kaylee, and he hadn't been looking forward to breaking the news that it looked to be a lean night for the two of them.

The sniffers' screams stopped after a few minutes, but that didn't matter. They were a call to arms for every terrible thing within twenty miles, maybe farther in a world as silent and still as this one. They'd come, and god help anything nearby when they did.

Kyle and Tim passed through the outskirts of town and back onto the remains of the highway. It took an hour to get back to the RV. The moon hung full in the sky by the time they returned, and Kyle saw the corpse from a distance. He stopped Tim with an outstretched arm.

"What?" Tim searched the highway. "Oh, shit. Is that Sara?" He pulled out his gun.

Whoever it was had been huge. An arrow appeared to be sticking out of their neck.

"I don't think so. And don't pull that out. You heard those screams. There's going to be a thousand monsters nearby that will hear a gunshot."

"What if we need it?" He put the gun away, but kept his hand on it.

Kyle stared at the corpse. "Then it's probably already too late for them." He shouldn't have left them alone. They should have stayed together.

He pulled out his machete. "I want you to go around in the woods to the far side. Keep an eye out; there could still be people nearby. Come in slow, and I'll do the same."

Tim vanished down the nearby embankment. Kyle didn't like relying on him—he didn't like relying on anyone except Sara—but he didn't have a choice. He waited in the darkness, staring at the corpse and expecting the worst. When he saw movement on the far side of the RV, he took a deep breath and stalked forward.

Sara's arrow had pierced the man's carotid artery. She wouldn't have done something like that unless she had to. Nothing emerged from the twisted wreckage of the cars around him. A moment later, he stood at the trailer door as Tim moved to the other side. Someone had kicked it in.

He eyed Tim from across the doorway, nodded, and stepped inside with his machete raised. Nothing had changed inside the RV. "Clear."

Tim looked around as he entered. "I didn't see anything else out there."

Blood soiled the walls and door. Sara's knife sat inside the door, a crimson stain on the blade. Still half wet. Kyle picked it up. "Look around."

The bags in the back remained undisturbed, but Kaylee and Sara were gone.

Everyone was dead. Richard, Karen, and all the others. Kyle limped away, the bullet in his leg sending bolts of pain shooting through him with every step.

"What the fuck is the point anymore?"

He sat at the edge of the road. He should get as far away as possible, but he didn't care. If some scavenging hell beast wanted to make him its lunch, so be it.

Tim pushed him. "We don't got time for that. Stay with me."

Kyle leaned against the counter, rubbing his eyes. Something moved in the cabinet beneath him. He spun, readying his machete.

"Kyle? Tim?"

Kyle opened the cupboard to reveal Kaylee, covered in cobwebs and curled into a ball. When she saw him, she started crying.

"What happened here?" Kyle pulled her out.

The first few words out of her mouth were inarticulate. Kyle lifted her face so she looked him in the eyes. "Where's Sara?"

"The men took her," she sobbed. "They want to hurt her." Another wave of sobs wracked her.

"What bad men? What happened? Where did they go?" He couldn't spare her feelings right now. Sara might be alive.

"I don't know. They said they were going to take her somewhere because she killed someone."

Kyle stood Kaylee up. "Watch her."

Nothing outside gave an immediate indication of where they'd gone. He leaned over the dead body. Sara's shot had been clean. She didn't miss with that bow. The pool of blood around the body had dried and started to crust in spots, but on the far side, red footprints led toward the edge of the highway. Kyle followed them. They proceeded down the road, away from the city, before they vanished.

It wasn't much, but it was a start. He walked back to the RV. "Strip Sara's bag and grab what we can carry. I think I know which way they went."

Tim, who had been holding Kaylee, set her down. "What are we gonna do?"

"What do you think? We're going to follow them. If they've got Sara, they'll have to go slow." He knelt next to Kaylee. "How long ago did they leave?"

She shook her head, tears falling onto the floor. "I don't know. A while ago?"

"Hurry up, Tim."

It took longer to go than Kyle planned. Kaylee wouldn't stop crying, and they couldn't leave her behind. Kyle pleaded, and finally commanded, that she be quiet. Tim asked him to step out so he could talk to her. With a hard glance, Kyle did as he asked.

Every passing second wasted time. He would find Sara and kill every person involved. He didn't consider himself violent, but he'd done what he had to do to survive. He'd do it again tonight if necessary. After a few more minutes, Tim emerged with Kaylee in hand. "We're ready."

They followed the trail. Not sticking to the trees, just keeping low behind ruined cars. In long spaces between wreckage, they walked down the embankment to avoid any eyes that might be watching. There was no way to tell how many people were out there.

Tim held Kaylee's hand in one of his and a pistol in the other. Kyle wanted to say something about that but thought better of it. The sniffers hadn't been close, but they hadn't been far either. They'd come from the other direction, but there was no telling if those creatures were closing on them even as they walked. But monsters didn't use guns. People did. And if people with guns showed up, you had better have one yourself.

The tracks vanished not far from the RV, but they'd held in a straight line. Tim was quick to point out that Kyle didn't know where they were going. "What if they went off into the trees?"

"Then we'll search the woods until we find them."

"That's crazy."

Kyle spun on him. "If you don't like it, feel free to leave. Good luck out there."

Tim's nostrils flared, but he held his temper in check. Kaylee sniffled, standing between them. "Hey, I wanna find her as bad as you—"

"I really doubt that." Kyle continued down the road.

"Whatever, man. I'm just sayin', we can't wander out here all night. Not with those sniffers around."

Kyle ignored him. It was no different than when Karen and Richard died. He didn't care what happened to him anymore.

Sara would though, and her words drifted up from the fog of memory. *These people look up to you, Kyle.* She wouldn't lose it if Kyle went missing. She wouldn't take it out on two children, one a terrified little girl.

"I'm sorry." He said it without turning around.

Kaylee kept sniffling as Tim spoke. "It's okay. I'm scared too."

"Let's keep looking. Another hour and we'll find somewhere to hole up for the night."

Tim nodded, and they continued. They didn't have to look much further. Several miles down stood an old barn. They might have passed it if Tim hadn't noticed all the new boards nailed to the outside, or the suspiciously well-kept truck nearby.

The smell of rotten eggs had been growing over the last mile. Kyle guessed a natural gas line had ruptured over the years. The stink overwhelmed everything else.

"You seein' that?" Tim asked as they passed the barn.

Kyle hadn't been looking that direction; he'd been watching the woods on the other side of the road, expecting whoever had Sara to be hiding there. Even when he did look, it took him a moment to realize what Tim saw. The place was in much better condition than anything else they'd seen. "Keep low. If that's where they're at, they could have a lookout."

"What about Kaylee?" Tim hunched behind a car.

She looked at Kyle, and he stared back at her. "I'm not leaving anyone alone again. If shooting starts, I want you to get as low to the ground as you can, okay?"

Her gaze was on him, but her slack expression said she was a million miles away. "Are you going to shoot them?"

"Yes, I am. I want you to stay as low as you can."

Her lip quivered, but she didn't respond. Wherever the hell she'd grown up, it certainly hadn't been out on the road.

"You two stay behind cover. I'm going to have a look." He moved off without another word.

"Be careful."

The road in front of the barn was devoid of hiding spots. Kyle crouched and tried to make himself as small as possible, but if anyone had been watching, they would have seen him.

He did a full circuit. A door stood at either end of the structure, and a large barn entrance, long since boarded up, dominated the center on one side. The wood was sun-bleached and dry. No light came through any cracks, but someone talked inside. More than one someone. He pressed his ear against the wood but couldn't make out what the voices were saying. As he pulled away, a woman spoke.

It took everything he had not to break down the door with his gun drawn. *Stay cool, Kyle. Stay nice and cool. You've got Tim. No need to go in guns blazing just yet.*

He checked the truck on the way back. An old diesel. The thing had to be seventy years old. Old trucks were the only things that ran. Anything that used electrical systems had been fried. By the time the catastrophes had started, most of these old wrecks had long since seen a junkyard. Many of those that hadn't didn't use diesel, so their fuel source had rotted with everything else. Still, even if you could use a truck, it was suicide. The noise drew everything for miles.

He could see no keys inside, and the door was locked. He returned to Tim and Kaylee. "There's a door on the far side."

"Locked?"

Kyle nodded.

"Well what are we gonna do, then? Knock?"

The tone of his voice said it was a joke, but that was exactly what Kyle had in mind..

Chapter 8

Sara

Two sniffers screamed, closer now. The other men in the barn noticed, shifting and glancing at one another. Wood wouldn't save them from whatever hell those things would rain down.

The man in front of Sara punched her in the gut again. She'd lost count of how many that was, but something inside her hurt with every breath. The barn around them, converted into a giant living room with two cots, a couch, and boxes full of who knew what, spun around and around with every hit. The rope digging into her hands hung from a support on the ceiling, placed there as if they expected this kind of thing to happen; the casual murder of a stranger.

Mark had stopped speaking. Every hit was nothing but rage. Two of the other three men watched. The third, the kid Pete, wasn't looking. He'd tried to get Mark to stop when he'd started pummeling her, but all that earned him was a punch in the face.

The entire walk back, Jerry had been a simmering pot of anger. "Oh, you're gonna get it, lady. You're gonna wish you'd never been born. He's gonna make the things those demons do look like a tickle fight, you cunt."

He'd insisted they were looking for supplies, but Sara knew better. She'd touched their minds. She wasn't the first woman they'd dragged back to this barn. The fact there were none around said everything she needed to know.

Her thoughts scattered as Mark punched her in the jaw. One of her teeth shifted in its socket, and a spray of blood flew from her mouth.

"Spittin' on me, bitch?" He hit her again.

She wasn't going to survive. Even if they didn't kill her, she felt the things coming. She'd never screamed with her mind before. She didn't know she could. It was a tornado warning turned up all the way. A signal broadcast through the minds of every living thing for fifty miles. That creature, that walking blight she'd felt after they'd found Kaylee, it heard too. She sensed it on the edge of her consciousness, growing closer with every minute.

She wished she hadn't done it. The thinking monster would bring a thousand other horrors with it, sweeping Kyle, Tim, and Kaylee away in the tide. She should have kept quiet. She should have died with dignity.

She was barely consciousness enough to form a sentence, but she tried anyway. "You hit…" Talking hurt. "You hit like my little sister." She smiled at Mark as blood ran down her chin.

A hurricane of wrath formed in his eyes. *Good. Maybe he'll just kill me.* She hoped so. If she had a thought to spare for God, she might have prayed for it. In a world where things could only get worse, she didn't see the point.

He hit her again, and—

It marched. The head of a formation of filth. The king of crusted disgust. Moving toward her. It felt her the same way she felt it.

It reached out to touch her, its mind swallowing hers. A toad catching a fly. Its thoughts were alien, but they were thoughts. It planned. It plotted. It knew where it was going, and its kind had machinations in the works that would bring a new night to humanity; a forever night. They wanted things. Needed things. They fed and devoured the same way humans did, but their hungers were terrible and huge on a scale Sara couldn't fathom.

Cold water hit her face, bringing her back around. She shivered already, her extremities numb. Blood ran between her lips and down her jaw. The water dropped in beads from her hair, making the chill in the air unbearable. She opened the one eye that could still see. Mark was staring back at her. Jerry stood nearby, the bucket in his hands.

"Oh, no, no, no. You don't get off that easy." He grabbed her cheeks in one hand and squeezed. Pain rippled through her face and down her neck. Something had to be broken for it to hurt like that.

"They was just gonna invite you back here. And you killed my brother." He squeezed harder. "You fuckin' killed my little brother!"

139

Pete spoke up from the back. "Jesus, Mark! He was coming at her like he was gonna rape her. You should of heard what—"

The fourth, nameless man slapped Pete in the back of the head, shutting him up. Too late. Mark rounded on him. Sara couldn't see his face, but his shoulders were hunched, and his posture stiff. He approached Pete slowly.

"You want to defend this bitch? She killed my little brother." Closer to Pete now, but Pete didn't move. His eyes screamed defiance, but he flinched with every step. "I been watching out for Jerry since we was knee-high. We kept each other alive when those demons showed up."

Closer.

"We built all of this to protect ungrateful shits like you." He closed the last of the distance and grabbed Pete by the shirt, lifting him off the ground. The guy had a hundred pounds on him easy, as big as his brother. "You think she did right killin' him?"

That defiance in Pete's eyes became fear. "N-no. I'm just saying she was scared." He looked Mark in the eyes. "You gonna kill her for defending herself?"

Sara wanted to tell the kid not to get himself killed for her, but that moment had already passed. Mark reared back and punched him in the gut, folding him in midair.

"You're out of here, you little faggot."

Pete unfurled and gasped only to be hit again. Pleasure radiated off Mark in waves. Sure, his brother was dead, but it wasn't about that. Mark liked to hurt people.

Watching as Daddy hit Mommy again and again. Mark hated him. Mark hated them both. She was so goddamn weak. *He took Gary by the hand and led him out of the room as his mother hit the floor and screamed.*

"You eat the food I provide and then talk to me like that? You ungrateful little shit!"

It made him feel like a man.

Susy Kessler said no, but she wanted it. He slid himself out of his pants and hit the lock on the car door.

Disgust welled up inside of her. This man was as much a monster as the things that ruled the world.

Gary held the guy while Mark watched him squirm. They hadn't seen a woman in almost a year. This piece of shit wanted to steal their guns while they slept.

"I just needed some ammo. I gotta stay alive too, you know?

He stole like a bitch, and he moved his hips like a bitch.

"What the hell are you doing?" Gary asked as Mark undid the button on his pants.

"Just hold him."

Sara sneered even though it hurt. "Your parents hated you too, Mark."

He slowed his fist mid-swing, but still hit Pete with enough force to make him sputter and groan. The poor kid gasped for air, the wind knocked out of him.

Mark stared back at Sara, Pete forgotten for a moment. "What did you say, bitch?"

"Your parents hated you as much as you hated them." She smiled, and the blood ran down her face.

Speaking was painful, but worth it. She hoped Pete had the good sense to slip out while he had a chance.

Mark's eyes went as wide as the moon, and he dropped Pete to the floor. "What?" The anger and bravado vanished from his voice. He was a puppy being told a command for the first time, not understanding. A little boy not knowing why his family hurt themselves so badly.

In an instant, the angry man was back. "What, bitch?"

"Oh?" Sara wanted it to end. "Big tough guy again?" She wanted a mercy, a bullet in the head. Maybe putting him over the edge would do it. "Your brother screamed while he died. He screamed and begged for his life."

His face turned dark red. The veins in the side of his neck stood out, pulsing with each beat of his heart. He picked up a crowbar leaning against the wall and stormed toward her.

"I'll kill you! I'll fuckin' kill you!"

Pete stirred on the ground. She felt sorry for the kid, and it struck her as ludicrous. She was the one strung from the ceiling by a bunch of hillbilly murderers, and she was worried about him.

Sara closed her eyes as Mark approached. Fine. So be it. She didn't care to stay in this world much longer anyway. She wanted to be brave and not cry out, but her lip quivered as he closed the distance. The old world hadn't been kind to her, and this one was worse. Dead would be better.

Please, Momma, don't let this hurt.

She focused on Kyle. With any luck, he'd find Kaylee and they'd get away, maybe to that bunker where her mother's friends hid. She squeezed her eyes shut and held her breath.

Three hard knocks came from the door at the end of the barn.

Sara's eyes flew open, and her breath came out in a baited gasp. Mark stood comically still, a cartoon of a man about to commit atrocious violence on a stranger. Everyone stared at the door. Even Pete strained his neck from where he lay gasping on the ground.

Again, three pounds. Slower this time, more deliberate.

"Who's there?" Mark called out. The bravado had vanished from his voice again.

Sara's heart skipped a beat. If Kyle had heard her scream, if he'd come after her, then they were all as good as dead.

In the distance, a sniffer's scream pierced the night.

Please don't be him. Let him be far away and running.

"I said who the fuck is out there?" He set the crowbar down and picked up a shotgun propped on a nearby cot, cocking it and holding it at the ready.

Sara tried to touch the world around her, but she could barely keep her eye open. Everything hurt.

"Get the door," Mark said.

Jerry and Fourth Man looked at one another, but neither moved. Bravery was in short supply among cowards. Jerry kicked Pete on the floor. The Fourth Man grabbed his shoulder, pulling him to his feet.

He could barely stand. Fear had replaced the defiant expression. He must have understood now the kind of people he'd taken up with, the kind of monsters he'd decided to follow. He grabbed his gut, each breath labored.

"Open the door." Fourth Man pushed him toward it.

Pete fought it for the first few steps, until Mark levelled the shotgun at him. "I'll kill you where you stand, kid. Walk."

The boy was a rabbit caught in a snare, and chewing his own leg off wasn't an option. His hands shook as he stared down the barrel of the shotgun. Jerry and Number Four had both pulled out guns, aiming them at the door; close enough to get a peek, but not close enough to be hurt by the something or someone outside.

Sara hung quietly, forgotten in the sudden excitement. She wished she had a knife, a piece of glass, a sharp stick; anything to cut herself down. She wished she could call out to Kyle as she had before. Maybe she could warn him about the armed gunmen waiting to shoot whatever was outside the door.

Pete lifted the bar across the entrance, grunting with the effort, and set it aside. He undid the locks, one at the top and one at the bottom. Hands still shaking, he turned the handle and opened the door inward. From where she was, Sara couldn't see anything. The world was a black void containing endless horror. Pete poked his head around, looking outside for whatever had knocked.

"What do you see?" Mark asked behind him.

Pete shook his head. "N-nothing."

"Then get out there and look." Jerry pushed him, and the kid tripped.

A gunshot rang out in the darkness. She flinched in her restraints, closing her eyes at the sudden roar from the darkness outside.

Pete bounced off the door and landed in the doorway, blood running from the hole in his face. Chaos reigned. The men started screaming, terrified to have their violence reflected back at them.

It had to be Kyle and Tim. "Kyle! There's three of them!"

A sniffer screamed somewhere close, and all hell broke loose.

Chapter 9

Kyle

.

Tim waited behind a car parked on the far side of the road. Kaylee was with him, hunched close to the ground.

Kyle was scared, but he wouldn't admit it. He had to be strong for them.

Tim would take the shot if it needed taking. Kyle's role in this incredibly stupid plan was to get close enough to draw them out. This was the place, and she might already be dead.

The world tilted sideways, and his thoughts tried to drag him down. Back into memories of the past, memories of everyone and everything gone by. He resisted. *Gotta stay clear. Gotta stay focused and cool if I'm going to be any use here.* Resisting hurt. His head pounded with each step. The ever-present keening in his ears rang louder.

The side of the highway closest to the barn was clear in either direction. Vehicles had been dragged to the side and dropped into the ditches or left on the side of the road. There was little cover. These people had been here a while. The smell of the busted gas line must have covered their scent.

A sniffer screeched in the distance. They were close, and getting closer.

He pulled out his gun as he crossed the road. The barn loomed over him like one of the monsters in the early days of the invasion. He'd made the comment before that they were as big as barns, but the truth was they'd been bigger. Standing close to this barn in the dark—

Little girl in the window.

He shook his head, clearing away the cobwebs and making it jolt in agony. This wasn't the time. Sara needed him. She was the only person left that mattered to him in this shit world. He couldn't lose her too. Not after North Fifteen.

Kyle glanced behind him, but Tim remained invisible in the dark.

Yelling rose from within. He couldn't make out what they were saying, but the tone was clear. Anger. Indignation. A smaller, weaker male voice spoke out. Kyle crept closer and pressed his ear to the door.

Sara spoke, too faint to hear, but clearly her. Adrenaline bled into his fingers and toes. He tingled with dread. Someone mumbled something inside, but the sound didn't carry through the thick wooden walls. The next voice chilled him to the bone.

"What, bitch?"

Sara replied, and—

The two men she was with weren't the friendly sort. She rolled her eyes half the time they spoke.

"How long have you been out here?" she asked.

Kyle leaned against the wall of the shed, gazing through the hole in the roof to the firmament above. "Two years."

She drew back from the bag she was digging through and examined him again. "By yourself?"

The two men with her looked at one another. They'd barely said a word since he walked up. Dogs pissing on their territory to let him know he wasn't welcome. The flat expression on her face spoke volumes. They hadn't been friends for long.

He didn't doubt they thought he was full of shit, and he didn't doubt she'd been the one to suggest they speak to him. He wondered how long they'd been watching him. Part of him wanted to be annoyed that he hadn't noticed. If they'd wanted to kill him, he'd be dead. Another part of him missed talking to people.

"Yes. Two years." He extended a hand. "Kyle."

She didn't look put off by the old world manners at all. She smiled, and it brightened up the room. "Sara."

She had a no-bullshit grip.

The world bled back into focus. He'd lost time again. Church bells rang in his head. He blinked hard, his ear still against the door. Panic rose and his stomach turned. He'd missed something. Every worst thought ran through his head. He didn't know how long he'd been standing there, eyes blank, mouth open. They could have killed her. Beaten her half to death.

Not knowing what else to do, he knocked. Three hard pounds. The sound rang into the darkness, vanishing in the night. He stood there stupidly, his hand pressed against the door, waiting for a response. Nothing. The inside remained as silent as the outside, even more so. In the cold twilight, bugs chirped. Birds sang. The world carried on as if it hadn't really ended; turned as if lives weren't in the balance and people didn't matter. Maybe they didn't.

He pounded again. Slower. Deliberate.

"Who's there?" The voice from inside wavered as it spoke. He wasn't thrilled about having a midnight visitor

Why would he be? What good news comes looking for kidnappers? His mind dipped low, away from Kyle the Sociology Professor. He was Kyle the Killer. Kyle the Survivor. A sniffer screamed off in the distance as if to agree with his grim resolve. He'd do what he had to. The jitters tapered off as he took a breath.

He made for the corner of the barn, ready for the door to open. Ready to save Sara and deliver a bloody death to anyone who tried to stop him. He pulled out his light, flashing it once toward Tim.

The midnight ride of Paul Revere came to mind. One if by land and two if by sea.

"A voice in the darkness, a knock at the door."

The insanity of such a thought brought a smile to his lips. Not a humorous smile. A dog's grin. A killing leer.

Kyle positioned himself at the corner of the barn. If the plan didn't work, he would have to bust in alone. Tim wouldn't last long alone in such a miserable world, but at least he and Kaylee would have a chance. That's how things went now. Families and friends torn apart. Nothing permanent. That had all gone out the window thirteen years ago.

"Hardly a man is now alive, who remembers that famous day and year."

He tightened his grip on his pistol and waited, crouched not ten feet from the door.

Locks popped. This was it. Now or never. Tim knew what to do, and Kyle hoped he had the courage to do it. They would get one chance to give up Sara. If they refused or tried to go back inside, Tim would take one out, and Kyle would move in. If there were more than two or three, it would almost certainly be suicide. Only in the old movies did one lone gunslinger take down an army singlehandedly.

"And the meeting-house windows, black and bare, gaze at him with a spectral glare, as if they already stood aghast, at the bloody work they would look upon."

The door opened, and a light spilled out into the world. These people had no caution. It was a wonder they'd survived this long.

"What do you see?" asked the big voice from inside.

A smaller voice, not more than a terrified child, replied. "N-nothing." That could have been Tim.

"Then get out there and look."

On the other side of the door was a small scuffle, someone being shoved.

This is it. Kyle readied himself, gun drawn.

Tim's shot rang out from the darkness. Maybe he'd gotten nervous, or maybe he'd seen something Kyle hadn't. The kid who'd poked his head out the door jerked back with the force of the round. Inside, the voices of at least three men started yelling.

"Fuck!"

"Close the door!"

"Get that fucker!"

Above it all, clear as day, came Sara's voice. "Kyle! There's three of them!"

Hearing her brought everything into narrow focus. Her voice was weak and her speech slurred. Kyle stepped out from around the corner, his gun pointed ahead.

Sniffers screamed, close now. The howls of dozens of crawlers drifted on the wind, the ghostly whispers of the damned coming for their flesh. Something bigger roared in the distance, a bass note Kyle felt as much as heard. One of the big ones. A behemoth. He hadn't seen them in years. He pushed the dread down. One problem at a time.

"Pull the kid out of the door!" yelled the big voice.

There was a moment of hesitation as Kyle closed on the entrance. A man's shadow blocked the light as he grabbed the lower half of the kid's body.

"No! Just grab his arms!"

Too late. The man saw him. His eyes widened as if he'd seen a ghost from the past, gun drawn, face set in fury.

Tim shot again, and another chorus of howls and roars answered. His sure aim from earlier had vanished, and the bullet slammed into the side of the barn.

Without saying a word, Kyle squeezed the trigger. The round hit the man in the face before he could draw his weapon. He fell on top of the other body. More swearing from inside. The jolt of the gun renewed the throbbing in Kyle's head.

Bullets ripped through the wood around him, and pistols roared. The first one flew close enough that splinters from the barn gashed his cheek. He hit the floor, his ears ringing, as the shots tapered off.

Over the ringing, someone yelled from inside. "Fuck! Fuck! Don't shoot!" It was the big voice.

Don't shoot. Kyle had heard and said that more times than he could remember over the last thirteen years. He crouched low, weapon ready. "You took one of my people." He didn't sound like the professor who'd once advised a student on how to pull off the perfect first date. That man was dead. "Let her go, and you walk away with your lives. There's a dozen of us out here, all armed."

The blackness threatened to seize the moment. He gritted his teeth and bore down. He had a job to do. Once Sara was safe, he could crawl away and die.

"She killed my brother. He wasn't going to hurt her, and she killed him."

Kyle had known Sara a long time. That was a bold-faced lie. "I'm not here to bargain. Give us our friend or die."

The crawlers' howls and the roar of the behemoth drew nearer. Odds were good they'd all be dead soon either way. Fine then. He'd die with Sara at his side.

Silence greeted his ultimatum. "I want an answer. Now."

A shotgun blast through the barn wall answered him, inches from his torso. Some of the buckshot dug into his ribs, searing painfully. Kyle rolled forward as another shot ripped apart the place where he'd been kneeling. The impact of the ground lit his brain with a galaxy of pain. Everything turned gray and distant as the wood shattered above him.

"Kyle! There's only—" Sara's words cut off with a meaty thwack of something striking flesh.

They'll kill her before I can get in.

He picked up a rock and crawled toward the door as two more shotgun rounds drove through the wall where he'd been. The ringing in his ears pierced the silence, and his headache pulsed dangerously, threatening to pull him under. It was now or never.

"Grenade!" He threw the rock through the door.

"Fuck!"

He jumped to his feet, weapon in hand. He was the specter of death, the unkillable spirit of vengeance come to rescue his friend.

A big man near Sara stared at the rock as if it would kill him.

He looked up as Kyle squeezed off two rounds as he rushed through the door. The first one hit him in the shoulder, spinning him. The second popped his head in a shower of gore. The second man, who'd been running toward the far end of the barn, whirled at the gunshots. Kyle trained the weapon on him.

"Don't shoot! Don't shoot!" The man dropped his pistol.

Sara hung from the ceiling, blood dripping from her mouth. He'd seen people hurt badly over the last thirteen years, but if he'd seen worse, he couldn't remember when. His heart broke. "Tim! Get in here!" The stacks of boxes, the cots—these men had turned the barn into a survival fortress.

"Kyle." Sara stared at him through a swollen eye. "You have to go." She could barely speak.

"Shh." He pulled the knife out of his belt and sawed at the rope. He didn't have the heart to tell her it was too late. The things outside would be on them soon. They couldn't outrun it all, and in truth, he was sick of running. He didn't have many years of hiding left in him, if he had any at all. There was no escaping what was coming. The cacophony outside grew louder as if to agree. Hundreds of feral voices crying out in unison for their blood. "Let's just get you down, Songbird."

The corners of her lips twitched. "Hate that name." A line of bloody drool ran from her mouth down her chin. He gently brushed it away with the back of his gun hand. The world blurred as hot tears filled his eyes.

"I didn't do nothin'! I was here the whole time!"

Kyle had forgotten about the man in the back. Tim rushed in with Kaylee in tow and two bags slung across his back. He stopped in the doorway when he saw Sara hanging from the rope. Kaylee let out a gasp as the behemoth roared loud enough that it echoed.

Kyle's tears vanished as quickly as they'd appeared. "Tim, keep your gun on him."

Tim stared at Kyle before he recalled the gun in his hand and trained it on the kidnapper.

The ever-tightening ring of monsters drew closer. The endless groans and howls outside were a zoo on a full moon.

The rope spiraled apart with a soft snap, and Kyle grabbed Sara before she could collapse. He set her on her feet and held her to make sure she wouldn't fall.

She leaned against him, throwing her arms over his shoulders. He wanted to be happy that they'd found her. He wanted them all to be okay. He wanted Kaylee's family friends to be real, and to have a place where they could live out the end of days in quiet. It didn't look like any of that was in the cards.

The first reverberations from the behemoth's stomping shook the ground. With paws big enough to crush a car, it would make short work of the barn. Maybe the silver rounds could kill it, but that wouldn't stop everything else. These things had wiped out humanity by crashing upon every defense they put up. Knocking down walls and crushing tanks. Killing the soldiers who'd tried to fight them a legion at a time.

The memories tried to claw their way up and take him back with them when Tim spoke up. "What about him?"

"It's a Phoebe. They're songbirds. The first picture I ever drew was one of them."

The other two men stared at him. They'd warmed up a bit, but they weren't overly polite.

"What?" Kyle couldn't focus. It was all too much.

"Does the songbird ever sing?" Kyle asked as they walked down the highway.

"Don't call me that." Sara brushed a piece of hair from her eyes. "It makes me sound like your sixteen-year-old girlfriend. I don't swing that way, and I'm not sixteen."

Kyle laughed. Not a chuckle but a good, genuine laugh. It had been a long time. Sara glanced sideways at him, but he just smiled back.

"You're too young for me anyway."

"I didn't do nothin'!" The man looked back and forth between Kyle and Sara.

Screeches and moans, closer and closer.

"Kyle." Tim eyed the door. His knuckles were white, the grip on his gun absolute. "What we gonna do?"

Sara leaned against him, barely able to stand on her own. "I'm sorry, Kyle. I'm so sorry." She whispered the words into his neck, and they chilled him. He'd expected Kaylee to start sobbing, but she didn't.

Kyle squeezed her as tight as he dared. No way of knowing how much damage those thugs had done. "It's alright. There's nobody I'd rather spend the last of my time with." That was the god's honest truth. She was the only family he'd had in a long time, and if they had to die, he wanted to do it together.

The remaining man fidgeted from foot to foot, ready to run, but there was nowhere to go. He didn't take his eyes off at Tim's gun. His eyes lit up. "The truck! We can get in—"

The behemoth's roar washed out the last of his words. Kyle stared at the man without blinking. "Truck's haven't worked in a decade. The gas went bad, and the electrics were fried." Kyle put his right hand onto the butt of his gun. "Your time is up."

"No! No! Wait!" Without asking, he walked toward the corpse of the big man with the shotgun.

"What the fuck are you doing?" The muscles in Tim's neck stood out.

"He keeps the keys on him. It's an old diesel. No electric parts. We kept it gassed up in case we needed to run away. Road's clear east of here for miles." He knelt next to the corpse and started digging in its jeans. He threw them an ingratiating smile that made Kyle want to vomit.

He wouldn't get his hopes up. When things seemed too good to be true, they usually were. The man's hand brushed the shotgun next to his friend's corpse as he dug in the dead man's pockets. A round burst from Tim's gun, drowning out the sound of the incoming horde.

"Jesus Christ, man!" He threw up his arms, the keys held high. A glance at Tim said it had been an accident, but he didn't look

157

upset. The muscles in his jaw were visible; his eyes cold as a killer's. He was harder than Kyle had given him credit for.

"Touch that again and you're dead." The barrel stared into the man's chest. The boy who'd panicked at the thought of starving to death had pulled together into something else.

The man stood slowly. "See? I ain't like them."

Kyle lifted Sara off her feet, cradling her in his arms. "Shut up and give him the keys." Kyle nodded to Tim.

Sara groaned, and her eyes rolled back. Kyle and her were the first ones out the door, Kaylee in tow. "Just leave me, Kyle," Sara whispered in his ear. The moonlight revealed a hulking shape growing ever closer.

Girl in the window. The behemoth sliding into the building as—

"Kyle," Sara whispered.

He shook his head, chasing away the ghosts of the past as they circled him. They were out of time. He ran around the side of the barn as the screams of the damned edged closer. The old truck wasn't in as bad a shape as it looked from a distance. Free of rust and damage. Salvation made by Ford eighty years before. He set Sara on her feet.

Tim opened the door as the bandit followed around the corner behind them. Kyle threw his backpack into the bed and stepped aside. The slamming feet of the behemoth sent bolts of agony through his skull..

"Get in." Kyle picked Kaylee up and threw her into the cab.

Sara climbed in after her, wincing and halting with every move.

"You want to stay alive?"

The kidnapper nodded as he glanced over his shoulder. The *tik tik tik* of dozens of claws tapping the pavement drifted from the road. A sniffer shrieked.

"Give him the keys, Tim, and get in the back with me." Kyle jumped over the edge of the truck and into the bed.

"Are you kidd—"

"Do what the fuck I say!" Kyle tore open his bag. Metal screeched under the feet of something impossibly large.

Tim opened his mouth to say something else as the first crawler barreled around the corner, followed by two more. His handgun rang out as the bandit, eyes wide and face pale, yanked open the truck and jumped behind the wheel.

The shots took the first crawler down. The one behind it tripped over its companion, its doglike head slamming into the pavement. The next shot caught the third one in the leg, knocking it down. Others would arrive any second.

Tim hopped into the back of the truck. "Go!" He pounded on the window separating the cab and the bed as Kyle found what he was looking for. Sniffers called to their brethren. An army of monsters converged on their position. The truck roared to life as Kyle dropped the old magazine from his gun and slammed the new one in.

The one with the silver-tipped bullets.

With a flick of his thumb, he locked the first round into place as an ape creature rounded the corner. Kyle saw it before Tim did. He let out a breath, aimed the weapon, and fired a round into the thing's misshapen head.

Its skull snapped back. The skin of its face melted away instantly. It clawed and scratched at the hole as bone and sinew bubbled and oozed. The screams ceased. The creature fell forward onto the crawler with the wounded leg. The silver worked faster than acid; within seconds, the upper part torso had dissolved into a puddle of black goo.

"Go! Go! Go!" Tim beat furiously on the side of the truck.

The engine screamed as it dropped into gear. Kyle had just enough time to think, *"Thank god the guy can drive a stick,"* before a dozen more crawlers careened around the edge of the barn.

Tim popped off one shot before the truck jerked forward. He fell, teetering on the edge of the gate as rocks sprayed at the creatures behind. Kyle had the presence of mind to grab the edge of the truck, and managed to get a handful of Tim's shirt. Instead of falling out, Tim flew face first into the rear gate. A tooth flew out in the spray of blood from his mouth.

The truck angled off the gravel and over the grass back toward the highway. The crawlers were fast, but they couldn't keep up with a vehicle.

Kyle pulled Tim closer. "Tim!" He could barely hear himself over the creatures around them and the engine's roar. The behemoth's stomps were right on top of them, but Kyle couldn't see it. He let go of the truck and flipped Tim onto his side. The kid could have killed himself. Snapped his neck on the gate. His face was a bloody wreck. Red ran from his nose and mouth in a thick stream. When he noticed the rise and fall of Tim's chest, he let out a breath he didn't realize he'd been holding.

The barn exploded.

The behemoth dwarfed the landscape, as if the Earth itself had risen to kill them. It didn't slow as pieces of timber flew off into the night in every direction. The horns on its head glinted in the starlight. It caught sight of their truck and let out a deafening bellow, a cry that challenged the gods.

Kyle's heart hammered a dirge for the remainder of humanity. Seeing that thing drained his will. There was no victory. A legion of monsters swarmed around it. Dozens. Hundreds. A thousand.

He couldn't look away from where that girl had been seconds before. The dust washed over him and stung his eyes, blocking out the little light left behind the red clouds. The emergency sirens kept wailing their useless warning. Five of those things had come and gone down the street, the lanes full of creatures ripping people out from under cars. He watched through the broken window as two of the creatures that reminded him of hairless apes threw a man off the roof of the building across from him. It caught sight of him and screamed, vanishing as it returned the way it had come.

Coming for him, no doubt. He didn't care anymore. He'd been so scared the last two months that he'd welcome the end. This last wave of creatures was a death he looked forward to after living in terror for so long. An expected friend hours overdue. The National

Guard hadn't been able to do anything. And now Kyle sat alone in his apartment, waiting.

Someone screamed in the hallway. They were in the building. The furniture he'd piled in front of the door wouldn't keep them out. He was going to die here.

A second earth-shaking rumble brought him around. Tim lay bleeding and unconscious next to him. Kaylee screamed his name from the cab.

"Kyle! Kyle!"

The leviathan gained on them with every second. The wind slapped Kyle's face. Monsters had closed in from all around on the highway in front of them; an infinite legion of death. The truck jerked to avoid two crawlers jumping out from behind a vehicle.

He could hear the labored breath as the giant grew ever closer. He could feel the heat, smell the stink of decay issuing from its mouth.

Kaylee screamed and the truck jerked again, nearly spilling Kyle from the back as they swerved to avoid a car. Tim slid across the bed and slammed his already damaged face into the vehicle's side. Kyle had to do something.

He became aware of it as its teeth chomped together.

But he couldn't.

Kyle looked up as he drew another gasp, trying desperately to catch his breath so he could flee further.

He couldn't save anybody.

The thing once called Betty shambled toward him.

He was as broken as the world they lived in.

Another swerve brought him back into the moment. Kaylee screamed as they ran something over.

The truck listed dangerously, and Kyle was sure they'd crash. They corrected back to the left. The bandit caught Kyle's gaze in the rearview.

"Do something, man!"

There was nothing to do. They were dead; the reaper just hadn't reached them yet. Kaylee buried her face in Sara's side, her little arms wrapped so tightly around her waist that it must have hurt them both.

Sara didn't move, just sat there facing the bandit without seeing him. Her eyes were half rolled into her skull, her expression slack. She focused and caught Kyle's gaze for a moment. No words passed between them, but they didn't need to.

He turned back to the thing behind them. It roared again, opening its maw wide enough to swallow a man whole. Endless darkness and teeth yawned before him.

He squeezed the trigger as the truck hit a bump in the road, and the shot went wide. Aiming more carefully, looking the behemoth in its dead eyes, he fired a second shot. It hit the thing in its exposed chest, but if it damaged the creature at all, it didn't show.

He unloaded eight rounds into it.

It didn't stop. If anything, it was closer now. The hot stink of its breath washed over him, recalling the memory of opening the curtain to a scalding shower, and the smell of rancid meat in a fridge.

His hands shook as he lowered the gun. He dropped to the floor of the truck and grabbed his bag, digging furiously for another set of silver rounds. His canteen, his blanket, his shelter half; all of it cast aside in a manic flurry, flying out of the truck into darkness.

They jolted right again to avoid something else in the road. Kyle grabbed metal near the bottom of the bag as a sniffer wailed from the highway in front of them, its cry piercing the night.

The truck swerved again, too late. For a split second, everything in the truck bed floated. The bag drifted away from him in slow motion. It flew over the tailgate, and the creature not twenty feet behind them trampled it.

But the last magazine of silver was in his hand.

He dropped the spent magazine from his .45 and slapped the new one in. The giant closed the last of the distance. Three stories of hate towered over him, looking down at its next meal.

The truck swayed back and forth.

The wind roared in Kyle's ears.

The sound of other creatures faded, left behind in their mad dash for something close to safety.

In the entire world, it was just the two of them.

He pointed his weapon into the thing's gaping maw and squeezed the trigger three times.

The roar that issued from its mouth wasn't one of rage and hunger but of pain and surprise. It slowed, stumbled, and fell a dozen yards behind the truck. The left side of its face, where Kyle's third bullet had caught it, bubbled and turned pink.

Its cries became high-pitched moans of pain. Even as they pulled farther away from its prone form, a horn fell off its melting head.

One of the things that had wiped out cities and armies was dead by his hand.

He dropped the gun as the truck jerked left to avoid another abomination, and stared slack-jawed at the world behind him. He'd overcome death again. He'd stared into the frigid eyes of the biggest enemy humanity had ever known and come out on the other side, killing it when even the mightiest soldiers could not.

Crazy. It was all crazy. Kyle the Professor had become Kyle the Monster Hunter. Kyle the Savior. Kyle the Survivor.

He laughed an insane sort of laugh. A loud, belly-shaking bellow that poured out as tears formed in his eyes.

Memories washed over him, and everything went black.

Chapter 10

Sara

The spots in her mind, the monsters, closed in as the shooting began. She didn't need to fall into a scanner trance to feel them, not when hundreds were all around. A rush of nightmares moving in to dine on them. Above it all, the cancerous thing she'd met on the highway shone as a black beacon making its way toward them. Already, its mind groped out to touch her, a slimy appendage on some unfathomable other seizing her. As the alien presence grazed the edges of her consciousness, a chill ran through her.

It noticed.

She didn't see the gunfight in the barn as the thing slid toward her.

She wasn't in her body anymore; she was in a hurricane. Pieces of pictures flew by; memories of alien worlds where the rules of the universe as she knew them no longer applied. Colors were wrong, or they weren't colors at all. Shapes without names zipped past her, and impossible geography rained all around. Above it all stood the Walking Cancer.

Stood wasn't right. It existed everywhere around her. It permeated this place and pulled her in. It was strong enough to rip her from her body and put her into its own. It had her under glass. The Sara slide to be dissected, studied, and put away.

She struggled in its grasp, but she was nothing. It didn't have hands, but it stilled her with a touch.

In the real world, she became aware of Kyle fighting for his life as shotgun blasts stung her ears. She had to get free and help him; she had to—

The connection broke. A car radio passing through a tunnel. The thing still lurked outside of her, but it had lost its grip.

Its displeasure was heat coming off a hot stove. It wasn't used to being outwitted.

She had to help Kyle, do something before these kidnappers killed him. A quick survey of the situation said things weren't going their way. Two dead men sat piled in the doorway. Mark unloaded round after round from his shotgun into the wall. Number Four stood next to him, holding a pistol and looking ready to run.

She didn't know if Kyle was alive. One of the giant creatures grew closer with every breath, and the countless smaller ones were a colony of wasps moving in to snuff out invaders. Above them all was the Walking Cancer. Circling. Gaining momentum to crash down on her again.

The utter hopelessness of the situation struck her all at once. After all that running, all that hiding, it was going to end here in a dirty barn, surrounded by people she didn't know. She thought she should be afraid, but deep down she wasn't. There was nothing to be afraid of anymore.

She'd felt the strange wiggle of her mother and sister leaving their bodies the first time she'd ever scanned. They didn't cease to be, just left. Went on. Moved elsewhere. Here at the end, it made everything less big, less scary. A few more minutes of pain, and everything would be okay again.

But Kaylee might still be out there. That little girl had gotten nothing but a few miserable years on a miserable planet.

"Kyle! There's only—" She'd wanted to shout a warning, but Mark turned around and socked her in the mouth with the butt of his gun. Her lip burst open, and her bottom teeth dug into her tongue.

The Walking Cancer swooped in as—

It was ill pleased. Nothing had ever gotten away before. It didn't know that people could walk in this place the same way it did. It hadn't foreseen that, and it wasn't often surprised. It swirled in a maelstrom around her, locking her in and keeping her still.

Questions assailed her, but not with words. Not with thoughts either. With emotion. Feelings that dragged up memories of her own.

A cloud in the sky. She was nine years old and wondering why she didn't fit in with the rest of the school. They all talked about Jesus as if he'd spoken to them personally, but she never heard anything. Not a whisper or a word. She looked at the cloud and wondered, "What are you?" when she really wanted to know what she *was*.

The Walking Cancer's filth coated the memory, ruining it forever. It made the thought into a shape and passed it to her through the blackness between them. It burned as it forced its way into her mind and put the question on her lap.

"WHAT ARE YOU?"

Things were happening outside of her. Kyle lived still, though not for long.

The eerie geography swept by faster. Circles without edges flew past. Squares that smelled like yellow and tasted like triangles moved by her, close enough to feel their wind. The Walking Cancer wanted answers, and it sensed her hesitation.

It didn't see people as people. They were animals. Food and nuisances. Things to be collected and set aside. She was new. It didn't snuff out her will to live as it did others, at least not right away.

It could though; she understood that much. It could shut down her brain and make her die on the spot. It could turn her into a meat puppet that danced on its strings. It had done it thousands of times before.

The window worked both ways. She could see it, and suddenly she understood. If it could do it, so could she. It was impossibly large, blanketing everything in this nowhere place, but the rules of the world didn't apply here.

She had power too.

She was an egg in the void. A thing of vast potential and infinite curiosity, the whole world contained within. The universe had started this way. All the promise of all reality held in one tiny spot before shooting outward to create everything.

It loomed closer. Curious. It hadn't learned so much about people from other minds it had invaded. It wanted their knowledge. It wanted to know what made them tick so it could savor them better; taste them fully and use them to their utmost potential.

She wasn't the universe though. She was a snake—big, red, and deadly, bursting from her shell.

She struck out as the shell fell aside. The thing reeled back. Not scared, just surprised.

Kyle's eyes widened at the sight of her. The slow drip of blood from her mouth patted against her chest. She'd never seen him cry, but he wanted to. She didn't need to be psychic to see that. Something about that hurt more than anything else.

He screamed for Tim over his shoulder.

"Kyle." She had to swallow blood before she could continue. "You have to go."

"Shh." He couldn't feel the Walking Cancer building up around them. She could. It drilled into her, tearing through her defenses and touching her soft center. "Let's just get you down, Songbird." He said it as if he were a stoic warrior from some Greek play. Any other time she would have rolled her eyes, but she didn't want to spoil the little time they had left.

"Hate that name."

Tears welled in his eyes. This was the end for him too. They'd had a good run. They'd gotten more out of their last years on the ruined Earth than most, little as it might be. She wanted to smile for him, to be brave and show him it was okay. They weren't dying; they were moving on.

The man in the back said something she didn't catch as Tim and Kaylee entered. Then Kyle, Tim, and the last remaining bandit spoke, but she didn't hear them. The Walking Cancer danced around her. It tingled across her skin. Static on a television. It wanted in. It wanted to tear her apart. It would take her piece by piece and see how everything worked. It was close enough that she imagined she could hear its steps approaching. If she were stronger, she would have put a bullet into Kaylee's head right there to keep her from suffering.

If they hadn't come to get her, they would be far away. They could have heard the monsters coming and gone the long way around.

Kyle placated her, but she didn't want to hear it. She had to focus everything inward to keep these last minutes. If she lost focus, that thing would shut her off and take her in.

Tim's gunshot almost let the Walking Cancer slip past her defenses. She wouldn't let it. She was the egg again, impenetrable even in the palm of a giant.

"Jesus Christ, man!" Fourth Man held up truck keys. The conversation played again in her mind. They had a truck. An escape.

But she couldn't get away. It had marked her. It knew her inside now, deep inside where nobody else could ever go. It slithered across her memories and left pieces of itself. It would find her again. It would track her down.

Sudden pain brought her around as Kyle carried her into the moonlight. Everything out here was a bad horror movie. The woods and distant terrain crawled as the beasts circled closer and closer. Something enormous approached, shaking the world.

"Just leave me, Kyle." He had to. If he didn't, they would be hunted no matter where they went. She was a beacon now.

His jaw slackened and his eyes dulled. He didn't fall into himself the same way she did. He didn't have extra parts; he was broken. A stalled machine winding down faster and faster.

"Kyle."

He came right back and took her around the side of the barn to the truck she hadn't seen on the way in. She hoped for their sake it worked, but it didn't look like salvation to her, it looked like another broken promise in the making.

Tim unlocked the door, and Kyle shoved Kaylee in. Sara climbed in after, her insides twisting painfully. The constant howling of their would-be killers drowned out everything, making it hard to focus. She had to though. She had to hold on long enough to find some space to breathe. Kyle wouldn't let her stay here. He'd die first. She had to make a plan. Had to think. Had to escape that goddamn noise.

"Are we going to get away?" Kaylee stared at her with eyes wide the way only a fearful child's could be.

"We'll be fine." The pain in her side blackened her vision, stealing her focus. Kaylee threw her arms around Sara's waist. She cried out as one of her broken ribs stabbed something inside. Her focus shattered.

The memory sat in her lap in a dark room. No doors, no windows, and no lights. The air hung heavy with the creature. It permeated everything. "WHAT ARE YOU?" The memory burned, but she couldn't move it.

It was done asking. It wanted answers, and it wanted them now. Its fingers crawled through her mind, paging through her files, browsing for her secrets. Her self-awareness stretched painfully as it forced itself inside.

Time ceased. The building exploded, Tim yelled, Kaylee screamed, and the giant creature grew ever closer.

Another memory came away from her, covered in the Walking Cancer's filth.

She knelt in the prayer closet, her dad standing over her. He hit her with the switch again.

"Pray! Pray God forgives you!"

She was caught kissing Jodie Miller behind the barn. The whole church knew. The whole town knew. Jodie was sent to live with her aunt and uncle in the city. Sara was stuck here.

But she wanted to go. More than anything, she wanted to be free of this place and the people in it. They hated her. They told her she was bad. To them, everything was bad. God wasn't a bastion of love and forgiveness; he was a font of wrath and rage. They took their God with a heavy serving of Old Testament.

But she wouldn't be free. She screamed as Daddy hit her on her bare back until it bled. Again, and again, and again.

"Pray, you little brat!"

Momma tried to stop him, and she got hit too. The truth was, she would never get away, and she knew it.

The Walking Cancer grabbed onto that last part and shoved her face in it. It held her nose under it so she could get a good whiff of the memory.

"NEVER GET AWAY!"

They were trying to run. Even now, the connection thinned as the distance between her and the thing grew. It wasn't going to let her. It stepped inside of her more fully, wearing her.

She looked at Number Four as they sped away. Through the window, an endless plague of monsters spread across the road. Kyle stood in the back, staring at the death closing in on them.

Looking for a hairbrush as a child.

"WHERE IS IT?"

Pictures of a silver cloud rising above Chicago and killing all the monsters there invaded her mind. It wanted to know where that thought went, where it came from. It set it on her lap for her to see. A piece of someone ripped out of them, kept by this thing and made into a, "Have You Seen Me?" poster.

She wasn't afraid to die, but the thought of being stuck like this forever terrified her. If there was a hell, this was it.

In the outside world, she lifted her arm to grab the wheel from the driver and crash their vehicle.

"NO!" She fought back, holding the arm in mid-air. "NO! NO! NO! NO!"

Daddy hitting her in the back over and over.

"NEVER GET AWAY!"

A cloud of silver rising above the world, raining down and cleansing it.

"WHERE IS IT?"

She didn't know. She couldn't tell it. But it saw things differently. It swept through the memories Sara had of Kaylee and her mother. Kaylee's father dying. The lab.

"Pacific Applied Biology Technology," Momma said. "The cutting edge in biological research. All those taxpayer dollars and we can't get one damn thing to work."

"Alchemists tried for a thousand years to turn lead to gold." Heather leaned back in her chair. "They never succeeded either, but they advanced science anyway."

The Walking Cancer saw something it liked and moved deeper in that direction.

"The biological compound has a ninety-eight-point-seven percent similarity to silver."

It walked through the memory and into the place where she kept her thoughts of Kaylee.

Sara sat in a chair in the bedroom they'd had when her mother had taken her away from the church. The first place where she might belong. This room had been hope.

Now the air oozed with the Walking Cancer. She could almost see it, a shifting glimmer at the edge of her vison in the nowhere place. A tall, gray thing. A caricature of an old movie alien. It had no mouth, just two great black eyes. Those eyes scanned the room, seeing past the walls into the things she kept there.

It sniffed deeply, breathing in Kaylee's scent as it grew farther away in the real world. Its intentions were clear. Sara didn't know what it was looking for, but Kaylee might. It would find Kaylee, and it would make her talk to it the same way it had countless people before.

She imagined what it would be like for Kaylee to have this thing in her head during her last moments. Worse than pain. Worse than anything that little girl could imagine. Sara wasn't going to let that happen. She hid the memories of Kaylee deeper, making lies to cover them up.

Miriam looked over at her companion, Heather. "We'll hide it at the bottom of the ocean. Only mermaids and madmen will be able to get to it."

The Walking Cancer stopped scanning through the memories of Kaylee and focused on the new thought. A dog that had caught a fresh scent.

Its hands, or whatever it used to invade her thoughts, rummaged around in the place where the new memory hid, away from the room where thoughts of Kaylee rested.

She slammed the door and locked it behind them as they drifted out.

"Here." Heather handed a flash drive to Miriam. "Everything we need is in here."

"Shit." The word bounced around the walls of her mind. She hadn't meant to do that. The fake hard drive, the one she'd invented to draw away the creature, stood next to the real one Kyle had found. Her duplicity became clear.

She had to buy more time. They were getting farther away by the second, but they were still too close for her to break free.

"NEVER GET AWAY!"

It reached deeper, going for her core. If it couldn't have her, it was going to shut her down. It would drag the information from Kaylee or Kyle.

Seizing her deepest mind, it plunged her under. Everything became ice.

It wasn't wrong. There was no escape. Even if they fled, they couldn't run forever. She hurt. Even in this dream world, she hurt terribly. It knew her now, and any small safety left to her on the dead Earth was gone.

"NEVER GET AWAY!" The voice came straight out of a nightmare. An alien drone free of any semblance of morality. It wasn't indifferent to her pain; it was curious. It enjoyed her

suffering as an experience. Even in its search for the source of the silver cloud, it took time to savor her agony.

Its appendage dug ever deeper, closer and closer to her secret heart. It would turn her off. A biological machine with the key removed. The soul neatly cut off from the body.

Its fingers touched the spot it sought. She held her breath.

But the end didn't come.

Something outside changed, and it hesitated. It looked outward as a silver round hit the giant creature in the eye, melting part of its face into a puddle of sludge.

She seized the moment. The door to her inner mind slammed closed. The Walking Cancer's mental arm, the thing it had used to probe inside her, came off with a snap and a shriek.

Pain. Fear. Pain. Fear.

It had never known either of those things. It had been born into the world with one purpose, and it served that purpose well. Find threats to the Horde and eliminate them. Give the Horde room to grow. Devour resistance.

Fear. Pain. Fear. Pain.

The tables had turned. It tried to pull out and get away again and again. The connection grew thin with distance. This giant alien other now tried to flee like a wounded animal. It couldn't kill her. It couldn't hurt her.

But she could hurt it.

The giant red snake at the center of the universe reared up, free of its shell.

Pain. Fear. Pain. Fear.

It wasn't just large, it was venomous. Hungry.

FEAR. PAIN. FEAR. PAIN.

A smile tweaked her lips. The things that had wiped out humanity could feel fear.

The connection grew weaker as the snake slithered toward its prey, the gray demon with its arm stuck in a door. She thought of her mother and sister as the galactic snake lunged forward.

She hoped it gave them some satisfaction in whatever afterlife they'd found.

The connection broke before the snake's teeth could dig in.

A hot flash of anger, not from the creature, but from herself, accompanied her back into her body. She wanted it dead. She'd been robbed of her recompense.

Her rage didn't last long. The world inside her had dulled the pain in her body, but in the real world, it returned in full force.

The truck sped along the highway going east. No sign of the damned in front of them, but…

"Where's Kyle?" The words came out as if she had a mouth full of cotton. Everything tipped sideways. Black spots swam before her.

Number Four glanced sidelong at her. Her arm still hovered halfway between them. The car slowed and weaved through several wrecked vehicles as she lowered it, the joints popping. She'd been holding it there as tight as a bar of steel.

"He fell down." Kaylee buried her face in Sara's side.

Sara turned quickly, bringing the spots back and hurting every muscle in her torso. Both Kyle and Tim lay prone in the bed. The hills and trees outside gave way to valleys and forests before opening onto breathtaking ravines. She'd forgotten what driving was like. Sara locked her gaze on the pool of blood in the back.

"I'm scared, Sara." Kaylee hadn't moved since they got in the truck. She exuded fear in great, stinking waves. Her every thought was of an early death. For someone so young to have such terrible concerns hurt Sara's heart. Her childhood had been awful, but she couldn't imagine what this world must be like for Kaylee.

"How much gas—" Sara swallowed, trying to force the dryness from her mouth. Her physical senses were slow to return. Every part of her conscious mind felt as if it had woken from a deep sleep suddenly disturbed. "How much gas is left?"

Number Four looked at the gauge and glanced at her again. He radiated fear as well, but not like Kaylee. His was the fear of consequences, of a man who'd done wrong and knew Johnny Law was coming.

"Fourth of a tank." His voice dripped with anxieties, not of the things behind them, but of the future.

"Pull over." She needed to know Kyle and Tim were still alive.

He stared at her, his mouth open.

"Pull over. Now."

"Them things are still close."

She was well aware. She could sense them as if she were scanning. In fact, she could feel Kyle and Tim as well, their unconsciousness pulsing with the pain in their bodies.

It hit her all at once. The piece of the Walking Cancer she'd slammed in her mental door still wriggled on the floor of her mind. It presented no danger. It had done something though. The taint of that thing had opened up another door inside her. She flexed outward, still in her body, but beyond it too.

The fear that Number Four radiated came from guilt, not monsters. He'd done a lot of bad things since the world ended, but deep down he considered himself a good man.

Kaylee's anxieties and wishes were a child's. Let everyone be okay. Let this end. Let it all be a bad dream.

In the back, Tim dreamt of nothing. Inadequacies shed off him. Flakes of perceived failures beyond his control chipped away and surrounded him.

Kyle dreamed bad dreams of dead friends and ended worlds. Something sick pulsed in his brain. A cancer or a growth that would have been treatable in the old world, but would kill him now.

The shock of finding the sickness hit her in the gut. He didn't have long. It was a wonder he could still stand. Spider webs of red and white growth laced the pink insides of his cerebral tissues. His pain must have been unbearable.

It all made sense. The blackouts. The mood swings. The headaches.

She closed her eyes to keep the tears away, but it did no good. She took a deep breath as the first salty drop formed. "Oh, Kyle."

She whispered it, but Number Four heard her. "Do you want me to pull over?"

A single tear ran down her dirty face. She watched it fall in the side mirror, leaving a streak of purity on her stained visage. "Just keep going."

There was no mistaking it. That thing in his brain would kill him as dead as the creatures behind them would.

"What's wrong, Sara?" For the first time, Kaylee removed her face from Sara's side. She must have sensed the sudden tension, the absolute certain dread that filled Sara as her breath caught in her chest.

Kyle didn't have long to live.

Chapter 11

Kyle

They sat under the apple tree, sunned and warm. His dark skin made a sharp contrast with her alabaster complexion as their bodies glistened in the afterglow of sex. The clouds overhead bore mute testimony to their tryst, paying it barely a glance as they swept by. They had more important things to do than bother two lovers in a perfect world. No blight reached here. It was a sanctuary. A Garden of Eden tucked away in the Smokey Mountains.

Karen kissed his chest, making an outline of his heart. "I love you."

He smiled one of his biggest and boldest smiles, the kind he reserved for lovers and bartenders. "Oh yeah?"

She stopped kissing him, turning her face up to look into his eyes. She wore a dangerous expression, the kind a woman scorned might have before slapping a mouthy lover. "That is not the correct response, Professor."

"Professor?" His smile widened. The ray of sunshine that illuminated them didn't shine as bright as that smile. "Am I to profess my love for you then?"

She slapped his chest. "I suppose I could find another man to kiss softly under an apple tree."

He erupted into laughter. He took her in his arms and lifted her gently to his face, kissing her for a long, tender moment. He loved her. He loved her so much it hurt, even if he wasn't sure why. "That would break my heart."

She pulled back and gazed at him. The apple tree. The mountains. The clouds and the sunshine. All of it highlighted her perfectly, but none of it could touch her.

There was more than love in her eyes though. There was sadness, deep and old. A pain she'd kept inside endlessly. It brought a frown to her lips. The sun hid behind the clouds as if to be spared her misery. "You're breaking *my* heart, Kyle."

He sat up on his elbows, taken aback by her serious tone. "What?" Those words didn't make sense here. This was a safe place. A refuge from the storm. A spot to contemplate one's next move.

"Watching you hurt so much breaks my heart. Come home. You don't have to suffer anymore. It's okay."

The air turned cold and sour. This wasn't the Garden of Eden, just another chilly mountaintop. Aches and pains sprouted all over his body. Or maybe they'd been there all along and he'd forgotten.

"Don't." He set her aside. They weren't naked anymore. He wore the same ratty shirt and pants he had for weeks. She wore that blue shirt she'd died in. The holes from the bullets remained, but the blood was gone. "I don't like that song you're singing, Songbird."

He knew the words were wrong the moment he'd spoken them, but she pointed it out anyway. "I'm not your Songbird. That's the other lady in your life. She doesn't need you anymore. None of them do. Come home."

Karen reached for his hand, but he pulled. He didn't know what she was talking about, but it felt wrong. Everything off this mountain was remembered through static. He couldn't recall what had happened before.

Footsteps on the grass crunched behind him. Kyle turned, and the sudden spin hurt his head, though he didn't know why.

Richard wore the bent glasses he had in the years Kyle knew him. His dark hair stuck to the side of his face the same way it had the day he'd been shot. No crimson stain there either, but something wasn't right.

Kyle could see through him. He could see through them both.

"She's right, man. You're hurting for nothing. You can't help. Just let go."

His friends' transparency didn't bother him, but Richard's words did. He was wrong. Someone needed him. A few people. He had to remember who. "Fuck you, Dick."

He'd said the words a thousand times, usually with a smile. When Richard would suggest going back to the city. *Fuck you, Dick.* When he tried to bargain for the chocolate they'd found in an old warehouse. *Fuck you, Dick.* When he'd suggest with a sly smile that Karen thought of him when she slept with Kyle. *Fuck you, Dick.*

That old humor was gone. Richard meant every word he said, and Kyle did too. He tried to stand up, but everything jumped, as if the world had taken a deep breath. He closed his eyes as his senses did a pirouette. When he opened them, he was on the ground, looking up at his dead friends. His dead family.

"Just don't get up, Kyle." He didn't know which one had spoken. Maybe all of them.

"Go away. Leave me alone." He closed his eyes as the pain inside his head revved up. A motorcycle about to be driven hard after a long winter. They shouldn't be saying this. He would have died to protect them. He'd killed all the people that killed them. He'd do anything to safeguard the people he loved. They knew that, or at least he hoped they did.

"You are alone, but you don't have to be." The phantom sensation of Karen's hand touching his cheek chilled him, and then it was gone.

The wind shrieked around him, and it grew cold. So damn cold. Everything hurt. His left leg. His right arm. His head and back. The shrapnel in his shoulder burned. Everything protested.

They weren't on a mountain, just near one. Still, his old friends looked on.

"Don't go back."

But he did. They vanished, a whisper in a storm, replaced by the sounds of an old diesel truck flying through Tennessee's cold dark.

Kyle opened his eyes and looked at the night sky. Clouds covered most of the moon, but some of its light shone on his situation. The scuffed truck bed under him shifted and shook as they drove over grass that had retaken parts of the road.

He stayed that way for a long time, staring at the moon. Not in appreciation for his recent brush with death, or even to savor being alive, but because everything hurt. His brain pulsed with every bump as if it might explode. Something wasn't right up there, but even that feeling took a back seat to the ache in his heart.

Richard and Karen. Karen and Richard. He tried not to think about them. Lamenting the death of close friends and lovers did nothing to keep him alive. But they'd been there. Right there. It had been so real he could still feel Karen kissing the outline on his chest. They'd begged him to stay, and he'd wanted to. Anything had to be better than this.

He stared at the big moon, bashful behind the wall of clouds. *Why not just go?* He didn't think he was far off anyway. Every day it became a little harder to wake up. Every minute he slowed a little.

Tim groaned nearby.

But right here, people were in trouble. Sara had saved his life a thousand times, and he hers. Maybe she could get by just fine without him, but he wouldn't gamble her life on it. Until they were safe, he wouldn't let them go. People relied on him. People still needed him.

After a decade without machinery, all of its clicks, whines, and growls were as alien as the creature he'd killed. In thirteen short years, humanity had gone from the dominant force on the planet, masters of both technology and biology, to rats hiding under the heels of giants. But on this lonely road, the old machinery whirred away, chugging toward an unknown fate.

"Sara." He called her name loudly as he sat up. He took it inch-by-inch, certain that if he tried to do it all at once, he would pass out. "Sara."

The little window into the cab clicked and slid open. A woman's face appeared, bruised and battered. Kyle stared at it, not understanding who this person was. Both eyes were black, and one had swollen closed. Her nose might have been broken, and blood stained everything below it. Her lips split in two spots, and a bruise on her cheek stood out in horrible contrast to her white skin.

He stared at Sara's face, his sadness mirrored there. Her eyes were moist, and her broken lips trembled. He touched her chin gently, not wanting to cause her further pain. "It'll be alright."

She sniffed back tears and pulled away to wipe them. He couldn't imagine what she must be going through. He knew damned well the things she'd suffered before the world turned up the pain. For her to have to relive all of that.

"I'm sorry. We should have stayed together." He had to yell to be heard over the wind.

She shook her head and took a deep breath. "You saved me, you big idiot."

Kyle stuck his head into the window. The noise of the rushing wind died away. The inside of the truck reeked of assholes and onions. Kaylee looked at him from Sara's side, her eyes wide and fearful. The remaining kidnapper glanced over, not taking his attention off the road. His posture said he feared retribution. The sight of him brought the adrenaline back full force, as if Kyle were staring down the Behemoth again.

"Yours is coming."

The man opened his mouth as terror lit his face, but Sara spoke first. "Is this the time for that?"

The bandit clamped his mouth closed.

"We're all alive, right?"

Again, the man's lips twitched as if he would speak, but he wisely decided against it.

"Is Tim all right?" Sara asked.

Kyle pulled his head back out and slid over to Tim. He was breathing regularly, but hadn't woken. Kyle turned him onto his back and looked as closely as he could in the moonlight. He hadn't knocked out one tooth on the gate of the truck, he'd knocked out several. His chin held a bruise even darker than the one on Sara's face. A small miracle he'd stayed on his side, otherwise he might have choked on all the blood caking his face.

Kyle returned to the window. "He's hurt, but he's alive. How long have I been out?"

"Half hour or so. We've been lucky. The road east hasn't been blocked yet."

Lucky indeed. The road outside grew wild and rugged. Long grass sprouted from in between the cracks in the cement, most of it blighted. Cars that looked ancient but had only been sitting for a decade dotted the landscape. Howls and roars echoed from the lightless wilderness in the hills and valleys.

Their good luck wouldn't hold; he was certain of that. It wasn't a matter of if they ran into something blocking the road, but when. Worse yet, the noise of the truck might attract creatures. It ran surprisingly smooth and quiet for such an old thing, but it wasn't worth the risk.

"We need to abandon the vehicle."

"What?" The man said. "No! We can get away with this."

Unbelievably stupid. "Like all of those people thirteen years ago who had guns and cars?" This guy was old enough to know better. "The noise draws too much attention."

The man licked his lips, and a manic gleam lit his eyes. "Not that it matters. You motherfuckers brought hell down on us. I ain't never seen one of those big ones before." His grip tightened on the steering wheel. If the vein in his neck beat any harder, it would pop.

Kyle's pulse flared as well. "We brought hell down on you, you fucking kidnapping pig?" He'd killed two men today; one more wasn't going to end the world again. He reached for his gun, determined to end the conversation in the most decisive way possible.

"Drop it, Kyle."

He stared at Sara in disbelief. "After what they did to you?" There was nice, and there was stupid. This was stupid. He endangered all of them while he remained alive. He couldn't be trusted to watch their backs or listen if given an order. A person you couldn't trust was worse than useless; they were a liability.

"I don't need no witch defending me."

"I said enough. If you want the goddamn truck, you can have it. Take us a little farther and we'll get out."

Kyle opened his mouth to protest. He didn't want the truck, but he didn't want this man getting anything from them either. But then again, if he took the truck, he'd draw away everything around them with his noise. With any luck, he'd been dead by dawn. Maybe that was Sara's plan.

He let out a sigh , expressing his displeasure and acquiescence in one swoop. "We're hurt badly." That was an understatement.

The bandit grumbled something under his breath that Kyle was glad not to catch.

"We'll be all right. We'll find someplace safe in Oak Ridge."

The certainty in her voice annoyed him, and protests bubbled up inside.

But what does it matter? The truth was, it didn't. He hadn't rummaged around in the remaining bag or the few scattered supplies in the bed of the truck, but they were out of second chances. Oak Ridge was as good a place to die as any.

"I'm going to check on Tim." Kyle grabbed his gun from the bed of the truck. Dropping the mag revealed six bullets left. Probably most of what they had between the four of them. He locked the rounds back into place and poked his head in the window again, handing the weapon to Sara. "Shoot him if he does anything stupid."

The widening of his eyes and straightening of his back said he wouldn't, but more surprising things had happened in the last several hours. Sara shook her head, but she took the gun.

He ducked back into the cold Tennessee wind, short on understanding and high on pain. The pulsing in his head hadn't abated; if anything, it was getting worse. What started as occasional headaches had coalesced into a throbbing knot of discomfort in the front of his skull that on occasion blossomed into agony. Thinking about what they were going to do worsened the pain.

"Nap's over, Tim." Kyle shook him gently. He narrowed his eyes when that didn't work and slapped him hard across the cheek. "No time to be sleeping on the job. There's gold in them thar hills."

Tim groaned and rolled over, immediately reaching for his broken face. "Wha—" He winced in agony and closed his mouth again. He mumbled and tried to scoot away, but Kyle held him down until he'd calmed. His eyes closed again, but he stayed awake.

"It's a misquote of an old story." Kyle leaned against the side of the truck. "A man who ran a gold mine said there would be millions in it, but everyone misquoted it as, 'gold in them thar hills'. It says a lot about education at the time." Kyle closed his eyes and tried to ride through the pain in his head that every bump elicited. "Of course, some would argue that education never got better, only more expensive."

They drove in silence. He reached into his pocket. His flashlight wasn't there. More than likely fallen out in the frantic panic of the last hour. Something else was though.

He pulled the flash drive out and turned it over in his hands. A little piece of nothing. A chunk of a life gone by that no longer had any relevance. He considered throwing it out of the truck. Instead, he shoved it back into his pocket.

"Where are we?" Tim mouthed the words carefully. He tried to sit up and failed.

Kyle put a hand on Tim's leg, surprising himself with the tenderness of the gesture. "Just stay down. You're hurt. We're in a truck moving on some clear road."

The behemoth bearing down on them. Glistening horns and heaving breath.

"Truck's dangerous." Tim didn't try to get up again. Kyle could barely hear him over the rushing air.

"Yes, it is. We're going to leave it soon."

"Everyone okay?"

"Everyone is—" He almost said fine, but that wasn't true. "We're all here."

Tim managed to prop himself on his elbows. "What'd they do to Sara?"

He wanted to spare him the details. He was already going to lose it when he found out one of them was along for the ride. Maybe Kyle would let him. "She's hurt too, but she'll live."

Tim stared into the cab. His eyes focused and unfocused. In the old days, he would have been checked for a concussion. Now it didn't matter any more than Kyle's frequent blackouts. He hoped the kid would be spared that.

193

"Who's drivin'?" His eyes went from hazy to alert to angry.

"One of the men who attacked Sara." Kyle's gaze mirrored Tim's. "He saved our lives, for what it's worth."

"It ain't worth shit. I'll put a goddamn bullet in his face."

An odd sense of pride surged through Kyle. Maybe because those words so closely echoed his own. "You might want to wait until we stop. You aren't old enough to remember what a car crash at fifty-five looks like, but I am."

"Why the hell would you let him—"

"If you'd like, we can ride off on a monster next time."

Tim pursed his lips and drew a deep breath in through his nose, blowing it out in a huff.

Kyle patted Tim's knee again, half-expecting him to brush his hand away. He didn't. "Don't let it bother you. If it hurts you that much, put a bullet in his head when we leave. Just remember two things: You can't take it back, and they're loud as hell."

Tim glared at Kyle with the same cold look he'd had in the barn. Those were the eyes of a killer, and it occurred to him that he didn't know half as much about this young man as he thought. He'd shit bricks when things grew tight, but when they got ugly, he nutted up like he'd been a hard-ass the whole time. A small voice in the back of his mind suggested that hadn't been the first time Tim pulled the trigger on someone.

He suspected it wasn't be the second either.

Kyle was right; it didn't take long for their luck to run out. As the truck turned onto I-40 heading east, the road became unpassable. Wreckage stretched as far as the eye could see. The remains of cars that had fled Knoxville spread everywhere, a silent testimony to humanity's impermanence. People had tried to go around on the grass. Vehicles were stuck between the trees of the forest that coated the hills around them. All of them were rusted now, overgrown with vegetation the headlights dimly illuminated.

Kyle poked his head back in the window. "Looks like this is where we part ways, asshole."

The man didn't rise to the bait, just stared straight ahead. Sara ignored it as well.

The dread in his stomach didn't match his tough words. They were all hurt. Sara could barely stand. Tim had done an inventory of the one bag they had left. No food, no water, and little to keep warm with.

Tim dropped the gate of the truck and eased himself down, grabbing the bag and sliding it off with him. He wobbled slightly as he stood, but tried to hide it. None of them would be able to hide their weakness soon.

Kyle jumped out as Sara opened the door. The world shook as his feet hit the ground, threatening to pull him back into his nightmare with Karen. Kaylee hopped out of the cab, standing by Tim and eyeing the decrepit remains of the old world. Kyle watched her and frowned. She wasn't wrong to be afraid. A thousand horrors hid in places like this. The longer they dragged out their goodbyes with this pig, the worse the odds became.

Sara didn't say a word as she got out. He wondered if she felt the same longing for things gone by after their little drive. "Can you stand?" He put out an arm to steady her.

She nodded and stared at him with the same sad eyes she had earlier. They'd hurt her badly. He wanted to drag that asshole out of the truck and make him share that misery, but the guy had helped save their lives, and the noise would draw too much attention.

Tim didn't care about any of that.

"Tim." Kaylee's voice commanded Sara and Kyle's attention. She'd stopped near the back of the truck, not following him to the driver's side. The bandit didn't notice either, until Tim yanked the door open.

He jumped in his seat as Tim put a gun in his face. "Why shouldn't I kill?" In the dim light, the blood running down his jaw painted a bandit's mask. A spark of insanity glowed behind his eyes; the same killing gleam Kyle had seen in the truck.

The man parted his lips to speak, but before he could, the 9mm was in his mouth.

"Trick question."

The sharp intake of Kaylee's breath was the only noise in the darkness. The man started to shake, his knuckles white on the steering wheel. He didn't move, and Kyle had no doubt that as soon as he did, Tim would blow his brains out.

"Tim," Sara said through swollen lips. She put her hands up in a placating gesture.

A sudden burning desire to see Tim splash this man's head all over the inside of the truck rose inside him. It wouldn't fix anything, but goddamn if it wouldn't make him feel better.

"Just put it down." She moved toward the front of the truck. The man whined through the metal barrel clenched between his teeth.

Kaylee ran around the back. She threw her arms around Kyle's waist and looked the other way.

"After everything they did?" Tim's upper lip curled, turning his bloody bandit mask into a crimson sneer. "He ought to get worse."

Sara shook her head. "I'm alive. We're all alive. If you shoot that gun here, that won't be the case." She glanced over her shoulder at Kyle, but he didn't take his gaze from the young man with murder on his mind.

It was all too familiar. Tim could be Richard's kid for all the attitude he threw around. Now he was pulling guns. With a sudden crystal clarity, Kyle saw it all again. Richard had let his temper get away from him. They'd tried to go back into the city and lost eight people. Eight. When the bandits came, he pulled his gun. He'd gone crazy, lost his temper after seeing his friend killed. He was quick, but they were quicker. Everyone paid the price, maybe Kyle most of all.

Across the truck, Kyle could see the tremor in Tim's hand. That kid wanted it bad, but it wouldn't help. It never did. The only purpose served by murder was that of the monsters.

197

"Let it go, son."

Tim jumped at Kyle's words as if they'd been gunshots. "I ain't your son."

"Fair enough. Let the man go. He's done as much harm as he can, and you don't want that on your conscience."

Seconds dragged on as if they were hours. The wind died, the howls stopped, and even the breath in Kyle's chest came out a little softer.

Tim pulled the piece out of the man's mouth. The glint of slobber on the barrel glowed in the moonlight. "Get the hell outta here."

The man fumbled with the keys as Tim stared at him through the open door. Kyle envisioned the man starting the vehicle and getting far enough away to turn around and run them down.

It didn't happen. With heaving breaths, he managed to turn the ignition back on. He threw the vehicle into gear and pulled a quick U-turn before speeding off back the way they'd come.

Tim watched him go, but everyone else watched Tim.

"It was the right thing to do," Kyle said at length.

With the truck's lights gone, the gloom of the world pressed in on all sides.

"'Right?' What the fuck does that word even mean? Right ain't shit but a way to turn anymore." He spit out the side of his mouth.

"Right never meant anything if you didn't let it. The world doesn't make the rules you live by, Tim; you do. If you start shooting people, you're no different than them." Kyle had hunted down and murdered all of Karen and Richard's killers. He'd murdered people who were infected or wounded. Those faces didn't haunt his dreams, but he never forgot them.

Tim grabbed the bag and slung it over his shoulder. "So what now?"

Sara didn't miss a beat. "Oak Ridge. We're closer now. We just need to get there."

And everything will be okay. But she didn't say it.

"We're at least two days away, and you can barely walk," Kyle said.

That sadness in her eyes reached out at him again, an alien look of absolute surrender.

"I'll manage."

She did manage for the next few hours. The choice was clear. Without food or water, and with so many of those things not far behind, staying still was suicide. The wreckage blocking the road continued alongside them. They walked in the trees next to the road, making their way slowly as much for Sara as to avoid breaking their ankles in a hole.

Kaylee hadn't said a word since Tim's episode. After proceeding in silence for the last few hours, he spoke up. "I'm sorry you had to see that, Kaylee."

She turned toward him, her small frame like a wisp of night in the deep shadows of the trees. "I wanted to hurt him too."

"But you're glad I didn't, right?"

199

She kept her gaze locked on him a little longer before she shrugged. A maybe yes, maybe no kind of answer. Not the sort of thing one expected out of a child.

A different world indeed.

Sara interrupted before the conversation could go any further. "We're going to need food. There's got to be an exit coming up we can check out."

More than food, they needed water, and a quiet place to rest. The sun would be coming up in a few hours, and it had been over a day since any of them had proper sleep. A tired mind led to mistakes, and mistakes led to death. Kyle desperately needed sleep more than he would admit aloud. A splitting headache beat in time with every step. He blacked out more than once, only to find himself still walking when he came around.

He looked over his shoulder after one episode to find Sara staring into his eyes. The dim moonlight didn't shine strong enough for him to see it, but he could imagine the concern there. It was absurd. Strangers had kidnapped and beaten her half to death, and yet she was looking at him as if he were the one in pain. He didn't think she'd ever scan him without permission, but the way she was watching at him...

"How are you feeling?" he asked.

She shrugged, but otherwise didn't respond. Even in the poor light, he could see the swollen eye and busted lips.

"We should rest a moment."

"After our refreshing car ride?" Her tone was jovial, but she didn't smile. She leaned against a tree, easing herself onto the ground. She winced and put a hand to her abdomen. If anything were ruptured or broken, there was nothing to be done. She could be slowly bleeding to death right now for all he knew. Unable to provide any relief, he sat next to her and gave up some of his warmth. Tim sat in front of them, facing out without a word. Kaylee sat next to him.

"We can stop here for the night if you like," Kyle said.

A howl—a wolf, not one of the creatures—pierced the stillness. Sara cocked her head and listened, her eyes glassing over. "Just a little further up the road. It'll be safe there, for a while at least."

"You're sure?"

She peered at him through the slit where one eye now hid. The bruises of her face said she was a war refugee. A woman on the run. In many ways, she was.

"It'll be fine."

She was correct, though whether that was through luck or something else, Kyle didn't know. Decaying cars covered the road past and into the exit off the highway.

The tornados that had plagued Tennessee had been particularly unkind here. They had utterly destroyed the to the left of the exit that passed back under the highway. A few vehicles had tried to brave the shattered pavement's carved-out remains and gotten stuck in the process. The street remained intact to the right of the ramp. A line of cars continued that way until it vanished behind trees when the road curved. The only remaining building on the street was a half-collapsed fast food joint.

The inside wasn't much better than the outside. The decayed remains of a drop ceiling hung over broken tables and chairs. Moss, thankfully unblighted, grew thick under their feet. One of the walls had been knocked over and now sat as nothing more than a shattered pile of masonry trying to meet the sagging roof. It was depressing and ugly, but it would keep some of the cold from the wind out.

Kyle and Tim went inside to check it while Kaylee and Sara waited. The angry buzz of Kyle's headache had turned into a wrathful swarm of bees. They poked and prodded inside his head, making it hard to focus, hard to see at all. By the time they cleared the restaurant, he needed to sit in order to quell the nausea. He waved Tim outside to get Sara and Kaylee while he settled onto the mossy ground behind the counter.

He closed his eyes and rubbed his temples with one weathered hand. It did nothing to stop the pain. White noise flooded his ears. An old radio between channels. There were almost voices in it, but not quite. Just snatches of missed conversation coming to him across the airwaves of time and space. Brief pictures of people long dead and places long destroyed.

"You okay?" Sara grasped her side as if she had a stitch, but Kyle knew better. They shouldn't have pushed so hard.

"I'm fine. Take a seat. You and Kaylee can share the blanket and bedroll we have left."

202

She sat next to him as Tim came around the counter with the bag and Kaylee. The gooseflesh on Tim's arms rose in small waves under his shirtsleeve. Kyle caught a glimpse of it as he sat. The wind didn't touch them in here, but the night's cold bit harder than the last few.

"No fire tonight."

Tim glared at Kyle. "Being sneaky ain't gonna do us much good if we freeze to death." That defensive posture of his. Amazing that the guy could be so bloodthirsty when the stakes were high and nothing but a scared kid when they weren't.

"We can't run. We've got nowhere to go. We've got nothing to fight with. We don't even have enough blankets to block the light. No fire. It'll be warmer in the morning."

Tim sat. He rubbed at the dried blood on his chin. Over the last several hours, he'd managed to flake a lot of it off, but even in the darkness, Kyle could see the outline of his angry red beard. He lisped when he spoke, trying not to aggravate his broken teeth. "What we gonna do about food? And water?"

Kyle rubbed at his temples, but it did nothing. "It may not be a bad idea to stick around here and check out the exits in the morning." It wasn't a solid plan, but it was something.

"No." Sara never took her gaze from the ground. "We keep moving. Those things will follow us out this way sooner or later."

Tim and Kyle glanced at one another. "How do you know that?" Kyle asked.

"Trust me."

He did trust her, but she was scattered right now. Hurt and scared. They couldn't make rash decisions based on emotions. Not for the first time, he thought of the food stores at North Fifteen. A year back, they'd lucked out and found a semi-truck filled with canned goods. Corned beef hash. Dried fruits. Jams. Some of it had spoiled, but a good chunk would last another few years. Between that and what they'd found running, they had a fortune in goods. Now it would all rot in a warehouse nobody would ever check, surrounded by the reanimated remains of his dead friends.

He leaned his head back against the counter. All that food and they were starving to death while their resident scanner ran spooked.

Sara interrupted the quiet. "I'm not spooked." She spit the words at him.

Tim shifted uncomfortably on Sara's far side.

Kyle couldn't believe his ears. "Did you scan me?"

She shook her head.

"Don't bullshit me, Sara. You know I don't like that." She'd done it once before. The only time they'd had a real argument. She had grazed the edge of his mind and then asked about Karen.

"I didn't." She bit off her words as she spoke. He'd never known her to lie, but they'd been through a lot over the last few hours.

"Just don't do it again."

A storm of rage passed over her face. She kicked him in the shin, and not softly. "I said I didn't do it. Something happened back there. Something's different now. I can—" Her expression said she was picking her words carefully. "I can hear more now. That's how I knew nothing was here." She glared at him, her words sheepish as they faded. "God, you're infuriating sometimes."

Kyle didn't give her the satisfaction of rubbing his shin. "Alright. Fine. I believe you. We can leave in the morning." He moved across the slick moss floor and sat against her. "But I don't know that it's going to matter. A few extra miles aren't going to do much if they follow us."

"They won't. I made sure of that. I just don't want to risk it."

The quiet anger in her voice sent a chill down his spine. She could hear more now.

That scared him.

Chapter 12

Sara

Number Four drove on, trying to ignore the impression that someone was sitting next to him. It wasn't warmth or an indent in the seat; it was eyes watching him. The absolute certainty that if he closed his own and reached to the right, he would find another person.

It was her. It was that goddamn witch.

Sara heard all his thoughts as clear as day. She *was* next to him. While they walked through the woods and he drove the other way, she was next to him. When they stopped for the night in the old grease trap, she was next to him. She moved around him, always keeping just out of arm's reach. He'd gone far away, but not far enough. She wasn't like the Walking Cancer. She wasn't stronger, just different. She stayed next to him long after the truck ran out of gas and he started walking.

He didn't know where he was going. He just wanted out. The howls all around him said those goddamn monsters were close.

Those demons. No earth-shaking sounds, but the horde's constant din frayed his nerves. They couldn't know where he was. They couldn't find him when he was alone and quiet in the middle of nowhere. He'd doubled back and started toward Knoxville. He hadn't gone anywhere near the highway leading to Murfreesboro. They couldn't know. They weren't that smart.

But they drew closer. The night came alive with their hunting, and Sara stuck right next to him. Calling them. Calling *it*.

And it came, like a stupid dog to the dinner bell.

He screamed when it found him, but it did no good. The thing ripped into his mind and tore him apart. Cutting him open and crawling inside, forever tainting him. It ravaged all his most precious memories and wore them out until he was nothing but a slobbering, jabbering sack of meat on the ground. It crammed itself inside his thoughts and ripped his mind open, tearing his self-awareness asunder. When it didn't find anything it liked, it gave up, feeding his violated remains to the crawlers as scrap.

It didn't know why she wasn't there; she got that much as she watched the event unfold. She lay in her bedroll, Kaylee curled up next to Tim while he kept watch, Kyle sleeping behind her. When the deed was done, she came back into herself, confident the thing wouldn't find them, at least not tonight.

She pursed her lips, and her swollen eyes filled with tears. *Fuck him. Fuck all of them. If Hell's real, I hope they burn there.*

She silently cried herself to sleep, trying not to wake the others.

She slept until shortly after the sun came up. Nightmares plagued her and chased her through dreams. The Walking Cancer riding one of the giant beasts chased her down the corridors of her mind, cornering her in her innermost thoughts and violating her until she died.

When she opened her eyes and the sun showed through the cracks in the ceiling, she didn't go back to sleep. Tim had dozed off on guard at some point. She'd keep that to herself when Kyle woke. Rather than move, she stayed on the ground, watching Kaylee as she groaned in her sleep with the doll clutched to her chest.

Kyle's back pressed against hers. He didn't like to be scanned, but she couldn't help it. When he touched her, she could feel his nerves rotting inside his body. She could smell the slow degradation of his consciousness and see where it would lead.

She took a deep breath, trying to fight back the tears. So many tears over the last week. So much death. There was no reprieve in the monsters' world.

She closed her eyes. Crying was as useless as all those prayers of the faithful. The ones they had sent to God before the monsters had gobbled them up. It didn't bring comfort, it didn't bring change; it made everyone else suffer. Better to keep it in and let everyone sleep.

She reached out in her new way, trying to distract herself from the black death coursing through Kyle. The sensation of flying out of her mind while remaining conscious disoriented her. Seeing through two pairs of eyes and feeling through two pairs of hands gave her vertigo. Bizarre, like the first time she realized she'd never seen her own face outside of a mirror. Now she could.

Nothing except for normal wildlife for miles around, but a few memories had imprinted themselves on things close by. A steel countertop still stood under the building's shattered half.

Rebecca tore off her shirt, one button flying against the carton of milk standing behind Carl. The lights were all out, the cars were all gone, and they were the only ones around for miles.

He nipped at her neck, and she let out a small moan. Goddamn, she wanted him inside her. He tore off his jeans, the bulge in his slightly yellowed tighty-whities proving how eager he—

She pulled herself out of the memory, shocked wide-awake by it. Her cheeks heated up. She hadn't expected *that*.

The giggling bubbled up without warning. The bruises on her face burned as she blushed. Laughing was juvenile, and being juvenile made her laugh more. It hurt her abdomen where the pain throbbed, and her swollen eye jolted in agony. It burst out of her, the laugh of a girl in her teens coming from a woman in her thirties. Slow and silly at first, but quickly escalating beyond control.

And for a second, it was all gone. Kyle's pain, the last day, the lack of food; it all vanished while she giggled at the fornicating teenagers who were probably long dead by now. Better than a porno.

Kyle stirred as she shook with laughter, and Kaylee rubbed her eyes. Tim was awake and looking at her as if she'd lost her mind. It only made her laugh more.

"What's funny?"

They wouldn't understand what it was like to take a backseat in someone else's memories. "Just a dream."

It tapered off, and the gravity of the situation set in again. She hadn't cared for a moment, and that was a rare gift.

"Really?" Tim raised an eyebrow, his serious expression unchanged. Kyle sat up her behind without a word. Kaylee snuggled against Tim, her face a stony mask. Sara wished she could share that momentary reprieve with them. Take away their pains for a little while. Instead, she put her own mirth away, back into the disused parts of her life.

"Yeah, really." She tried to sit up. Any remaining humor vanished as the pain in her abdomen sent her back to the ground.

She hadn't realized she'd let out a moan until Kyle hovered over her. "What is it?"

"I'm fine." But that was a lie. All the walking the night before had taken it out of her, and she was in no shape to keep going.

Unfortunately, they didn't have a choice.

"We can wait here another day."

Another day wasn't going to fix whatever damage those people had done. "I'm fine. I just need to stretch a little. Help me up, Tim."

Tim did as she said. It didn't hurt nearly as much with the help. The others were silent as she bent carefully at the waist. Halfway down, the first twinges of pain pulsed near her stomach. *Guess I know my limits there.* She twisted around slowly, trying to get the stiffness to leave.

Kyle stood as well. "We'll, if we're going, we should leave. We'll need to find someplace to scavenge something before we lose daylight."

Sara reached out for one last peak at the mirth she'd found on that steel table, but it was gone.

They continued following the highway east. It wasn't a choice anymore but an imperative. A holy mission. Reach the Promised Land or die horribly. The decision was already made, their path set in stone.

The endless stalled cars tapered off and then vanished as the day wore on. The weather hadn't been kind to this stretch of road. Cracks, dirt, and weeds buried the pavement. The blight covering most of the wildlife over the past miles slowly faded, then disappeared altogether. The diseased trees that hung overhead gave way to beech and pine, barren from the winter cold. The black limbs that reached toward them retreated, and the air sweetened.

Traces of creatures both natural and unnatural brushed the edges of Sara's mind. Some were close, others far away. She stayed inside of her own head to try to ignore the growing pain in her guts. Fear filled her, pushing everything else away. She wouldn't let it take root. Couldn't. They might all be dying for all she knew. That didn't mean she would give up and lie down.

Instead, she flexed her new limits. She could reach out impossibly far with her mind, so far that it scared her. She didn't know if she would become lost if she wandered too distantly, and she didn't want to find out. She tried to feel forward to Oak Ridge and find some trace of Kaylee's family friends, but it didn't work. Everything looked unreal in her mind's eye when she travelled too far from her body, as if the whole world were made of porcelain. It unsettled her, and she chose instead to touch the world nearby.

Someone had dropped a ring in the grass. It called to her from the dirt, when she turned her mind to it—

"Do you think it's far?"

"I don't know."

"You think they're there already?"

"I don't fucking know, Megan."

He was agitated. That was understandable. Their town hadn't been attacked; it had been wiped off the map. But they couldn't give up. As long as they had one another, they could make it through.

But other memories were attached to it, ugly ones.

"Roger!" She screamed his name again and again into the darkness. The howls of the night things drifted on the wind all around her.

He'd left her. He wasn't coming back. She huddled in the cab of the old sedan, scared and alone. She would have done anything for him, and now he was gone.

Sara withdrew from it, not wanting to see any more. It whispered to her, trying to pull her back. A lonely memory in the middle of nowhere that hadn't seen people in years. She moved past, having no desire to witness the ending.

She wanted to tell the others what she could do now, but this was a time for survival, not revelation. Far more concerning was the thing looking for her, looking for Kaylee. She couldn't tell them about that either. Knowing wouldn't make them move any faster, and fear wouldn't keep them alive longer.

They trudged on. Hunger pains were frequent enough that it didn't bother her, but the thirst did. By the time noon rolled around, her mouth was dry and her throat parched.

"We're going to need to find water soon." She was worried about Kaylee more than herself.

Kyle looked up at the sky then turned to the mountains in the distance around them. Soon the trees would taper off, and they'd be out in the open for miles and miles. "Unless it rains, I'm not sure what we can do."

It didn't look as though rain was in the cards. One of the unfortunate casualties of the lost bag was the map. They could be two miles from a lake for all she knew. She looked back at Tim. His features betrayed nothing as he shrugged.

"We can stop at the next exit," Kyle said. "Maybe we'll find a stream."

"This goddamn state has water everywhere. We'll find some." In deserts and places without fresh water, people must have died early on. The thought followed her down the road to the next exit. No liquid. Nowhere to hide. There were places in the world devoid of human life when they'd coated it by the billions just over a decade ago.

213

Tim and Kyle left to explore and, with a little luck, bring back some food and water.

After two hours searching collapsing buildings for food and tree lines for water, Tim sat on the ground. "Nothin'. Again." His head thunked on the tree behind him as he leaned back.

"Not nothing." Kyle pulled out a half-crushed pack of cigarettes from his pocket, tossing them to Sara. They flipped through the air and landed in her hands.

"Where the hell did you find these?"

Kyle smiled. "In a break room in the motel across the road."

She stared at the smokes. The plastic on the pack hadn't been broken yet, and the Marlboro name, faded with age, was still legible. She hadn't seen her favorites in years. She tore off the plastic and ripped away the tin foil packaging inside. The smell of decade-stale tobacco wafted up. She pulled one out and dug the book of matches out of her pocket, lighting it and taking a delicate drag. "Kyle, this is better than water." Fifteen years ago the stale tobacco would have been unpalatable; now it was amazing. The nicotine buzz set in at once.

Kyle laughed, but neither Tim nor Kaylee did. Kaylee had barely spoken all day.

When she finished, she tucked the cigarettes in the bag before they returned to the highway. The trees gave way to open fields. The homes were beaten and dilapidated, the fields overgrown with blighted weeds. Red and ugly things the size of bushes, limbs slick as if they were perspiring. The openness of the road offered no place to hide. When the highway rose up on hills, they were visible for miles around.

Her sore muscles screamed, and the pain in her gut rumbled, angry and sharp.

"We're gonna get nailed if we keep walkin' in the open like this."

Kyle glanced over his shoulder, his expression inscrutable. "You wanted to see the cities. This is the only way."

"We're gonna get killed before we get there."

Kaylee squeezed Sara's hand.

"Enough of that," Sara said.

Moody silence answered her. He was scared; that was apparent. But spreading it around wouldn't help. Kaylee stared up at Sara with her big blue eyes. They had to keep it together. If not for themselves, then for her.

"You were on your own for a long time, right?" When Tim didn't respond, Kyle continued, "How'd you get by?"

Sara had to admit, the question had been bothering her for a while too. People who were all nerves didn't last long, and Tim had been a bundle of them since they met.

"You want my story?" He bit off each word.

"We've got time."

"I'll tell you what; you tell me every awful thing that got you here, and I'll do the same."

Sara shook her head. Again with the pissing-contest bullshit. Tim radiated resentment and angst, much like any teenager. Kyle felt…empty.

What he said next surprised her. "Alright."

Chapter 13

Kyle

He hadn't told anyone but Sara about his past since Karen and Richard died, but the words were out of his mouth before he had time to think. The way things were going, he didn't have long anyway. If the monsters or the dehydration didn't get him, whatever was wrong with his head would. The headache had been pounding against his temples all day, worsening with each step. He didn't need the old world's doctors to tell him he was a dead man.

"I taught sociology in Memphis, which is a few hundred miles that way." He pointed back down I-40 in the opposite direction. "No kids, no wife, no family. I was just a job."

Tim was looking forward at him, his attention focused. Good. If he could keep their minds off their troubles for an hour, it was worth it.

"What's sociology?" Kaylee asked.

Kyle smiled a humorless smile. "It's something people used to care about that means absolutely nothing now." Not entirely true but not far off the mark. "I was in Memphis when the army came through. They stopped for a few days, set up soldiers and roadblocks, and then moved on. It didn't do anything to slow the creatures down. When they showed up, they picked everything off a little at a time, then they came in force. By then the power had been out for weeks, and we'd stopped getting any news. When a thousand of those things appeared, they wiped out most of the city in two days. I hid in my apartment for a month, until I was out of food and water." He remembered the sour taste of his urine, drunk again and again until it stunk so bad it made him sick.

Talking about it made his head swim, and the images floated by in his mind, threatening to make him black out again. He closed his eyes and blew out a deep breath. The ghosts could have him later.

"I'd hear them in the halls or out in the streets. They'd break in doors and tear people out of their homes, eating them if the big ones didn't crush them first. I don't know why they never found me. I thought they would. They would walk along the hallways of my apartment building, sniffing at the doors. Looking." He stared up into the sky, now lightly overcast. "I finally stopped caring if I lived or died. I could either starve to death or run. I left my apartment and made it down to the street without anything seeing me." He glanced at Tim and Kaylee. Both stared at him in rapt attention. "The quiet. You two couldn't understand. Downtown cities weren't quiet; they were loud. You had music, people screaming, horns blaring; there was never a second of peace. But right then, everything was as quiet as it is now."

He let that sink in for a moment. The only sound in the world was their feet on ruined pavement and the hushed rustle of the fallen leaves in the wind. The tintinnabulation of the new world to mark the passing of a Sunday afternoon, if indeed it was Sunday.

"I'd heard them just hours before. The growls, howls, and gunshots let me know I wasn't the last man on Earth. I didn't make it far before they saw me. Three of them. I ran, but I wouldn't have made it if…"

Kyle huffed as he ran, out of gas from four days with no food. The click of claws on pavement gained on him. Just ahead, a head poked out of an alley.

"Kyle." Sara's voice pulled him out of his darkness. "You don't have to go on."

"No, it's fine. I want to tell him." It might be the last chance he ever had to tell his story. He needed to, though he hadn't realized it until he started. "The crawlers found someone else, and I hid in another building. There was food there, and other people. That's where I met Richard."

He didn't know what to say about Richard. It was impossible to condense half a decade's worth of memories into a story, or at least impossible for him. They'd been through so much, and almost died so many times, that to tell anything but the whole felt cheap. A disservice to Richard's memory.

"He was my best friend. We escaped the city and went to his family's farm. We met some other people on the way. A woman named Karen. If I'd met her ten years before that, I would have married her." It all flooded back. The blood on his hands. The bullet in his leg. The first time he and Karen ever got drunk off warm two-year-old wine and danced under the stars in a dead world.

They were his memories, his baubles to fawn and treasure inside his head. It was as rude to ask about Tim's treasures as it was for anyone to ask about his.

"They all died. I met Sara later, and we wound up in North Fifteen a few years after that." He walked slightly faster, needing to distance himself from his sudden burst of honesty. It made him lightheaded, and his empty stomach churned. All of it gone now. The world. Karen. North fifteen. Everything. He'd join it all soon in whatever came after. It had to be better than this.

The highway curved out of sight a mile ahead of them, lost in the trees. He focused on the vanishing road, not wanting to touch the raw emotions swirling inside of him.

Kaylee wasn't finished though. "What happened?" The words were innocent. A curious girl wanting to know the details of a curious story.

"Bad men shot them, like the ones that took Sara. I found and killed all of them, and then I spent a long time alone." But not really alone. Nobody chased by the ghosts of their past was ever really alone.

The scrapes of worn out shoes and boots on pavement filled the silence.

"I'm sorry," Tim said.

"Don't be."

He wanted to look over his shoulder, but he already knew what he'd see. Sara and Kaylee staring at him with their sad eyes, Tim unable to hold his gaze. It wouldn't make anything better. It wouldn't give him a sense of validation. There was none of that anymore and no place for it.

The road vanished around the curve, gently turning so that it was never out of sight, but never visible more than a few hundred yards ahead.

"My family got killed too."

The words were quiet, an afterthought spoken aloud. The lisp in Tim's voice from his missing teeth made it pathetic. The voice of a young man barely out of puberty meekly sharing a secret.

Kyle looked back and caught the sadness in Sara's eyes before she gave her attention to Tim.

"We had a farm in Texas. When it all happened, my dad took us into the bomb shelter that grandpa kept in case the Russians ever attacked. Nothin' came that far out though, at least not that we saw. We was in the middle of nowhere." He looked up into the sky the same way Kyle had not long before, struggling to keep a straight face. "We'd seen some of those things from time to time, but there was seven of us with the hands, and we all had guns. Some men showed up winter two years back. A lot of them. We let them in 'cause Pa said it was the right thing to do. They looked mean, but we didn't see people for so long… We thought we were the last ones in the world. Pa said it was the end times."

"Tim, you don't have to talk about it. I'm sorry." Kyle didn't want to hear anymore. It was too familiar.

"They killed everyone but me. I was out in the fields checking the traps."

His gaze met Kyle's before looking away. He hid the tears with his hand. "I killed four of them that night when they slept, and when the rest ran off, I killed two more." He sucked in a deep breath.

Sara wrapped her arms around him. "Shh."

But he talked over her. "I tried to bury my family, but I couldn't. Frost came and the ground got hard. I wanted to, but I couldn't." Tears fell down his cheeks and onto Sara's head. "They killed my whole family for food and guns. Killed them like it was nothin'. And I had to just leave them there. My little sister. She was just Kaylee's age, and they… They…"

Kyle looked away, ashamed at having made the kid relive that. Ashamed of having treated him like something other than a scared boy with no family and no place to go.

"I walked by myself for a long time. I had lots of food, but it ran out eventually. I met other people who said they didn't have space for another mouth, but they told me the cities was safe. They said New York hadn't been taken yet, but that in the winters they ran out of food." He sniffed back a fresh wave of tears, the look of determination on his face stating he would get through his story. "I came up here, and when I passed North Fifteen I saw the signs. I didn't want to be alone no more."

Lost and alone in a world full of monsters. The same story as everyone else. Earth had indeed become a cold place when even kids shared nothing but tragedies.

"It's alright, man." Kyle walked over to Tim and Sara as Kaylee grabbed hold of Tim's hand. "You aren't alone. We're going to be okay." He put a hand on Tim's shoulder.

Tim sobbed into Sara's neck for a long time. Kyle stood there, ashamed and quiet.

The road continued, first free of trees then thick with them. Car pileups dotted the landscape, but there were few signs anyone had tried to flee here when the calamity struck. The big highway narrowed to country proportions, and open countryside gave way to houses, fields, and barns. Some homes were nothing more than wrecks, others only in need of lawn care and new siding.

They stopped for the night at one such house hidden by weeds and tall grass. Kyle eyed it from a distance as the first fingers of twilight reached across the sky. "We'll camp here tonight. Tim, let's check it out."

Tim hadn't spoken or made eye contact since his sobs tapered off. The apocalypse hadn't softened the old world's outrageous rules about masculinity. That sat wrong with Kyle as he moved quietly through the grass. Things shouldn't have been like that before, and they certainly shouldn't now.

Sara and Kaylee vanished from sight behind them as they approached the house. The first signs of blight, a sickly yellow tinge that marked the beginning of their planet's terraforming, showed at the grass' roots. Soon the crap would cover the Earth.

An overgrown stone walkway appeared out of the weeds. They followed it to the remains of the front door. The windows gave no indication of what was inside. Kyle loosened his machete and pulled it out before looking back at Tim. They stepped in.

Shafts of sunlight illuminated the years of dust in the air. The Tennessee moisture had stripped the paint from the walls, and the moldy furniture was dilapidated to the point of being unrecognizable. But the rest of the house—the pictures on the walls, the old vases, the light fixture hanging from the ceiling—stood intact.

Kyle nodded toward the kitchen, and Tim stalked in that direction. The smell reminded Kyle of an old woman's attic as he entered the short hallway at the back. Bedroom and bathroom doors stood ajar, and he moved slowly past each one, his senses straining for any signs of danger. Hunger and the headache had made him lightheaded throughout the day, and his thoughts drifted to the people who'd lived there.

Then he found them. Two weathered skeletons, the leathery remains of skin and soft tissues still stuck to their bones, embracing forever on a king size bed. The man gripped a rusted gun, the woman's face buried in his chest. No infection. No monsters. A clean exit from the world to spare themselves the pain of watching it rot away.

The smell wasn't bad, likely thanks to the windows that had long since been broken. They didn't look as if they'd struggled with the decision. He wondered if the man had even told her. Maybe he'd pulled the trigger when she closed her eyes. Maybe an infected had bitten them and they never stood a chance. Maybe they couldn't bear to face what the world was becoming. One of the thousands, maybe millions of people who'd seen where everything was headed and took the easy way out.

Two smart people who'd gotten off the bus before it drove off the cliff.

Tim's footsteps approached from the living room. "Anything?"

Kyle pulled the door closed, taking one last look at the couple before sealing their tomb. "No."

The decaying mattress in the other bedroom was little better than the ground. Their shelter half and a blanket blocked the view from both the door and the window, and they lit a small fire. No water or food. Another hungry night.

The day's aches settled over Kyle. Judging from the way Sara winced as she turned onto her side, it was bad for her too. Not as bad as the morning, but what dawn would bring might be a different story. Kaylee sat against Tim, whose back was to the wall. He stared into the fire as if it held answers.

Part of Kyle wanted to comfort him, but some things couldn't be fixed. No amount of soothing noises and placating words would give Kaylee or Tim their families back. Nothing they could do would make the world a better place. That was as true as it ever had been.

"Next town we pass, we need to find food," Tim said.

Idly picking at the dry grass he'd brought in for kindling, Kyle looked at him across the fire. "We'll see what we can find."

"No." His voice was calm, not the unreasonable, hungry thing he'd been earlier. "Everyone's in a bad way. We need to find something soon."

The longest Kyle had ever gone without food was a week and a half. That had been after Karen and Richard died. His leg had become infected. Not by monsters, but by good old-fashioned bacteria. The world passed in a dream as he wandered roads and fields looking for the things he'd lost, his gun in his grip and the blood of killers on his hands. He'd found a scummy pond with fish in it and lit a fire, not caring what found him. He survived, but barely. "We'll get by."

Tim closed his eyes, but Kaylee didn't look away. A child's bold stare, without a highly evolved sense of shame or old world propriety. She feared, yes, but not him.

"How are you, little lady?"

She shrugged, never taking her gaze off him.

Kyle threw the pieces of kindling into the fire. "When we find your mother's friends, things will get better." Maybe yes, maybe no. A little lie wasn't going to kill her. But Sara had to scan that girl again, and soon. They couldn't walk into a city with no clue about where to go. If they did that, they might as well blow their brains out like the couple in the other room. Another four ghosts in a house full of them.

Kyle rolled over to sleep, letting Tim take the first watch and hoping things wouldn't be so bleak in the morning.

The dreams were unpleasant, but the pain in his head on waking was worse. The gnawing, biting ache in his temples pressed in on all sides. He basked in the fire's warmth, trying to let it ease the hurt. It didn't. Bells rang in time with his heartbeat. Karen had been calling out to him.

"Come home, Kyle." She waved at him, begging him to stop hurting. And he did hurt. He hurt terribly.

He opened his eyes to stare into the embers. Shapes and shadows blurred and wiggled from more than just sleep. His headache raged, shrinking the world to a pinpoint.

"Kyle, are you okay?"

Sara's words barely registered above the keening in his ears. He understood them, but when he tried to form a response, the grayness threatened to overcome him.

"Don't fight it anymore, baby. Just go to sleep."

"No. Shut up." He said it louder than he intended. Tim stirred but didn't wake.

"Shh. What's wrong?"

"My head. It hurts." An understatement. This was Hell condensed into his brain and trying to break free. It throbbed from the front of his temples to the roots of his teeth.

Sara scooted over to him. "It's alright."

"Goddamn. This hurts so much." He squeezed his eyes shut, trying to keep the tears back. They oozed from between his lids and fell to the ground. "I don't know if I'm going to make it."

"Stop." She was crying, too. "Stop fighting it, please. It kills me to see you like this."

Those weren't the right words.

They were dancing in the barn as her skirt twirled in the moonlight. Not really a skirt, just some flimsy little thing she'd found and worn for him. It was all theirs though. That skirt, that moonlight, that dance, and that wine; all of it was theirs, taken back from the monsters for one night.

"You can have that again."

"Shut up." He grunted through gritted teeth as Sara rested his head in her lap. The movement killed him with every jolt, but her hands caressing his beard and hair chased the phantoms away. "Just leave me alone."

"Shh. It's okay. I'm here for you."

"Why won't they leave me alone?"

"Shh. It's alright, Kyle. You're okay."

He wasn't. Nothing was.

He fell asleep again hours later, Karen's whispers in his ears.

The morning sun made things better, but not much. He opened his eyes to find Sara leaning against the wall, his head still in her lap. Kaylee and Tim were already awake and packing the bags.

"You think he's okay?"

"He's fine."

"Did you hear him last night?"

Tim didn't respond, just kept folding the shelter half before putting it into the bag.

Sara stirred. Kyle feared last night's pain would wash over him and leave him a gibbering mess on the floor. A head full of broken glass sloshed as he sat upright.

Tim didn't look up, but Kaylee did. She sat still while holding the bag open for Tim, never taking her gaze off Kyle. "Are you okay?"

Nothing had been okay in a long time, and odds were good that wouldn't change anytime soon. "I'm fine." Water would help. His throat hurt from dryness, and saliva wasn't doing much.

Tim sighed as if reading his thoughts. "We need to find some supplies today."

"We're only a day and change from Oak Ridge. We can make it."

Tim pursed his lips and shook his head. "Are we gonna pretend like I ain't missing teeth and the two of you are right as rain?"

Sara blew out a sigh. "If that's what it takes to keep going, then yes, that's exactly what we'll do." She stood slowly before helping Kyle to his feet.

Kyle tried to smile. "Worst comes to worst you can eat me." The off-color joke might have been funny if people hadn't been doing worse to survive.

"Food and water." Sara pulled the shelter half down from the window. "We'll check everywhere that looks like a maybe."

Dizziness, great wracking waves of it, assailed him. All he wanted was to lie back down and sleep. Maybe never wake up.

Sara watched him through bruised eyes. As long as she needed him, as long as any of them were still around, he'd hold on. "Can you walk another day?"

She forced a smile. "I'm game to try if you are."

They left the house and returned to the highway. Kyle took the lead, but that didn't last more than five minutes. He stumbled and leaned against the remains of a car.

"Kyle?" Sara put a hand on his shoulder.

"I think you'd better take point, Sara." His vision swam, expanding and contracting with every breath. Walking was difficult. Everything was difficult. The crushing pain of broken glass in his head became a steamroller, flattening everything inside, threatening to pop his eyes from their sockets.

"Shit." Tim spit onto the pavement. Kyle imagined he must look pretty damn pathetic. He couldn't blame the kid if he wanted to leave him behind, though Sara would never go for it. "Why don't I go ahead and get food and water, and the three of y'all stay back."

He'd been expecting the big axe. *I'm sorry, old man, but it isn't working out. Time to send you off to the farm. Maybe you'll get tenure next year, if your brain doesn't explode or you aren't eaten.*

He wouldn't be the reason they slowed until they died. "I can keep going."

Tim opened his mouth to speak, but Sara beat him to it. "He's right. We need to keep moving." She stared off into space as if listening to something.

They should leave him behind. If he had any courage at all, he'd put his gun in his mouth and waste a bullet. He didn't. Even with all the hurt, he didn't want to leave them alone.

"You're fucked up, and he can't hardly walk. What are we killin' ourselves for?"

Sara's anger rose to meet his. "A week ago you couldn't find a city fast enough!"

"If there's somethin' there, it won't matter if it takes us a few more days to find it."

"Those things are right behind us, do you understand?"

Kaylee watched it go back and forth like a tennis match, unblinking.

Their bickering drove nails into Kyle's brain. "Enough. Enough! We'll keep going. If I can't keep up, you'll leave me."

Sara and Tim opened their mouths to speak, but Kyle wasn't having it. "This isn't a matter for discussion. The three of you have a real chance at a safe place."

A lie.

"We're going to get you there." The ever-present 'if' rang in his mind. *If* monsters didn't find them. *If* they didn't starve. *If* they weren't shot. "You aren't going to let some busted old man slow you down. I'll put a bullet in my goddamn head before I let that happen."

He didn't know if he'd have the balls to do it. He'd always imagined he could if things grew bad enough. But he'd held onto every second of life with an iron grip, even when it seemed utterly hopeless to do so.

Tim broke the silence. "Alright."

Kyle's gaze fell on Sara. That sadness behind her eyes. The look that said goodbye. She already knew what she had to do. She was strong. She could do it if she had to.

She finally nodded.

"Fantastic. Now that it's settled, let's keep moving. Tim, take point. Kaylee, help an old man walk." He held his hand out to her, but she watched Sara.

"How do you know monsters are coming?"

Her eyes glassed over again, seeing the things nobody else would ever see. "I can hear them."

Chapter 14

Sara

The disease and pain inside Kyle radiated outward, impossible for Sara not to notice. It had been bad for a long time. Only his stubborn, bullshit personality had allowed him to barrel through it. A lesser man would have given up and died.

She brushed the hair from her swollen eye, slightly ashamed for spying into his pain. She watched as he plugged along, holding Kaylee's hand, his vision always set on the next horizon. Nobody had spoken since her spat with Tim that morning. There had been no exits and no signs of civilization in eight hours. They were in the middle of nowhere, but closing on their goal.

The things behind them were closing too. Three steps closer for their every one. Maybe the Walking Cancer saw them in its mind, but she suspected it was dumb luck.

"Next place we see, we need to stop for the night," she said. The things had gotten much nearer while they slept the night before, but they couldn't keep on. She ached with every step, her insides still feeling out of place, and Kyle could barely stand.

Tim turned around. "You think we're close?"

Kyle was more out of breath than he should be, but he answered for her. "Yes. Another five or six hours."

An old truck weighing station stood largely intact a few miles up the road. In the woods behind it, the partial remains of old warehouses leaned against the trees.

"I'll go check it out," Tim said as they approached.

Kyle rested against what was left of an old road blockade, his hands on his knees. Kaylee didn't move from him, as if her presence could make him well. "Go peek around those two cars." He gestured at a pair of sedans a hundred yards away in the parking lot. "See if there's anything we can use in them. Be careful."

"Is it safe?"

Sara wanted to tell her everything was safe, everything would be okay, but she didn't.

"It'll be fine," Kyle said. "Go." He waited until she was out of earshot before he turned to Sara. "You need to scan her tonight."

One of his pupils was dilated. Only one. That terrified her. "I will."

"If there's anything to find, we need to do so before we get there." He rubbed his temples.

Watching him hurt broke her insides worse than any punches could. "Are you going to make it?"

He shrugged, but said no more. She grabbed one of his hands and held it for a long while, wishing she could take some of his pain away.

Tim, grinning, returned the same time as Kaylee. He hadn't smiled since North Fifteen.

"Guess what I found?" He turned over his canteen, and dirty water poured onto the pavement.

The stream behind the building slaked their thirst, even if it did nothing for their hunger. They boiled the water in the steel canteens and let it cool. Blight usually showed as an orange tint to the water, but it was better to be safe than sorry. The first drink Sara took was still warm, but she didn't care.

The firelight in the tiny bathroom, the only room not exposed to the outside, cast Kyle's face in shadow. "Sip it slowly. We don't want you throwing up from dehydration."

She drank it quickly, heedless of his warnings. All day she'd told herself she wasn't thirsty, fooling her body into ceasing its constant demand for sustenance. An old trick she'd picked up on the road.

Within an hour, they'd made four runs for water, and the last was cooling. Her stomach still growled, but it was easier to think about what she had to do when she wasn't dying for a drink. She pulled out a cigarette. Her internal alarms about the smell went off before she lit it, but nothing touched her mind. They'd been lucky since their midnight flight, but that luck wouldn't last. The Walking Cancer would find them.

She brushed her fingers through Kaylee's hair, gently untangling any knots she found. "Kaylee, I need to try and see your memories again."

Kaylee stiffened in her lap.

"We need to find out if you saw anything about your mother's friends." She blew a puff of smoke to the side.

"It scared me."

"I know it did, but we have to try. We need to know where we're going when we get there. If we don't, it could be bad."

Bad didn't cover it. They'd all die wandering in a city, especially in their state.

Kaylee kept silent until the cigarette burned out and Sara cast it into the fire. "Okay." She nodded, her face set in a stoic mask that wouldn't have looked out of place on Kyle. "Right now?"

"We should, yeah. We're getting really close."

Kaylee took a deep breath and blew it out. "Okay."

Sara focused inward, willing herself to loosen up for the process as she placed a hand on either side of Kaylee's head. The aches in her body protested. "This won't hurt."

She could feel everything Kyle, Kaylee, and Tim were feeling already, but she focused on Kaylee. The tiny hole she entered through the first time was in the same—

She fell into Kaylee's mind like water. It was easier than last time. No effort at all. Kaylee felt as shocked as Sara at the simplicity of her mental intrusion.

"Sara?" The word echoed off the walls-that-weren't-walls around her.

"It's just me. It's okay." The walls fell away, and she stood at the bottom of a crystal-clear lake, seeing everything for miles. Each of the rooms here contained a thought or memory replaying endlessly. She'd never seen anything like it. The water around her was tinted yellow, the color of caution. A giant version of her rag doll hung just below the surface, dangling from a chain that led all the way back to the sun high above.

"This looks different," Kaylee said.

The other visit to Kaylee's mind had been a dark cave. This was a wide-open field, every memory available at a touch. "I know. I think I'm different now."

Different because of the Walking Cancer.

Thinking about it tore a piece of her out of Kaylee's mind and launched it down the road. She flew past the landscape to the place where the world turned to porcelain. There it stood. It didn't have a human face in the waking world, but here it did; a delicate glass mask shrouded in shadow. Its smile curled upward, cracking its countenance apart as it grinned at her.

Glad. It was glad to know she was still close enough to be seen.

She snapped back to the undersea landscape and shuddered. Her new abilities were dangerous.

"Sara, are you there?" The water turned a deeper shade of yellow, bordering on orange.

"It's all right, I'm here." Sara dropped all thoughts of the Walking Cancer, not wanting it to pollute this place. She imagined herself grabbing Kaylee's hand. "Can you feel that?"

"I can." Sara's imaginary hand grasped Kaylee's, comforting her. The water faded back to yellow and then lightened to green.

"Everything's all right. I'll be here the whole time."

She gazed at the endless little rooms filled with the pieces that made up Kaylee. She could see them all, even the ones far, far away. She closed her eyes and waded through them, looking for Oak Ridge or Pacific Applied Biology Technology. There were many.

One drifted out of the darkness and consumed her.

"So you and Daddy work for the government?" Kaylee sat on Miriam's lap and stared at her. She couldn't have been older than four.

"Well, a little bit. We worked for a company that the government paid." Momma stroked her hair the same way Sara did.

"Why?"

"So we can help people. We were going to change the world. We still might."

The image melted away to another room at another time. Kaylee couldn't play outside, but she wanted to. The bunker's sterile, melancholy lights beat down on every waking moment. She was tired of them. She'd never seen the sun outside of pictures, but some part of her demanded it.

"There are monsters, Kaylee. Big, scary monsters are everywhere out there."

Momma wore her no-nonsense look, but Kaylee could tell she was scared. Her eyes were narrow, her hands on her hips. She thought Kaylee would try to get outside one of these days.

"We've got guns. Maybe there aren't a lot of monsters."

The scene shifted to a few minutes in the future. Tears glistened in Kaylee's eyes as she watched a picture on the monitor. A map of the world with red circles expanding outward glowed on the screen.

"They're everywhere. The guns and bombs didn't even slow them down. That's why we're here, sweetheart. We have to find a way to stop them."

Sara pulled back into the undersea world between thoughts. They'd been working on a way to stop the monsters. A way to take the world back. After thirteen years of wandering the wastelands that had once been the United States, it seemed like nothing but fantasy.

Indignation oozed across the link from Kaylee. "It wasn't made up. Momma said they were close."

Miriam's words whispered out of the darkness. "The biological compound has a ninety-eight-point-seven percent similarity to silver." She laughed into the phone. "I know, I know. It isn't all good news. All the digital lines have been severed. We need to make the trip in person to get you the data." She laughed again. "I think we did it."

Sara spoke to Kaylee in the underwater memory room. "Is that right before you left?"

The room's green drifted to pink and then to blue. "Yes."

Other memories approached from the water unbidden. Kaylee and her mother playing in a makeshift nursery that had once been a small, ugly dorm. Miriam coming home drunk after celebrating New Years in the lab lobby. A memorial service for a man who'd gone out to take readings on the surface and never come back. That last memory stuck around longer than the rest.

Momma grabbed her arm tighter than ever before. Her eyes were red and puffy. "Do you see what it's like out there, baby? Do you see why we can never, ever leave?"

Another woman touched her on the shoulder. "Miriam."

"They'll get anybody who goes out there, do you understand? Never, ever go out there."

Kaylee quaked in fear. She understood. The world outside was a land of death, and only in this place could she ever hope to survive.

"Miriam!"

"I'm sorry. I'm sorry, I just don't—" The rest faded away into fog as the water shifted colors.

Sara wanted to cry, but she needed to get control of the situation before Kaylee became emotionally unstable. If her head turned into a storm, they weren't going to accomplish anything.

"I need you to relax, Kaylee."

The words had no effect. The water continued to darken, and Kaylee made no reply. The world deepened to blue and then started shifting to red.

"I don't want to be here anymore."

"Just calm down."

"No! I don't want to see this anymore."

A memory blurred past Sara. Her head spun. Miriam balled her hand and stared at Kaylee. Momma had never been this mad. The scribbles from Kaylee's marker covered the pages of the biology textbook like little red accusations. Momma reared back and slapped Kaylee across the face.

The slap hit Sara so hard her head jerked back in the real world. Her ears rang with the impact. Things could hurt here. Her stomach dropped.

Kaylee cried in the void. "Please, let's go! Please!"

It broke her heart, but they couldn't leave. "No, Kaylee."

The world started to spin into something different, some exit she could escape through.

Sara held up a finger, and the spinning ceased. The water became clear as day. "I'm sorry."

Sara had control here. She was strong now. Stronger with her mind than she had ever been. All their lives depended on the information this girl might have. Dirty as it might be, she had to hold her ground. Oak Ridge. She needed to find information on Oak Ridge.

Another memory emerged from the inner recesses of the girl's mind, this one after they'd already left the safety of the bunker.

The fading daylight cast the world in crimson and gold. Miriam huddled over a map, Kaylee at her side. Two soldiers chatted quietly nearby. Kaylee gazed at the map for a moment.

That was all Sara needed. She froze the moment in time and looked through Kaylee's eyes. Pacific Applied Biology Technology was scribbled on the right hand side with an address. She could only make out the words 'Gullman Road', but a circle was drawn on Oak Ridge's eastern edge, right outside the city.

"Is this where you were going, Kaylee?" Sara asked from behind the girls eyes.

Sobs echoed across the stillness. "I don't know."

"Your mother didn't mention any names, did she?"

The world dissolved into a billion tiny specks and reshaped in Miriam's office. She spoke into a monstrously large phone. "Dr. Stern for Dr. Chambers."

"Is that her friend's name, Kaylee? Is it Dr. Chambers?"

Only cries answered her. Forcing her way around inside the girl's head could be hurting her for all Sara knew. There was no manual for scanning, no instruction booklet to glance over the dos and don'ts. She was doing something to this girl that the men in the barn couldn't have done to her.

It no longer felt like a friendly meeting of the mind; it felt like an invasion. "I'm sorry. Let's get out."

Kaylee sobbed in response, reliving the most painful moments of her life. Some hadn't even had a chance to scar over yet. Time didn't heal shit, but it did offer a chance to forget. Sara should have at least given her as much.

She stepped backward out of the memory and into ocean of Kaylee's mind. From there, she swam to the surface and the way out. The doll floating above rocked back and forth in time with Kaylee's tears.

Kaylee started to cry the moment they were free of her mind. Sara blinked back the firelight as her eyes readjusted. She put her arms around Kaylee as Tim and Kyle looked on from the corner. "I'm sorry, Kaylee. I'm sorry. Shh."

Kyle grabbed Tim's arm. "Remember what I said."

Tim walked over to Kaylee, rubbing her leg and trying to soothe her. They had what they needed, even if the price was steep.

Kaylee insisted she was fine as they packed up in the morning, but she wouldn't look Sara in the eyes. Young as she might be, she understood what was at stake.

Still, Sara burned with guilt. The poor girl could never have a normal life. Even if everything was okay in Oak Ridge, and they had warm meals and hot showers the rest of their lives, that girl would always have monsters in her closet. As Sara limped out of the truck station, her limbs sore from cold, she supposed they all would.

Kyle didn't appear to be in as much pain today. The disease inside him still drifted through the air to her extra senses, but everything else was in check. Whether he was hiding it well or actually feeling better, she didn't know, and she wouldn't scan him to find out.

Tim's spirits were higher than they'd been in a while. She suspected he'd already concluded that Oak Ridge was indeed a safe place. She hoped he was right.

"Do you know anything about this Oak Ridge place?" he asked as they turned onto the remains of the highway.

Kyle's gaze was still glued to the horizon. "They made nuclear bombs there a long time ago. Weapons made to kill people and structures on a scale the world had never seen. There were bombs that could wipe whole cities off the map."

Tim looked over his shoulder, shock stamped across his face. "Why?"

"That's not even the worst of it. Within eighty years of that, almost every nation on the planet had them. People thought we were going to blow ourselves up before the year 2050." For the first time, he took his gaze off the road and stared into the sky. "And they did it because people are scared and stupid. Mostly stupid. The smart people tended to be the stupidest of all, and so they came together and made weapons instead of finding methods to prevent war."

As a kid, Sara had known about Oak Ridge too, but she'd forgotten. The irony of going to the town where the bombs were made in order to find salvation wasn't lost on her.

Kyle's answer shut Tim down, and they walked in silence. In the quiet that followed, a shadow passed over Sara's mind, as if a hand had reached across the sun and cast darkness on the land. Not a cloud marred the sky. It persisted for a long minute before it bled away behind her.

She glanced over her shoulder, and her vision was stretched back. Back beyond the truck stop and beyond the wreckage of a dozen houses they'd passed. It zipped by the line where her *other* sight turned the world to glass. There, in the far distance, the Walking Cancer leered at her. It saw her this time as much as she saw it.

Too far away to do anything, it released her. She rubberbanded into herself so hard her head snapped back. She moaned as vertigo pulled her toward the Earth, collapsing her onto the ground.

Tim and Kaylee stood over her. "Sara, are you all right?" Kaylee asked.

It took her a second to get her bearings. The Walking Cancer knew where they were, and it wasn't far behind. "Tim?" She stared up at him, his silhouette blocking the sun. For a moment, she thought it was the creature come for her.

He helped her up. "What's wrong? You look like you seen a ghost."

She had. Worse. A ghost couldn't get inside and wear you. "We need to keep going."

"Slow down. What's wrong?" Kyle brushed dirt off her back.

"It's coming. The thing from the barn is coming." She stared over his shoulder, expecting it to show itself any second.

"The big one? It's dead, Sara. I killed it."

"No. It's something else. Something like me. The thing from last week after we found Kaylee. It's coming for us, Kyle. We need to go." She moved forward, not waiting for a response. There wasn't time. It would be a miracle if they reached Oak Ridge and the PABT building before it did.

It wouldn't be alone either. Of that, she was certain.

"Slow down." Tim jogged to catch up as Kyle and Kaylee fell in behind. "We're all hurtin' here." He'd washed the blood from his face, but two gory holes remained where some of his teeth had been. When she didn't stop, he put a hand on her shoulder. "Sara?"

He didn't understand. It hadn't touched him like it had her. That thing was worse than death. It was mental invasion. It soiled memories, making them a part of itself. It didn't just want to kill and devour people like the other monsters; it wanted to know what made them tick.

"It saw me. It's coming for us."

He stared at her stupidly.

"You were right all along, Kyle. They think. They have a hierarchy. It's on the top of theirs, and it wants to see what's inside of us. It tears people open and pokes around inside, looking for things it likes up here." She tapped her head.

Kyle opened his mouth to speak, but she sensed his protest the same way she sensed the creature.

"I know what you're going to say, because I can feel it. 'Are you sure you aren't still hurting from the barn'? Yes, I am, but that isn't what this is. It touched me when I was hanging in that place. It heard me when I screamed for you. It wants something from us, but I don't know what. What I do know is that if it finds us, we won't die fast."

Tim began to say something, but she snatched that out of the air too. "It ain't gonna do us no good if we all pass out on the road.'"

Kyle gazed into her eyes. The pain was still there, barely hiding. Something else was with it too. He was searching for honesty, curious if she had come unhinged over the last few days.

"Alright. We move faster. Can you handle that?"

She nodded. Tim shook his head, but protested no further. He took Kaylee's hand as Sara led the way down the dilapidated highway. The only witnesses to their passing were the birds in the sky and the hollowed husks of buildings.

Chapter 15

Kyle

The Tennessee countryside had once called to him. Its voice had been as smooth as silk in those days, its song pleasant. Now it hid dangers around every corner, and nothing it said sounded anything but threatening.

Blighted grass sprouted up between cracks in the broken ground beneath his feet. The trees on either side of the road were black and red, but not dead. The blight didn't kill; it just changed. Made the world into some unidentifiable other. A sea of red as far back and forward as the eyes could see, the air sour.

The decayed remains of buildings echoed with the moans of infected, but the creatures never showed themselves. Sara urged them onward, not slowing even when it was obvious her own pain was mounting.

Kyle tried to bury his as well, but it became more difficult by the moment. Each step sent a reverberation through his skull. A small pebble on the mountain of discomfort, rolling down to create a landslide of agony. He was squeezing Kaylee's hand too hard.

"You're hurting." She wiggled free of his grasp, staring up with her soulful blues.

The response was on his tongue, but he couldn't get it out. The words jumbled in his head. He wanted to say, "I'm sorry," but every time he tried, he could only mumble. Terrified, he tried again, but only mumbled louder.

Sara caught up with them and grabbed Kaylee's hand. "Let's keep moving." She'd said nothing else since her earlier outburst. She stopped long enough to look into his eyes.

She knew. He could tell from the glint in her stare, the threat of tears wanting to spill out. He was coming unraveled. He didn't have weeks or months. He had days at best.

Fine. Then he had days. He'd help them reach Oak Ridge; be it salvation or more heartache. He took a moment to compose himself, trying to focus only on his feet and block everything else out. One foot at a time. That's all he could do. Slowly, his legs started to obey, and the terror eased up as the familiar pain of walking reasserted itself.

The road here grew wild, but the buildings hadn't been hit as badly. A dozen intact homes watched them as they fled. An old western ghost town transplanted to the east. All the people up and gone, moved on to better prospects once the world went mad.

"It's like all the people just drove home for the day." Karen couldn't tear her gaze from the subdivision below. Only four short

years before they would have looked like psychopaths sitting on a hill in the woods, staring at the community below. Not anymore. Now community was a rare word, and an entire block where all the houses still stood even rarer.

"Think there's anyone down there?" Richard gazed through his binoculars, but they couldn't tell him what he wanted to know.

They had enough food for themselves, but there were other mouths to feed back on the farm. "I know one way to find out." Kyle pulled out the machete Richard had given him. It glinted in the sunlight.

"Do you hear that?"

Kyle blinked twice at Tim before he realized Sara was speaking to him. "What?" The word formed without trouble.

"That sound. Do you hear it?"

Something drifted to him on the wind. The low murmur of a crowd. He'd heard it before.

"Infected. A lot of them."

The curvature of the Tennessee hills blocked the road out of sight a hundred yards ahead, but the sound came from that direction.

"Lemme go check it out." Tim skulked off towards the moans, crouching low in the blighted grass. He vanished within seconds.

Kyle leaned against an old Toyota whose white color was still visible. The throbbing in his head didn't abate. He wondered what it would be like at the end. It had to be leading to an end, after all. He didn't mind pain, but given the choice, he'd have preferred to go quietly in his sleep.

"Jesus Christ, that's morbid." Sara peeked at him between her hands as she rubbed her face. Kaylee looked baffled but kept watching the spot where Tim had disappeared.

"Are you scanning me again?" He couldn't get a moment's peace, even in his head.

"You're putting it out there; I'm just picking it up."

He didn't respond right away, just gave the implication a moment to sink in. "You know then?"

She only nodded, but her expression spoke volumes. All the sad looks over the last three days added up.

"I'll be fine."

Again, she didn't respond, but her face said it all. *No, you won't.*

A shuffle in the grass marked Tim's return. "There's a lot of 'em."

Kaylee squeezed closer to Sara.

"Define, 'a lot,'" Sara said.

"Highway goes over an overpass. The roads full of 'em under. Looks like they might have wandered from some camp you can see from the pass."

"Camp?"

"Yeah. There's a fence around what's left of a bunch of tents."

An old Army evacuation camp. All those places had turned into deathtraps overnight. Hundreds of people with nothing but a few dozen soldiers and a fence to protect them must have looked like a buffet to the crawlers and apes wandering around the forests.

251

"Was the overpass clear?" Sara asked.

He shrugged. "A few on the road, but most of them were below, just standin' there and moanin'."

Sara looked at Kyle, her eyes hard. "We need to keep going. That one from the barn isn't far behind us, and we don't have time to lose. I say we cross the bridge."

Infected weren't fast, but they were persistent. If a big enough group started in one direction, they'd move forever. They'd see the ones around them going one way and follow suit. An endless cycle. A living dead perpetual motion machine.

If they were seen, there would be no rest until they were far, far away. "Are you sure?" Kyle asked.

"Yes. We need to move." She grabbed Kaylee's hand and stalked into the tall grass.

With a glance at Tim, Kyle followed. The hill rose above them, and the wails of the damned grew noticeably louder, a hundred of them judging by the sound. They crested the hill, and the earth sloped downward slightly, giving a view of the overpass on the other side.

There weren't a hundred, but hundreds, packing the road below the overpass. Not a few on the overpass either but a dozen. Cars littered the bridge, creating a series of narrow paths with a big open space in the middle. Between the top of the hill and the legion of the dead, the blighted grass grew taller than their heads.

They would be blind down there.

Kyle's heart skipped a beat, and his vision darkened dangerously. *Not now. Not now.* He bit hard on his cheek, willing himself to focus. The taste of blood filled his mouth.

Sara had stopped at the top of the hill as well. She crouched and scanned the path ahead. "I think we can move around the ones on the road. The other side of the overpass is mostly clear. If we can cut through the ones up top, we'll be fine after."

"Cut through?" Kyle raised an eyebrow as if she'd lost her mind. "We'll draw everything on us. They'll chase us all the way to Oak Ridge."

Her eyes cold, she stared at him. As if to punctuate her sincerity, the howl of a crawler glided out of the woods north of the road. The whisper of a ghost, gone as quick as it started. "What's behind us is worse."

Kyle nodded. Tim started down the hill, picking the path of least resistance. Sara followed with Kaylee in hand, Kyle just behind.

The smell hit him before anything else. Meat left out in the sun. An animal dying in the summer under the porch. Something about the transformation prevented them from rotting correctly. They stayed putrid long after the time they should have been dust and bones. The smell never faded, just lingered and built with time. One day, the whole world would reek of them.

The first three were only a hundred yards from the bridge. The group made it past without being noticed, the tall grass hiding them from sight. Kyle's breath caught every time the grass swayed and rustled under his step, but he soldiered on.

Something shifted on the ground only a few feet away, scraping against the dirt. The grass parted, and a decayed hand reached from the ground.

He saw it in time to avoid it grabbing his wrist. He brought his machete down in an instant, severing the arm from the half-destroyed infected's upper body. The gaping mouth behind it let out a loud moan, but it had no eyes.

A million swaying bodies in the streets. A thousand dead for every monster they'd killed. This was it. There was no taking back the cites. Karen squeezed his hand.

Kyle snapped out of it as a dozen moans answered, then more. Soon the choir of the undead screamed in reply all around him.

The grass came alive with more crawling shapes. Some had legs that didn't work, while others were desiccated and still; only their eyes following him . One crawled at him, nothing more than a grayed shoulder, head, and arm reaching for him from the filth of the road.

He jumped back. The sudden movement swayed him as if the world had stopped turning. "Shit."

He'd lost sight of Sara and Kaylee. The grass crunched all around him.

"Sara?"

Moans answered. Then, only a few dozen feet in front of him, a gunshot rang out.

"Run!" Tim yelled.

Panic seized him, and he took off. A decayed hand reached out of the grass in front of him. He ducked his shoulder and plowed past, avoiding a snapping set of teeth on his ears by inches as an infected loomed out of the foliage.

Their lack of caution was going to get them all killed.

"Kyle!" Sara yelled somewhere ahead of him.

If he could see the damned overpass—

The grass vanished, and the road across the overpass appeared. Tim was halfway over already, gesturing for Sara and Kaylee to hurry as two infected closed behind them. The undead on the bridge drifted in, blocking the choke point on the far side of the open section.

The things beneath the bridge roared in deafening outrage at the transgressions of the living. The grass moved behind him as Kyle took off.

Kaylee screamed as the infected shuffled closer. Tim shot another behind him between the eyes. Sara picked Kaylee up, but they weren't going to get away. They were stuck in a choke point.

Kyle reached them as the first of the infected grasped at Sara's hair. His machete arced in a flash, cutting the arm from the body. It turned to him but caught his fist in its face, sending it sailing onto its back before it could react. He shoulder checked the second one and grabbed Sara's free hand, dashing between the cars and into the open space with her.

Tim shot a third infected.

Sara seized Tim with her free hand and fell in behind as Kyle let go and barreled toward the infected at the far end of the bridge.

The cars left only a narrow alley to pass through. The monsters from below were already climbing their way up the embankment on both sides. He was a dead man walking too, and he would get the people he cared about to Oak Ridge.

He swung his machete as if the wrath of God possessed his arm. Skulls split, pieces of leathery flesh flew, and death became permanent for the things in his path. Infected lunged at him. Teeth snapped. Hands reached. He cut through until the path was cleared.

"Go!" He stood to the side and let Sara and Kaylee run past as he struggled for breath.

Tim came last, dragging Kyle by the shirt as he ran past. The infected on the far side of the bridge were spread out further, and the ones down the embankment hadn't gotten topside yet.

Blight grass, hills, and wrecked cars obscured their vision beyond a dozen yards ahead. The foliage there moved too. The world had come alive to kill them.

The black spots returned to Kyle's vision as he tried to catch his wind, the din of the infected not far behind. His arms and legs burned.

"Come on, man," Tim yelled. He kept pulling Kyle by the shirt, but they ran slower with every step.

The lack of food and sleep would have taken its toll on anyone, and his illness only made it worse. "I think I'm done."

"The fuck you are. Sara, slow down. They ain't that fast; they won't catch us."

She stopped and turned to them. "We have to keep going."

"Leave me." He didn't say it to be heroic or brave, but because it needed to be done. They had to leave him if they wanted to get to Oak Ridge alive.

The infected inched closer with every passing second. The grass rattled.

Tim started walking again, his grip set around Kyle's arm. "Fuck that, old man. Get your ass movin'."

Kyle walked a few feet, and his vision blurred. He stumbled, and the Earth rose at him. He didn't realize he was falling before he hit the ground.

"Shit." Tim glanced back at the bridge. The moans were still too close. They had to move. "Come on." He pulled on Kyle's arm, trying to drag him to his feet. "Get the fuck up!"

Kyle tried, but the dizziness wouldn't abate. Those old memories called to him from the edges, waiting to swoop in. Maybe that was all dying was; being sucked into your memories like Alice falling down the rabbit hole. Maybe Heaven or Hell was walking the hallways of your mind forever.

"So that's it?" Tim asked. "You just fuckin' quit? Easy as pie?"

The audacity of this kid. "Fuck you."

A sudden pain shot through Kyle's ribs as Tim kicked him. "Get the fuck up!"

"Stop!" Kaylee yelled, but Tim paid her no mind.

Sara kept silent. One look told him she knew what had to be done but couldn't do it.

Tim stared at Kyle as the moans grew closer and closer. "Fine." He removed his backpack and handed it to Sara. She took it without question and put it on.

Tim reached under Kyle, lifting him off the ground and putting him across his shoulders. The guy couldn't have weighed more than a buck fifty. If Tim struggled under the load, he didn't show it.

"Let's go."

This was stupid. Trying to save everybody only got them killed. Sometimes surviving meant letting go. He was dying anyway, and he was goddamn tired of living. He opened his mouth to say as much, but nothing came out. The orange and black grass and broken vehicles were as miserable as the overcast sky that was settling into afternoon. He didn't want it anymore. Maybe Tim was right, and maybe he was a coward, but he'd done his duty. He'd survived longer than most, and kept everyone around him alive when he could.

Richard couldn't even load a damn gun. The guy wouldn't last long.

He'd done his best..

"You want to put up signs? Why not put up a big one that says, 'Hey, come get all our food'?"

Karen wanted him to come home with her and Richard. Things had to be better on the other side. Maybe there was nothing, but even that would be better. He stared at Tim's legs as they plodded along, their progress slowed. He glanced over at Kaylee, who still held the doll Kyle had almost died for.

Maybe things would be better once his generation was dead and gone. These kids didn't know anything about the old world. They couldn't lament the things no longer around, or the ignorant comfort of knowing monsters weren't real. They would move on in a world where survival was all they understood until the last human died or took back the Earth. Maybe that was better.

Kaylee looked back at him. She half-smiled and furrowed her eyebrows, trying to comfort him. An expression too adult for such a small face. She knew too much about death.

He faded in and out of consciousness. Richard and Karen called to him as he ran through the hills and forests of Tennessee. A horde of infected followed him constantly. They called his name, and their roars became an endless ocean.

He jerked awake as Tim set him on the ground none too gently. No blight anywhere, and the buildings on the roadsides said they were closer to a city than when Kyle had passed out. Howls had replaced the moans in the distance, monsters calling to one another in the mid-afternoon sunlight.

"Where are we?"

Tim sat nearby, panting and red-faced. He took a long drink of water as Sara answered. "Just outside of Oak Ridge. You've been out for almost two hours." She didn't look much better than Tim did.

He sat up. The same old pains presented themselves, and the black spots floated in his vision. He felt better, but not much. "Are we close to where we need to be?" His stomach rumbled painfully.

Sara took the canteen from Tim and dropped the pack to the ground, wincing. "Gullman Road. If the map I saw was right, it'll branch off this highway."

Another howl answered the first, and a faraway roar drowned out both. "When the hell did that start? What's going on?"

"It just started. The thing from the barn is getting closer. I can feel it. We haven't heard the infected behind us for half an hour, but we need to keep moving."

Kyle tried to stand, but Tim was over him in a flash, helping him to his feet. "Can you walk?"

Standing made him lightheaded, but he didn't fall. "I think so." Another noise in the distance made certain he understood it was walk or die. "I'll be fine."

Tim held his gaze for a moment before throwing the pack onto his back. "Alright. Come on."

Kaylee took his hand as they started walking.

"I didn't mean to scare you," he said.

She looked up at him but didn't respond, just took everything in with those big blue eyes.

The farms had mostly given way to industrial complexes and warehouses. Rusted hulks of buildings with tin roofs that had caved in over the years replaced country views. Among the rubble, shapes moved in the shadows. Infected, like the legion that couldn't be far behind. That was what they'd have to look forward to if they entered the city.

Sara wore an expression somewhere between determination and expectancy. She wanted this safe place to be true. She needed it. If it wasn't real or they couldn't find it, he didn't know what was going to happen. He wasn't scared for himself, but for them.

The roars and bellows, more now than before, drew closer.

"This is like the night in the barn," Tim said. "Is it the same thing?"

"Yes. It knows we're here. It's coming."

"How?" Kyle asked. "How can it know?"

Kaylee squeezed his hand.

"It knows the same way I do. I can see it like a beacon on the horizon, and I think it can see me."

That answered the question. If there was no sanctuary in Oak Ridge, they were dead. "We'll make it." He offered reassurances he didn't feel. "We'll get there in time."

Kaylee squeezed his hand harder.

They walked faster than four people who hadn't eaten in days should have, faster than three people with serious injuries normally could. Still, the sounds grew closer. The sun moved across the sky. The number of infected trailing them increased. The things took notice of their passing and fell in line behind. A few more soldiers in the army of the damned lining up to do their genocidal duty.

Kaylee whined under her breath as two of them not ten feet off the road spotted the group and shambled toward them. She held

Kyle's hand so tightly it hurt, and held her doll equally hard. On the other side of the road, an infected chomped its rotted teeth together. She whined again and squeezed her eyes shut. He wanted nothing more than to shut his own eyes and remain blissfully ignorant of their surroundings. "Keep them open. You can't see where you're going with your eyes closed."

She didn't respond.

In the distance, a road branched off the ragged highway. "I think we're close." Sara walked even faster, almost jogging.

Kyle ignored the pain as best he could. He didn't often consider suicide. When everything had happened with Karen and Richard, he'd flirted with the idea, but never seriously. If they couldn't find this road, he would. A thousand terrible things were making their way toward them, and he didn't have the strength or the courage to face it anymore. He wouldn't become an infected.

He wouldn't let any of them become infected either.

"There's no sign," Tim said, pulling Kyle from his grim musings. "There's no fuckin' sign on the road."

He was right. They weren't more than a few hundred yards from the turn, and nothing stood nearby.

"It might be in the grass," Sara said as another howl pierced the still November air. That same hope he'd seen on her face called out from her voice. "We'll be alright."

They closed the last of the distance, no infected blocking their path. The unblighted grass stood to their waist.

Tim fished for the phantom sign. "I don't see shit." He looked back at the dozen or so infected they'd picked up in the last twenty minutes. "What do we do, Sara? Do we just go?"

Sara looked from him to Kyle and back again, idly picking at a string on her pants. Her eyes glassed over as if she were seeing something they couldn't, something far away. It lasted only a second. "I don't know."

Bestial cries echoed down the road behind them. "Now ain't a good time for 'I don't know.'"

Kyle stared into that desperate need in Sara's eyes. They had to be right. Stalling now would be fatal. "It's Gullman. Let's go." Without another word, he started down the new road. The others fell in line behind him.

The weeds and foliage weren't as tall here. Trees surrounded them. Kaylee tripped and nearly fell, but Kyle caught her and helped her back up.

"Are we going to be safe?" She asked it quietly, as if she didn't want the others to overhear.

"Yes. We'll be fine."

"How do you know?" She fixed her vision on the point where the road curved into the woods and out of sight.

"We made it this far, right?" He wanted to sound self-assured, but it fell flat. An apology of sorts. *Well fuck, we didn't win the prize, but at least we got this great big bill for it.*

"I'm scared." Her voice quavered. She had the unaffected air of a little girl choked full of insecurities, but with the shield of absolute certainty that those around her knew what they were doing. The childish confidence that adults couldn't lead her astray. In the old world, kidnappers thrived on that. Here though, here it was another heartbreaking reminder of what the world now was.

"I know you are. I am too."

She looked up at him, her eyes rimmed with tears that hadn't fallen yet.

He wanted to say something full of self-assurance and swagger. "*Save the water, kiddo,*" or "*Don't cry until the fat lady sings.*" Instead, he watched the path ahead. It curved through the woods, going deeper and farther from the main highway. Straggling infected pursued them around the bend. If they wanted to stop to rest, they'd have to deal with that.

A sniffer screamed in the distance. Rest wasn't in the cards. There was no turning back now.

The buildings off the highway had vanished, but the concrete beneath their feet looked newer than that of the other road. He kept his eyes locked to it, hoping it was a good sign, when Sara spoke up. "Oh my god."

Kyle's hand went to his machete on instinct, but he dropped it when he saw the sign.

Pacific Applied Biology and Technology Testing Center. Authorized Personnel Only. Display ID at All Times.

He read it three times before it registered. They might have missed it leaning against a tree. It didn't seem real. It couldn't actually say that. That meant this wasn't a fantasy. It was true, and if it was true, everything else might be too.

Sara put her hand over her mouth, her eyes wide as saucers.

They might actually make it. They might actually be okay.

Chapter 16

Sara

She stared at the sign as if it would vanish.

"Kyle," Kaylee said. The infected trailing them were getting closer. The remains of previously human beings shambling toward them soured her mood, but not by much.

"Let's go. We're close now." She couldn't feel other people, but that didn't mean anything. Scanning didn't always work like radar, and this new type of scanning was more alien than ever.

But not as alien as the thing behind.

It had been growing in her mind all day. An ugly shape on the farthest part of her vision where the world turned to glass. A hot piece of iron moving steadily closer, radiating heat and trying to burn her. An army of monsters hovered around it, a swarm of carrion flies waiting to feast on any scraps it left behind. It called, and they came. The alpha dog monster. The Walking Cancer wasn't going to let them escape so easily, but maybe they could hide for a while. Bury themselves under the earth and hope it couldn't reach them.

She tried to put it out of her mind as its legion closed on them. The sparse forest ceased altogether after another mile. A hill, an ever-present commodity in Tennessee, blocked the road from view.

She held her breath as they approached the top. It would be destroyed. A wreck. There wouldn't be enough to identify it as a human construct. There would be a thousand times a thousand infected waiting for them on the other side.

None of that was correct.

Over the hill stood the largest intact building Sara had seen in thirteen years, but the four-story office had seen better days. The roof sagged over the edges in spots, and the red brick gave way to a massive hole in one side.

"Holy fuck. Is this real?"

Tim's thoughts mirrored hers perfectly. It had to be a dream. There were no safe places or four-story buildings anymore. It certainly didn't look like a sanctuary. In fact, a strong breeze might knock the place over.

"Do you think this is it?" She silently chastised herself for sounding like a child.

"One way to find out." Kyle continued down the hill, his hand wrapped around Kaylee's.

She'd wondered all day how he was still standing with the waves of pain that expanded out from him, but she forgot those thoughts as they followed the shattered road. They passed a knocked-over guard shack on the right. On the left, a car had been turned onto its top, and all the tires were gone. The closer they drew, the dingier the building appeared.

Doubt crept into her mind, a soul-crushing certainty that they hadn't found anything but a wrecked office building. Nothing worth a damn except a few filing cabinets filled with rotted paper. The Walking Cancer or the infected would find them and make a meal of them in this ghost of a place.

But somewhere ahead, she sensed other people. One second, nothing, and the next, life. Dozens of them. More even. "There are others here." The words were foreign to her ears. "Other people."

Tim's face became a mask of incredulity. "Where?"

"Inside somewhere."

Ants in a colony, going about their business as if giants didn't stalk the land overhead.

"I don't know how many."

Tim stared at the building as if it would bite him. "Are we sure it isn't just more bandits?"

There came a point when you had to bite the bullet and find out. She continued toward the building. "What if it is?" If they were wrong, and this place wasn't safe, they would die anyway. The Walking Cancer drew closer with every passing second. Already the occasional howls and screeches had turned into a constant roar.

"Was the place you and your mother stayed like this?" Kyle asked Kaylee as they walked.

Kaylee shook her head. "There was a door that led up to a road. It opened under a bridge."

"Was it hidden?" Sara asked.

"Momma told me nobody could find it if they didn't know where to look."

Sara's blood ran cold. She hadn't thought of that. *What if they're underground, and there's no way to contact them?* "Do you remember anything else?" A stupid question. If she remembered anything else, Sara would have seen it in her mind.

Kaylee shook her head as the shadow of the building consumed them.

Up close, it looked much worse than from a distance. The remains of cars littered the parking lot. Some of them remained neatly parked in their spots, as if the owners had gone home from work one day and forgotten them. Others were like the one near the guard shack, broken and dismembered. Even all these years later, seeing cars so casually tossed aside by some unseen force made her stomach spin.

Most of the windows in the building were gone too, and it wasn't hard to get in through the first floor's glass walls. Wires hung from the ceiling, and what must have been a nice hardwood floor at some point was a fractured mess. It looked as though it had been abandoned for decades.

"I don't think anyone lives here." Tim stepped over the broken windowpane and into the building.

Kyle was slowing noticeably. He glanced at Sara as he stepped inside, but his eyes didn't focus. He could have passed for an infected. "They'll be here." No assurances came through in his voice. It was mechanical. A man saying what he had to.

A scream of rage rose higher than the rest. All heads turned.

"We don't have time to discuss this." Not waiting for a response, Sara fell into herself, opening her mind to the unseen energies around her.

Crawling in their little tunnels, leading their little lives. Blissfully unaware of their lack of relevance. A production facility without a product. Ants fought for food. These busy little ants wanted answers and solutions, and that was much harder fare to forage.

She tore herself away and became aware of something watching her. It dragged her mind in the direction of the incoming horde, leading her away in chains.

No.

She thought the word, and the chains vanished. The Walking Cancer couldn't hold her here. She was still too far away, and the leash it pulled stretched too thin.

It wasn't in the porcelain faraway land anymore though. It could take its chosen form here. A shadow on the wall. An unseen hand in the dark. It operated behind the scenes, not out in the open.

She pushed it away as best she could, but its fingers, if they could be called fingers, reached for her. She had to find the ants.

They went marching in one by one and two by two, ("Hurrah, Hurrah") but never came back out. They'd gotten the green light and sealed the colony. These little ants had neat little tricks, pieces of the old world that left them in better shape than anyone up top.*

There was no time to search for the mound. The Walking Cancer was getting too close.

"NEVER GET AWAY!"

"Pray, you little brat!"

Tim held her by both arms while Kaylee and Kyle looked on. "Jesus, Sara. Are you back?"

"What?"

"You kept moaning and saying 'hurrah'."

She raised an eyebrow as if Tim had lost his mind.

"You've been out for ten minutes."

The infected that had followed them from the highway stumbled through the parking lot, making their sure but steady way toward the building.

The Walking Cancer. It had grabbed her. "They're below us. The people here are all below us, like ants."

"What?"

"When everything happened thirteen years ago, they sealed themselves up. They build things here, or they're supposed to." She walked over to Kaylee, her gait unsteady. "Did you know that, honey? Can you remember?"

Kaylee stared into Sara's eyes. Guilt danced across her features. "I don't remember. Momma said it was safe here, and that we had to find them. She said I had to come with her because we'd be safe here." Tears welled in her eyes. "Are we going to find it, Sara?"

Sara pulled Kaylee's head to her chest. "It's okay. We'll find it." She stroked the crimson streak that dyed the golden wheat. The infected didn't afford them much of a reprieve. "We have to keep moving." She gently pushed Kaylee away and grabbed her hand. Already the infected had reached the building's outer edges. "They've got to be here somewhere."

"So, what? We wander around until we find the fuckers and knock on a door?"

She shook her head. "The basement." The nightmare concert loomed ever nearer, and the infected shambled closer. "If there's a secret anything still left in this place, it'll be in the basement."

Tim helped Kyle to his feet as Sara walked deeper into the lobby. "You want to dig through the floor?" Tim said, catching up. "We need to go!"

She pressed on.

"Don't you hear that? Them things are close. We need to hide or get the hell away from here."

She dropped her voice so Kyle and Kaylee wouldn't hear. "And go where? Huh? There's nowhere to go, and even if there was, Kyle can hardly walk. You have to trust me. Those people are below us, I can feel it."

He doubted it. She could feel it as clearly as if he'd said it.

She passed through the lobby and into a hallway that stank of mold. An old building like this would have an elevator or a stairwell, something to let them get down.

She didn't have to search long. The third door she checked in the decrepit hallway contained stairs leading both up and down. "Here!"

"Are you kidding me? It's pitch black down there." Tim shook his head.

They could get by on starlight at night if there were no clouds, but natural light couldn't pierce the darkness inside. The men in the barn had taken her flashlight. "You have your light?"

Tim shook his head. "It's gone."

Sara turned Tim around and dug inside the pack. She grabbed an extra shirt and the lighter from the bottom, then snatched Kyle's machete from its sheath and fashioned a makeshift torch.

"I can't believe you're gonna waste lighter fluid on this."

Kyle slapped the back of his head. Tim turned, squaring up, but backed down when he saw Kyle's expression. "You've been bitching constantly. Either help or shut your damn yap."

He opened his mouth to speak, but closed it immediately.

"We're all scared, but that doesn't help anyone."

Sara walked into the stairwell and made her way down. Parts of the stone walls had fallen away, leaving the stairs rubble-strewn. Grime and dirt covered everything, and cobwebs filled the cracks and corners. Every instinct that had kept her alive over the last decade screamed that this was a mistake. She pushed the warning down. The people were here. She felt them growing closer with every step.

The others followed her. The stairs continued past the point where they'd be one floor down. Down here, the pieces of brick and debris littering the first floor vanished, replaced by a thick layer of dust.

"This is down pretty far," Kyle said when they were a full three stories under.

That would have been proof enough something was under this place, but more than that, she could feel it. The desperate ember of hope in her chest glowed a little brighter, even as noises from the things outside drifted down the stairwell.

"We're close."

It ended in a nondescript stone corridor. Only dust and spiders occupied the building this deep. There were six wooden doors in the hall, with a seventh at the end.

"Which one?" Tim asked.

Kaylee winced as a wail, louder than the others, carried down the stairwell and echoed against the stone.

"I don't know. Check them all." She tugged on the door at the end. Locked. "Shit."

The lock clicked as Tim pulled his door. "This one's locked."

Kyle pulled on his. "This one, too."

She tugged frantically on the door. "Damn! Damn! Damn!"

"Sara?" Kaylee trembled in the corner, her voice just above a whisper.

"It's alright." She tossed their makeshift torch onto the ground. Bracing her foot on the wall, she tried to force the door open. A sharp pain in her abdomen stabbed her. She let out a soft cry and fell to the ground.

"Are you okay?" Kyle asked.

"I'm fine." Something had torn in her gut. The warmth radiated inside her. "Tim, get this one open." She didn't know if it was the right door, but they wouldn't have time to bust them all down.

Tim did the same thing she had, bracing a foot on the door and tugging. The lock screeched but didn't break. "Come on." Tim continued to struggle, but it didn't budge.

The sound of a foot scuffing stone emanated from the stairwell. Something fell down a set of stairs, followed by a low moan.

Sara's heart leapt into her throat. The infected would be on them in minutes and everything else not far behind. That ember of hope started to grow cold. She may have lured everyone to their deaths. Pulled them from the open road where they had a chance to run, into a deserted building from which there could be no escape.

"Move." Kyle pulled his gun from his belt. He took aim at the door handle and fired until he'd spent the last of his ammo. The door handle was damaged, but intact. "Try again."

Tim tugged on the door with all his might. More noises of things falling down the stairs, several this time.

"Sara," Kaylee moaned, joining her on the floor and pressing her face into Sara's neck.

"It's going to be fine." Kyle flung the burning shirt onto the ground near the entrance to the hallway. It wouldn't last long. Soon they'd be alone in the dark with nothing but the damned to keep them company. He stared at Kaylee and Sara on the floor. "It's all going to be fine."

Sara dropped inside of herself, searching for the other people.

The ants in the hill didn't hear the gunshots. The memories of this place reached out at her, but above that, the Walking Cancer bore down, too close for comfort.

"Please! If anyone can hear me, open the door!"

The ants in the hill continued on as if they'd heard nothing. Then, slowly, several stopped and looked around.

"Yes! Yes! We're outside with Miriam Stern's daughter! Help! We're in danger!"

Several more stopped and talked. They were still too far away for her to enter their minds and speak to them directly, but they appeared to have heard.

Closer than them, the dead spots dropped to the bottom of the stairwell. Fear radiated from Kaylee and Tim like fireworks. From Kyle came some sort of sad determination. A feeling of shame and guilt, worse than what she usually sensed from him. The sickness consumed him. He was nearly as virulent as one of the monsters.

The Walking Cancer grabbed onto her thoughts. It was close now, as close as it had been in the barn. How had it gotten so near so fast?

Back in her body, Tim lifted her to her feet. "Come on, get up!"

She did as he bade, but the pain in her abdomen doubled her over. She gasped and tumbled backward. Tim saved her from spilling onto the floor and dragged her through the now open door as Kyle slammed his machete into the skull of an infected. As it fell to the ground, he retrieved the burning shirt with the tip of his machete and followed.

Sara looked around the large storeroom as Kyle closed the door behind them. A row of shelves covered in boxes spread out left and right. Tim pulled her to the left side of the room, following the bare wall to the end of the shelves. Around the corner, they could see six similar shelves and another faceless wall twenty feet away. No entrance to any underground facility that she could see. "Let's check the back wall. Kyle, check the other side."

Kyle walked to the other end of the room, Kaylee in hand.

Tim helped her limp toward the rear. She and Kyle had been in bad situations before, but nothing like this. They were trapped. Vermin in a room with nothing but neatly stacked boxes and rows of paperwork. They were so damn close to safe that she ached, but they couldn't reach it.

The ever-dimming light from Kyle's torch shone through the spaces between boxes, casting shadows across the wall. She prayed as they approached the back of the room.

God, if you're up there, you owe me one. You know damn well you do. Let this be the right room. Let us find these people and get the hell away from these things. Please. Please. I'll pray to you every night if you just make us safe.

They turned the corner, but she saw only Kyle and Kaylee on the far side of the room. "Was there anything?" Sara asked.

Kyle shook his head as the makeshift torch in his hand guttered, nearly spent. A crawler's howling closely followed a moan from the hallway.

Tim grabbed the pistol from his belt and checked the load. "I don't have much ammo."

Kyle stared into the flame. "It doesn't matter."

Tim opened his mouth to say something but looked away instead. A creature collided with the door to the room, but it didn't open.

"Okay, go block the door." Sara's mind raced. They couldn't get out, but they could hold off. Maybe the things would leave if they couldn't get in. "Collapse all the shelves on the door, and we'll wait them out."

Tim let out a long sigh and dropped his arms. He didn't have to say it; she already knew. There was no escaping. The end had caught them. All that running. All that surviving. It meant nothing.

A loud, mechanical groan emanated from the wall. Seams she hadn't noticed before ground together as a section of concrete moved back two inches.

Light, not the gentle light of the sun but that of harsh fluorescents, poured from the spaces. The hidden room's steel door slammed up and open as the piece of wall locked into place.

"Who are you?"

Sara had to look away, unable to stand the brilliance. When she regained her light vision, she was staring down the barrels of two rifles. The corridor behind them was painted white, had a steel grate floor. More shocking was the lost wonder of the old world— electricity.

"I said who are you?"

278

Something crashed into the shelves behind them as a creature burst into the room. Two moans and another howl followed from somewhere in the building.

Sara spoke first, the other two struck dumb. "Please. We came here looking for you, but there's no time to explain."

The younger of the two stared past her into the darkness as the monsters moved closer. Something thrashed around in the blackness. The rifle shook in his hands. He hesitated for half a second longer before he pointed his weapon down. "Get in, quick."

Sara grabbed Kaylee and went in first, followed by Kyle. Tim entered last as a set of shelves crumbled.

A piercing, inhuman scream blasted from the hallway with the doors. The young man pounded a red button on the wall, and the invisible door began sliding back into place.

A crawler crashed across the remaining shelves. It screamed again, and the older of the two men stepped back. "My god!"

The steel door slammed down, putting an impassable barrier between monster and man.

The light hurt her eyes. The atmosphere was sterile, and the stale air smelled unnatural to her after more than a decade outside. The light and the taste, the stink of metal and clean people, it was too much.

"Where the hell did you people come from?"

She let out a shaking breath as tears fell down her face.

The two men stared at the group as if they were alien lifeforms. To people who'd lived the last thirteen years underground, they were.

Sara cupped her hands against the one-way window, trying to see the people on the far side. Quarantine, they said. They had no way of knowing what anyone had been exposed to on the outside. They were right, in an old world sensibility kind of way. They'd gone to get the administrator of the facility, but that had been nearly an hour ago.

She was certain she would wake up soon. There were no safe places in the world. You lived and died by the whims of fate. The total lack of sound unnerved her. The whole thing had to be an elaborate joke.

The walls closed in a little more with every thought. Outside, the Walking Cancer hovered nearby. It didn't understand why it couldn't find them. This close, it radiated curiosity and hunger. Black spots of death covered the entire building upstairs. There were hundreds of infected and monsters. Down here might be an ant colony, but up there was a wasp's nest.

It reached out to her, but she brushed it away. As long as she didn't go into a scanning trance, she didn't think it could touch her.

Tim sat in the corner, his back to the wall. *This must seem like a fairytale to him.* He wouldn't be old enough to remember much, and he'd grown up in the country. Barely blinking, he stared at everything as if it would bite.

Kyle sat next to Kaylee, his head in his hands. He hadn't spoken a word since they came in.

Kaylee appeared to be taking it in stride. She kicked her legs off the bench they sat on, her feet not touching the ground. "How much longer are we going to have to wait?"

"Good question." Sara pounded on the glass. "Are we prisoners?"

No response from the other side.

"This is bullshit!" She slammed her fist against the glass again, harder than before. The pain in her abdomen flared up, and she doubled over. She didn't want to be trapped. Thirteen years of expecting the worst made even safety feel like danger.

Kyle and Tim both looked up. Sara shook her head and limped slowly back to the bench.

Without warning, an intercom blared overhead. "Are you wounded?"

What a goddamn stupid question. The bruises on her face had healed slightly, but they were still dark. Tim had washed the blood from his jaw, but his bottom lip was still split where his teeth had pressed through. He still had that ridiculous lisp.

"What do you think? Do you know what it's like out there?"

No response for a full minute. Then a different voice, older and more serious. "No, ma'am, I'm afraid we don't. We haven't had contact with anyone outside of this and our other facilities for quite some time. Why are you here? How did you find us?" The tone of his voice made it an accusation.

Her temper flared at the audacity. They sat here in positions of supreme comfort as the whole world died. These people hoarded ten thousand years of human evolution and technology, collecting it underground while others survived on scraps, if they survived at all.

Part of her thought she should be grateful they'd been rescued, but another part of her resented this. "I already told you, this little girl and her mother were looking for you. They came from another place like this."

"And where is her mother now?"

"Where do you think?"

"Charming. We can keep you in there until you're feeling more cooperative then."

She'd dropped Miriam's name and told them about her mission, but they wanted proof. She had that.

"Kyle, give me the flash drive."

Kyle pulled it from his pocket. She hadn't wanted to play all her cards so early. This was their only leverage if those people tried to turn them loose back on the surface. Paranoid, maybe, but paranoia was a valuable survival skill.

She held up the thumb drive. "Dr. Miriam Stern was looking for Dr. Chambers to deliver this. She and her soldiers were killed, and only her daughter survived. We found her and came here looking for a safe place." It was the fourth time she'd said it, but maybe they'd listen when they saw the goods.

She held the drive up for half a minute before she gave up. They were scared, and they should be. Hiding underground forever wouldn't solve any problems, and an army of monsters had been dropped on their front door.

The Walking Cancer scanned through the ground one more time and vanished. She jumped at the sudden disappearance.

The door leading deeper into the facility slid open before she had time to consider it. The older man in front wore a gray beard and a lab coat. The younger man from earlier stood just behind, his rifle slung over his shoulder.

"You have Miriam's research?"

The sight of him, impeccably clean and neatly shaven, made her head spin. She'd thought luxuries like that were extinct.

"And this is Kaylee?"

"How do you know my name?"

The man knelt before her, eye to eye. "I'm a friend of your mother." He extended a hand. "It's a pleasure to meet you. I'm Dr. Chambers."

Kaylee shook it, serious as a judge. He stood slowly, his knees popping, and extended an open hand to Sara. "May I have that?"

She hesitated. Their only advantage would vanish the second he had that flash drive. She glanced at the man with the gun behind him, knowing they were out of options, and dropped it into his open palm.

He turned it over, staring at it as if it held answers to some great mystery. For all she knew, it did. A smile spread across his face, softening it. He threw his head back and laughed. Sara looked over at Tim and Kyle, but they were as lost as she was.

"Do you know what this is?" Delight lit up his eyes.

Sara shrugged.

"This is the key to saving the world."

Chapter 17

Kyle

The lights burned Kyle's eyes after all that time without them. He couldn't focus on anything without searing pain, and so they stayed closed as much as he could manage. His stomach grumbled at the unfamiliar smells and the hint of food somewhere. He wanted to lie down and sleep more than anything, but he didn't think he'd be able to after the lottery they'd won.

"Miriam's was the only biochemical research team left after the Event. They worked around the clock for more than a decade to finish their work. Many of us thought it couldn't be done. After the Event, things were bleak." He glanced back at the group. "I'm sure you can appreciate that." As they walked deeper into the facility, he kept looking at the object in his hands as if it would vanish.

Fascinating as the conversation was, what was going on around them was more so. The scenery didn't change except for more doors, but heads poked out of many of them. Clean, healthy looking people curious to see the filthy, ragged topsiders that had found a way into their secret fort gawked and pointed.

Kyle hated them. "We haven't eaten in days," he said, interrupting the doctor mid-sentence.

Chambers blinked twice before the words registered. "Of course, of course. How rude of me. As you can imagine, we don't get a lot of visitors." He smiled as if he'd told a joke, but neither Kyle nor anyone else smiled back. Dr. Chambers continued, "The digital lines were severed ages ago, and we lost contact with everyone outside of the East Coast on land lines six years ago. For all we knew, Miriam's was the last research station left. Our little production facility wouldn't be much good without those." He laughed, giddy with delight.

"What the hell is this place?" Tim looked over his shoulder and through every open door they passed. Waiting. Expecting.

"We house a huge array of biochemical and engineering supplies. Our parent company set up a dozen places like this in case of an event of cataclysmic significance. As you can see, prudence paid off."

Kyle shook his head, and his stomach lurched. He nearly tripped over his own feet when he closed his eyes to get a moment's reprieve. "What the hell are you talking about? Why have you been down here this whole time?"

Chambers stared at Kyle as if he'd gone mad. "We're here to prevent the extinction of humanity." He stated it as if it were the most natural thing in the world.

"By what? Sitting here on unlimited supplies and weapons while people died by the billions above your head?"

Chamber's mouth dropped open and closed a few times, but Kyle didn't give him a chance to speak.

"Do you have any idea what it's like up there? Do you know what people are doing to survive?" Kyle balled his hand into a fist. Sara touched his arm, but it did nothing to stop his anger. "How the fuck would you know if you aren't the last people on the planet with your heads buried in your asses?"

Chambers surprise turned to a stony mask. He clenched his jaw. He clearly wasn't used to being spoken to like that. "Our estimates placed the survival rate of the human species at point-five percent. We are doing what we have to do to ensure the remaining five million people on this planet rise back to dominance. Now, mister, I know—"

"Not 'mister', 'professor', and you don't know a goddamn thing."

The stony mask broke, and his mouth hung open. The surprise vanished as quickly as it appeared. "Well, Professor, you should understand. It isn't about saving individuals anymore. We're playing for keeps. This is survival of the species. Vincent."

The young man with the gun jumped to when his name was called. "Take this to Dr. Charles and tell him to begin synthesis in both liquid and solid form immediately." He handed the flash drive to the young man reverently, a sacred object to be treated with the utmost respect. Vincent turned back the way they'd come without a word.

Dr. Chambers continued walking without looking back at Kyle. "He was six when all of this started." He let it hang in the air for a moment. "Two years ago he told me he couldn't remember what the sun felt like anymore. We stay here for safety and secrecy, of course, but more than that, we stay because our work is important. Work you've helped us accomplish. We keep the doors sealed to save one of the few repositories of thousands of years of civilization left on the planet. If we died or allowed this to be destroyed like the rest of the world, then humanity will truly have lost the Earth. When all of this is over, you'll be heroes."

The idea of heroes or villains was a luxury from a life where people assumed they wouldn't be eaten or shot. Kyle glanced at Sara, her face still bruised from their near-death experience. One of a thousand since they'd met.

They walked in silence for a moment before Sara spoke up. "The whole world is like this?"

"Russia and Europe were hit hours before the United States had their first sightings. South America went dark two days after the biologicals were reported in Nebraska." He met her gaze. "The United States was the last to fall. The call came in two days before Detroit was destroyed. Emergency lockdown was initiated for PABT employees and their families. High-ranking government and military officials had their own facilities. We lost contact with them within three weeks. I suspected an intelligence belied our enemies' true capabilities, but barring any direct contact with them, we never had the chance to find out. The one East Coast facility designated to study an extraterrestrial threat went dark within six months of lockdown."

They'd had no sense of things on the surface. Judging by what he was telling them, maybe that had been for the best. The news dampened Kyle's anger, but didn't dissolve it. Sara's mouth hung open though, her reaction stamped across her face.

"I always hoped—thought—there might be places that were still…"

"If there are, we've had no word. New York held off for six months before it was destroyed."

"Destroyed?"

A somber silence settled over them. To think something was one thing, but to know it was different. Everything had been crushed under the heel of the greatest threat humanity had ever known. The great bastions of civilization were all gone.

"What's an extraterrestrial threat?" Tim asked.

Chambers turned another corner that opened into a cafeteria. Small, cramped, and plain, it wouldn't have been out of place in a high school. The smell of cooked food hurt Kyle's stomach.

"Anything that has origins off the Earth. We know they didn't come from space, but baring any knowledge of where they originated, it seemed appropriate to label it as such."

A line of pans on the other side of the room sat half-full with what looked like mashed potatoes, corn, beef, and gravy. Real food. Hot food.

It all came crashing down on him. They weren't outside anymore. Nothing could get them down here. The treasure at the end of the rainbow. The Garden of Eden buried forty feet under the dirt. After everything they'd been through, they were safe.

Of the four, only Kaylee continued looking around unaffected, though her gaze remained locked on the food.

"You're more than welcome to as much as you like. There's plenty."

Tim approached it immediately.

"How?" Sara asked. "After all these years?"

"The facility was meant to last as long as two decades at one hundred ten percent capacity. After that…" After that, if whatever problems they'd been locked away to solve still existed, it wouldn't matter.

Tim grabbed a piece of beef from the pan and shoved it into his mouth. "It's hot!" He smiled as he chewed it, grabbing another piece with his grimy hand.

A laugh escaped Sara's lips. Chambers watched with no judgment in his eyes, as if seeing a filthy teenager eat with his bare hands was a daily occurrence.

"Holy shit. This is amazing!" He laughed around a mouthful of half-chewed food.

It reminded Kyle of how far they'd come from civilized, and overwhelmed him. The headache, the background noise of his life, rose to a fever pitch. White noise on the edge of hearing grew louder until it blocked out all other sound.

"Are you alright, Professor?" Chambers put a hand on Kyle's shoulder. He wanted to brush it away, to tell the guy to keep his fucking hand to himself. Instead, he mumbled something indecipherable and fell against the wall behind him, sliding down to the floor. Shapes moved in front of him as his vision blurred. The ringing in his ears grew.

"Are you alright?"

"Are you alright?" Big Mama knelt beside him. The smell of cookies and cigarettes had become a part of her over the years. Her own wonderful scent.

The scrape on his knee oozed. He wanted to cry, but Big Momma might think he was a sissy. He didn't want her to look down on him. "I'm fine."

She scooped him up in her big arms and walked up the steps into the house. "What do you say we clean that up?"

The alcohol she used to clean it stung, but he wouldn't cry. Not in front of her. Not in front of anybody.

"Kyle." Someone shook him. "Kyle."

"How long has he been this way?"

"You got tenure because you're black!" The color in her cheeks darkened past red to purple. Her jowls quivered as she screamed at him.

"My, my, things have come a long way over the last sixty years, haven't they?" He asked it casually, the way a man might ask the time. A slow smile spread across his lips.

"You know it's true!"

Everyone in the office stopped to stare, but nobody intervened. They never did.

"Maybe it is. You should try it sometime."

Half a dozen blurry shapes stood around him. A hand rested on his arm.

"We aren't equipped to deal with this kind of issue." The words were soft, apologetic.

"Reports are coming in of looting in Atlanta and Washington DC. We don't... Hold on... I'm getting word that our correspondents in DC have gone offline. Last word from DC was that there were creatures in the streets. Again, the president has been killed..."

He peeked out the window at the soldiers in the streets. Kids, all of them. Half his grad students were older than them. Not one of them knew what the hell was going on any more than the news did. They parroted the same shit day after day, not helping anything, only scaring people.

The power cut out and the broadcast died repeating what they'd been saying for three hours. The United States was going to shit, and monsters were to blame.

The bed under him moved. No, not a bed, a gurney. He tried to say something, but it didn't come out right, just a gurgle and a moan.

Tim, a scared kid in a place as alien as the moon, stood over him. Sara held his hand as two strangers wheeled him down a hallway.

"Where?" He mumbled the word as best he could.

Sara glanced at Tim. "We found the bunker, remember? You're safe. It's going to be okay." She squeezed his hand.

"We're safe, Kyle." Karen squeezed his hand the way she always did. Her eyes glinted in the starlight. It might have been the wine, but in that moment he knew with a certainty only the young normally possessed that she was the most beautiful woman on the planet.

She smiled her sad smile, the same one she'd smiled at him every day since they'd had to kill the kid. The kid. He didn't even have a name anymore.

Jesse. His name was Jesse. *Someone would remember him.*

"What's wrong?" She stroked his chin.

He grabbed a handful of the chestnuts they'd scavenged and shoved them into his mouth.

"It's going to be okay." Her head found the crook of his neck. "I promise; it's going to be fine."

But only a year later she'd be dead, and nothing would be alright. Everything would always be terrible, even if they found some magical underground kingdom. Up there, above their heads, people would be struggling and dying. People like Karen and Richard.

293

Others moved around him. Something pricked his arm. A light went on and off over his head.

And then blackness. The shapeless void of dreamless sleep. No nightmares. No memories rising up like living tar to drag him back into the muck.

Peace.

"Is he gonna be okay?"

Silence. "I don't think so."

Another silence, longer.

"Is he your father?"

Kyle chuckled under his breath, and all the talking stopped. "Does he look like my kid?"

"Kyle?" Sara's voice. "Are you awake?"

He opened his eyes to find a tiled ceiling above his head. The soft give of a mattress under him was as foreign as if it had fallen out of the sky. Some kindhearted soul had the decency to keep the lights low, but the sudden brightness pained him. He stomach lurched as if he would vomit.

"I'm here, Songbird. Can't get rid of me that easy." His eyes adjusted, and he cast his gaze around the room. It could have been any hospital, right down to the curtains on one wall blocking a window that couldn't be there. A small bathroom stood opposite a door to the hallway. Other than that, the room was bare. The industrial scent of cleaning solution permeated the air.

Tim and Sara sat by his bedside. An older man he didn't recognize was at his feet. Kaylee stood next to him. Thirteen years of dirt had been scrubbed off everyone's faces, and Tim and Sara wore new clothes.

"Holy shit." Not an exaggeration. After a decade of filth, seeing her clean startled him. "Look at you."

Sara laughed and brushed her hair over her ear. He'd never seen it untangled. "I told them to burn our old clothes. I didn't want them anymore."

"There isn't enough soap left in the world to clean those." He looked at himself, still filthy. "You could have given a guy a bath you know."

She smiled. "Tim wouldn't let anyone near you unless both of us were here. He took a shower in your bathroom." She glanced back and smiled at him too. "He can't remember if he's ever taken a hot shower before."

"Hot showers." Kyle said it with awe. Hot showers. Hot food. For a moment, everything was okay. He forgot about his disgust at the decadence of safety and electricity.

But only for a moment. He didn't feel right. The whole room wobbled as he turned his head. He hadn't been drunk in a long time, but goddamn if this wasn't drunk.

"How long have I been out? What's going on?" He tried to sit up, but Sara put a hand on his chest, gently pushing him back down.

"Relax. It's okay. They gave you something for the pain. You were yelling. Coming in and out of it and screaming." The sad eyes of the woman he'd always known replaced the smile of the clean woman with the bruised face. "They think you're really sick."

"We don't think you're sick, we know you are. I'm Dr. Gabble." He extended a hand, which Kyle ignored. He didn't like these people with their old world manners. That kind of shit hadn't mattered then, and it certainly didn't now.

He held it for a second longer before he dropped it to his side. Unperturbed, he continued, "We did a scan while you were under, and it confirmed my suspicions. You have a tumor on the right side of your brain. It's not benign."

The wobbly world stopped. It wasn't a great shock, but it was a small one. He'd seen it coming for a long time.

The doctor stared at him from above the foot of his bed. His friends sat to his side, waiting as if he would have questions, as if he would cry or curse the fates. He didn't. He lived with death every day. It didn't scare him one bit. Like the samurai of old, he'd been dead since the day the world stopped turning; his body just hadn't finished moving yet.

"Can you fix it?"

The doctor opened his mouth, but Tim spoke first. "They got all this fancy shit and can't do a fuckin' thing."

"If we had a hospital with a surgical suite and medication to treat cancer, we might be able to buy you some time. As it stands, we don't have any of those things. This facility wasn't designed for long term care."

"Fine." He wanted to care more than he did but couldn't bring himself to do it. When those things had been breaking down the door to get them, when it looked like there wouldn't be another five minutes before a painful death, he'd considered taking his friends' lives. Death would be better than coming back as one of those infected.

Dying didn't even register as a blip on his radar anymore. As long as his remaining family was safe, he'd die with a smile on his lips. That much was done already.

Sara clearly didn't feel the same. "You could muster a little give-a-damn."

He shrugged. "It is what it is. I assume I'm not going to die today?"

"It's hard to tell anything with the tools we have. The cancer is pervasive. It's almost certainly metastasized, but our analysis of your bloodwork will take some time. You could have months, days, or hours."

At least he wasn't a bullshitter. "Mind giving us some time alone." It wasn't a question.

Without another word, he left, shutting the door behind him.

"Jesus Christ, Kyle." Sara rolled her eyes the way she always did when she meant to put her foot down.

The drugs and wobbles slowed his thoughts, but not his temper. "Just drop it. It doesn't matter anyway. What do we know about this place? How long have I been out?"

"You were out for a day. And I think this place is exactly what it looks like. But—"

"What exactly does it look like?" Even now, sitting there, he couldn't believe it was real.

Sara clenched her jaw. Tim sat still as a stone, not looking at him. Kaylee played with a string on the mattress.

"They can make silver. Kaylee's mom found a way to make silver out of other things. They're scientists that got locked away when everything happened."

"Do you believe them?"

She pursed her lips. "Am I clean and full of hot food that wasn't expired?"

It couldn't be. Not after all this time.

Tim slapped his foot. "What do you say we get you up and into a hot shower?"

He sat up slowly, Sara helping him. "Hot shower, huh?"

"Yeah, they've got clothes in your size. It's insane, man." He pointed at the bedside table where a plate of beef, corn, and greens awaited him. Food piled on top of food. More than he had seen even at North Fifteen's most decadent times.

He wolfed it down as if he'd never eaten before. It came out of a can, like everything else over the last decade, but when hot, it was a sight better. He swallowed the water that wasn't rotten then boiled, and licked the inside rim after. Heaven. Pure heaven after not eating or sleeping for days. If this was how he would leave the world, he didn't mind at all.

Sara smiled at him. It must have been how friend's looked at one another after their first meal outside of a concentration camp. Having dodges the Reaper. The monsters that looked like men and the men who looked like monsters.

"They have coffee too," she said. But he was too busy wolfing down the best meal he'd ever tasted to give a damn.

By the time he finished, his stomach ached. Food gave him strength, but he wasn't going to risk standing on his own and bashing his head on the floor. "Sara, how about you and Kaylee take a walk? Tim, help me get in the shower."

Sara kissed his cheek and walked out, Kaylee's hand in hers.

The small bathroom shined in a way Kyle hadn't seen in years. He sat on the toilet and stared at the knobs that would turn on the shower.

"What's wrong?"

Hell and the world had become one and the same. There were no more hot showers. Those went as extinct as the dinosaurs, and in a less spectacular fashion.

He touched the steel knobs. They were as cold as he'd expected. He twisted the one with the *H* stenciled on it. Water shot out of the showerhead, hard as a jet. Within seconds, steam filled the room.

"Holy shit." His eyes widened as moisture settled on his face.

Tim laughed. "I know, right? Let's get that shirt off. You smell like ass."

Kyle let Tim help him up. The steamy room didn't help the wobbling. For a while up top, he was certain he'd never be warm again. His toes and fingers had achieved a state of near-permanent numbness he always feared would turn into frostbite come winters. But here, as if sent from on high, was a hot shower. A steaming bath gifted from the gods.

He adjusted the water as Tim helped him out of his road clothes. They had been patched a dozen times and were ugly as sin. At one point, the shirt had been green, but that color had long since faded to a dull gray. He threw it and his pants on the floor. If he never wore them again, it would be fine by him.

Tim held him steady as he stepped under the spray. It burned his feet. The steam made him feel as if he were underwater. A decade of shit vanished, and a million memories flooded him as water touched skin.

"I don't wanna take a shower, Big Mama, I wanna take a bath."

"Baths are for babies. You're a man."

Well, that much was true. Seven he might be, but a man he was.

Endless memories of water and a world no longer living.

"Ugh. I stink like smoke," she said as they walked into his apartment.

He stood on somewhat unsteady legs. He probably shouldn't have driven home. "Well, if you like, I can show you to the shower and give you a hand with that."

Her smile turned devilish, and she tossed her purse onto the couch. He didn't know her name.

The good and the bad.

He stayed in the shower until it turned cold. Big Mama was dead. Dead and in the ground. His tears mixed with the water as it swirled the drain and vanished.

"You okay?"

The hot water ran over him, washing away a decade of filth, but doing nothing for thirteen years of ugly memories. "I'll be fine."

Dr. Chambers sat across the table from him. Sara, Tim, and Kaylee were there as well, along with a man and a woman he hadn't been introduced to. A meeting, they'd called it. A chance to explain things. More old world bullshit.

The young man who had greeted them at the door, Vincent, had escorted them around the facility. It stretched on much larger than Kyle would have guessed, but the whole thing was hollow and lifeless, as devoid of people as the streets above. Most of the building stored chemicals or housed monstrous construction engines for god knew what.

Consoles full of buttons, blinking lights, and monitors covered all the control room's walls. A table big enough to seat twenty dominated the center of the room. The whole thing came straight out of a cheesy sci-fi movie.

Sara stared into the middle distance the whole time, distracted.

"What's wrong?" He nudged her shoulder.

"Nothing. The things above us are waiting. A whole lot of them. The one from the barn though… It's like it vanished."

Before he had time to think about it, Chambers spoke up. "I trust you're feeling better?"

He nodded.

"Good. There's something we want you to see." He gestured to a man at the central console.

His fingers flew across the buttons, and the big screen lit up. A camera feed from outside dominated the picture. The angle changed several times, but the image was clear; thousands of monsters were out there, maybe tens of thousands. Infected, crawlers, and even some behemoths, stomped around where the building had been. Nothing more than a crater remained. They hadn't just torn the building down; they were looking for where Kyle and the others had vanished to.

They were thinking.

Kaylee and Tim gasped audibly. Sara's eyes widened, but she didn't make a sound.

"Are we trapped down here?" Kyle asked.

"No. We have several entrances."

"Can they get in?"

Chambers shook his head. "I highly doubt it. The entrances in the building above have four feet of steel locked into the floor for doors. Even if they do find it, they won't be able to breach it."

"Then why show us at all?" A threat loomed over it. *Look what you've done!*

Dr. Chambers nodded to the man at the console, and the images vanished. "Our camera coverage isn't as complete as it once was, but

I want you to see what we're dealing with. I want you to understand the significance of what it is you've brought us."

The controller brought up a lab on the screen. Two women hovered over a petri dish filled with black ooze. The same black ooze the creatures bled.

"We've already synthesized the alchemical silver you brought us." He grabbed Kaylee's hand and squeezed it as she stared at the screen. "We've named it after your mother. We call it Miriam's Silver. Watch."

One of the women sprinkled a pinch of silvery powder onto the black ooze. It bubbled and smoked, turning gray and hardening in the dish. The other woman clapped and laughed, ecstatic with the results.

The screen shut off a few seconds later. "Silver was only brought into the production facility in small supplies, and nuclear production of it was out of the question. We had nowhere near enough to use on a mass scale, and no way to make more. The research labs concerned themselves with finding a way to change the materials we did have into something chemically similar to silver after we discovered the biological's intolerance to it. A task you might image as untenable, Professor."

Kyle couldn't take his eyes off the screen where they'd just witnessed the impossible. "It was just regular silver." It had to be.

Chambers smiled without a hint of condescension. "I understand it might be hard to accept, but it isn't. We've created a weapon to use against the enemy. For the first time since the Event, we have a way to stop this madness and take back our planet."

He let the words hang in the air. The man at the console started clapping, and soon the whole room had joined in. Others stood. One man hooted. Sara turned red, and Tim looked around as if everyone had lost their minds.

Chambers spoke over the noise. "By this time tomorrow, we will have made enough to put it into the air filtration system. If we purge it with the right amount of Miriam's Silver, it will blow through the intake vents on the surface, and we'll put this material to a real test." He started clapping himself. "You're heroes."

Kyle shook his head, the applause digging into his temple as if it had claws. Heroes. An outdated concept in a world where only survival mattered. By this time tomorrow, these people would be cursing the fates that had raised their hopes. He couldn't believe it. He wouldn't.

It took the better part of two hours to convince Tim they could sleep in separate rooms. In the end, he'd settled for sharing a room with Kyle as long as Kaylee and Sara were next door.

Kyle's earlier anger had cooled, but he still couldn't accept their cozy logic. He needed to be mad at something. All the years spent on the surface struggling, when who knew how many of these places were scattered around the world, hording countless resources. He couldn't blame them for their ignorance, but he could hold them accountable for their casual disregard.

He told Sara as much as she sat on the foot of his bed in the cramped bedroom, Kaylee and Tim having gone for food.

"If it works, can you imagine? Do you know what that could mean?" Her eyes lit up as she spoke. Even with all the damage those bastards in the barn had done to her face, she looked like a kid just then.

"And if it doesn't?" He rubbed his temples. They'd given him another painkiller and something the doctor said would relieve the pressure, but it wasn't doing much. Trapped in a small room with no escape didn't help. He couldn't relax.

"Stop it. Please. This is the first time in a long time we've had something to be excited about." She pulled the pack of cigarettes from her pocket that she'd saved from the bag, lighting one. Almost everything else had been incinerated. Kyle had threatened to throw Vincent in after it if he laid a hand on his machete.

He wondered if this was a non-smoking building before deciding that heroes could do what they damn well please. "Give me one of those."

She scrunched up her face. "You don't smoke."

"It isn't as if my health is an issue anymore." He tried to grab the pack from her, but she pulled it back. "If you don't want to share, you could just say so."

She smiled at him and extended the box.

Every muscle in her body stiffened, and her eyes widened. The cigarette dropped from her hand, and for half a second, she looked as if she were scanning.

He grabbed her shoulders. "Whoo! What's wrong?"

She shook it off, relaxing as suddenly as she had tensed. "I... I don't know. There was this feeling...The thing, the smart one from the barn, it's up to something." She swallowed hard. "My god, that scared the piss out of me. It was like it tried to grab me." She'd squeezed the smokes in her hand. Opening the box revealed only a few unbroken.

"Damn." A tear fell down her face.

"Hey." He rubbed her knee. "Are you okay? Can it get to you down here?"

She shook her head and wiped away the tears, picking up the fallen cigarette. "No, I don't think so. We're safe here." Her breath hitched. "We're finally safe."

Chapter 18

Sara

Sara stroked Kaylee's hair as they tried to sleep. She hadn't been able to get comfortable in her own bed, so she'd crawled into Kaylee's after tossing and turning for an hour. It wasn't that she didn't feel safe. Kyle might have his misgivings, but she sensed the genuine gratitude of these people. Miriam's Silver was a godsend, the culmination of their life's work. It might even work.

It was the memories that kept her awake. The place reeked of a cold war. Always waiting for the bombs to drop. Always waiting to find out it was too late to save your loved ones. Living your whole life minutes to midnight in a bunker underground. Tension dripped from every surface, and the legion prowling above didn't help.

No, they were safe, but she didn't want to feel their worries anymore, and she didn't want to feel the creatures on the surface. In the quiet of the night, once all the lights had been dimmed, it was hard not to.

"So is this like the place where you and your momma lived?"

Kaylee nodded. "It's just like it. This one is bigger though." She clutched the doll in her arms.

"Are there more people?"

"No."

Silence filled the space for a few heartbeats. "I bet she'd be happy to know you're safe."

No response, and maybe that was for the best. Kaylee dealt with loss better than Sara expected a child to, but there was no way it hadn't left scars. There were no people without scars anymore.

The Walking Cancer drifted through the halls, touching and tasting everything. It wasn't that it couldn't reach her; it just didn't need to. This strange underground shell filled with people untouched by its kind fascinated enough.

It savored the paranoia and fear that echoed through the halls. It walked through the building, scanning people, chilling them as they slept or worked.

It floated into the control room, stopping above the woman running the panels. For a second her hand froze, hovering as if she would move.

Then outrage. Great sweeping waves of it. An ocean of wrath. The creatures above howled in fear and madness. It screamed too, shooting Sara out of her dream.

Sara sat bolt upright in her bed, forgetting why the mattress was soft and the air was warm. Kaylee squealed and woke just as quickly. Sara instinctively put her hand on the girl to comfort her. "It's okay. I had a bad dream."

Not just a dream though. Even now, the waves of rage the creatures above them felt pierced the ground. The Walking Cancer moved through the halls. It had found something it didn't like.

It knew what they had planned.

Tim threw the door open and rushed in. They'd taken his gun, but he had the bedside lamp from the room next door grasped in his hands.

"What's wrong? What's happenin'?" He lowered his makeshift weapon. "Why were you screamin'?"

Kaylee's breath was deeper than normal. "Sara had a bad dream."

No. Not a bad dream. "Something's not right."

Tim peeked at the corners of the room. "What?"

She shook her head. "I don't know. Something above us. They're—"

Kyle rounded the corner, his eyes bloodshot. He grabbed onto the wall to steady himself. The bags under his eyes were dark and heavy, and his skin pale. "Are you alright?"

"I'm fine. But I think something—"

The lights went out. When they came back on, they were a dim red. A single loud *beep* emanated from hidden speakers in the rooms and hallways, and a recording followed.

"An emergency evacuation order has been initiated. All safety protocols have been overridden. Please exit the facility immediately and report to your pre-assigned rendezvous point."

Silence, then the noise and the voice repeated.

"What the fuck?" Tim said. "What does that mean?"

Murmurs rose from the hall. Kyle vanished from the doorway. Sara jumped out of bed and put her shoes on.

"Put yours on too, Kaylee."

The girl stared at her, a deer in the headlights.

"Do it now."

She sprang into action as Tim poked his head into the hall, flabbergasted. "What the fuck, Sara?"

Kyle reappeared in the doorway, machete in hand. "Get your things together."

"But… What the hell?"

Kyle grabbed him by the shirt with his free hand. "Tim. Get your things."

"No. No, man. We're safe." But he ran into the hallway.

"We need weapons." Sara dropped right into survival mode. Fight or flight. Flight was always the better option.

"We'll get some. Come on, Kaylee." He held out a hand.

She took it. The tears had already started. "Are we safe?"

"I'll keep you safe, don't worry."

Chambers appeared in the doorway right before Tim. "There's been a breach."

"We gathered," Sara said.

"We'll go to the control room and see what this is about."

The first scream echoed from somewhere in the building, followed by an unearthly howl.

"This can't be happening."

Sara met Kyle's eyes. It was happening. Their safe place, their Eden, had let in the snakes.

Chambers moved into the hall. The red lights cast everything in a sinister glow. People cluttered the halls, lost.

"What do we do, Dr. Chambers?" one woman asked.

"Get a weapon and lock yourself into your rooms."

More howls filled the air. The things were in the building. A lot of them. The black spots drifted across Sara's mind.

"How many entrances are there?" Kyle asked. They moved out of the dorm area and toward the control room.

"Seven."

Two armed men ran by them in the opposite direction. "And how many are open during an evacuation?"

He looked at Kyle as they fled down the halls. "All of them."

Vincent ran out of a nearby doorway. "Dr. Chambers, we're being invaded!"

The perfect word for it. This was a coordinated strike. The Walking Cancer had found some way in.

"Escort us to the control room."

The screams began again, more of them. The sound of a body hitting a steel grate banged around a corner in the hallway.

"Gimme your pistol," Tim said to Vincent. He did as he was told.

One of the hairless apes bounded around the corner. Blood stained its mouth, its black eyes brimming with malice. Vincent leveled his rifle just after Tim fired three shots into the thing's skull, putting it on the ground.

"Headshots." Panic shone in Tim's eyes, but his voice was cold as ice. "Keep movin'."

Gunshots echoed off the walls all around them. Kaylee wept openly. Sara wanted to carry her, but her injuries still throbbed. Kyle scooped the girl up, his machete still in one hand.

"I don't know how this could have happened. There's no outside access to the facility."

They approached the door. More rifles shot. Someone screamed, but they were alone at the entrance. Something touched the edge of her mind. Louder than the black spots around her. Louder than the absence of the Walking Cancer.

Something behind that door.

"Stop!"

Too late; Chambers had already touched the button on the wall.

A red-eyed man stood over the bodies of six others in the room, swaying back and forth, a gun in his hands. He pulled the trigger.

The round hit Chambers in the chest. Tim raised his gun half a second too late, putting four rounds into the man and spilling him back into the console.

A crawler charged down the hallway behind them as more anguished cries and gunshots filled the facility. Tim pointed his weapon and pulled the trigger, but the click of an empty chamber answered.

Vincent lifted his rifle and sprayed bullets down the hallway. He screamed as he shot, his voice wavering and cracking. One caught the crawler in leg, and it tumbled to the ground.

"Get him in here!" With Kaylee in his arms, Kyle stepped over the prone Chambers.

Tim and Vincent grabbed the doctor's shirt and pulled him into the room. Another crawler ran around the corner. Vincent hit the close button on the wall as the beast sprinted toward them, the door shutting soundlessly.

Blood covered everything inside.

"Shit," Vincent whispered. "Shit, shit, shit." He knelt beside Chambers and put his hands over the wound.

Veins bulged all over the head and neck of the man with the red eyes. Sara could feel the taint of the Walking Cancer on him. It had taken control of him, forced him to open the outside doors. His lifeless corpse stared up at her, accusing her. They had brought this here. They were responsible.

Out there somewhere, the Walking Cancer swooped down to grab someone else, taking them over and vanishing from her mind. "Kyle, we need to get out of here."

Kyle knelt next to Chambers, who gasped for air. "How do we get out? Where's the exit?" He said it gently, but the message was clear: They weren't going down with the ship.

Chambers had other ideas. "No. Silver. Enough silver to put into the vents."

Kyle shook his head. "We need to go."

Get out. Run away. Find some other hole to hide in until the inevitable end. Sara let out a deep breath. This was supposed to be a sanctuary.

Kaylee cried. Tim sat on the floor next to her and pulled her into an embrace. "I'll keep you safe, Kaylee. I swear to God, I'll keep you safe."

"Too many. Can't make it. Put the silver in the vents and purge. Purge the system."

The plan from the meeting. The one that had been a pipe dream at best.

"Enough silver already." He coughed, and blood splattered Kyle's face. His breath came in ragged gasps.

"Enough silver?"

Chambers nodded. They'd worked fast for their crazy plan. They'd seen what it could do already. The silver worked.

They were out of options. Sara watched Kaylee cry. She wanted to cry too. "Kyle, the surface is covered. We can't get out. There's no way."

Trapped. Their safe haven had become their prison and their execution grounds. Getting through the compound to the engineering section and then to wherever the hell the vent system was would be a Hail Mary plan, but she didn't see another way.

"Can you close the doors?" Kyle asked Vincent.

With blood covering his arms and hands, he ran to the console. He typed fast, information popping up all over the screen. "No. There's been an administrative override. The facility is locked into its orders for twenty-four hours."

"What about the vents? Can you make that happen?"

More furious typing. "Yes. Ventilation is on a separate system."

Chambers mouthed something more, but the words wouldn't come out. He coughed again.

"Can you take us to the engineering section? Can you show us where all of this is?"

"Someone has to stay here to purge the ventilation system to the exterior. You can't do it from facilities."

Someone pounded on the door, but something bashed into it, cutting off their screams.

"I don't know where the hell this shit is at, man!"

"I…" He ran more commands on the console. "I still have access to comms and camera feeds. I can guide you." He stared at Kyle across the blood-spattered room.

And there it was. They had one choice in front of them. Sara opened her mouth to volunteer, but the Walking Cancer swooped in.

Insects. Images of bugs crawling across the ground bombarded her. They were as beneath humans as humans were beneath the

Walking Cancer. It ripped images from her brain, putting together a picture.

Her daddy beating her.

The church praying over her.

Momma screaming. "This is all your fault!"

She had transgressed. She had tried to rise above her meager existence and bring harm to the creature and its kind. She would pay. It would bring hell raining down upon their heads and devour them from the inside.

It seized her, attempting to get inside and make her eat the other people in the room. Images of her ripping the flesh from Kaylee's bones with bloodstained teeth flooded her mind. She recoiled in terror from the creature as it moved in to take her.

NO!

The word boomed out of her mind, echoing off the layers of fear and paranoia that covered the building. The image of the creature turned into one she could understand. Ten feet tall with gray skin covering its body. It put its clawed hands over its ears.

NO! NO! NO!

The creature ran.

Tim shook her. "Sara!" He swallowed hard, rattling her as if she were a rag doll. "This ain't the time for that! Sara!"

"It's in the building. The thing from the barn is here. You have to hurry."

Kyle stood over Dr. Chambers, staring at his still form.

The Walking Cancer rushed her mind again, but she blocked it out, screaming at it.

NO! NO! NO!

"Kyle!"

Tim grabbed the rifle next to Vincent as Kaylee cried. "I'm going. You can come or not."

Kyle looked up from the body and tightened his grip on the machete. "Alright. Let's do this."

Chapter 19

Kyle

The door slid up, revealing a hallway covered in blood and bits of people. The creature was nowhere to be seen. Kyle moved out first, followed by Tim with his rifle at the ready. Sara took one last look at them before shutting the door.

The gunshots and screams had quieted, but the stillness was worse. The certainty that every terrible thing that had ever lived under his bed as a child was here, hunting for them, closed in around him and cut off the air. He took a deep breath and closed his eyes, trying to calm himself. When he opened them again, his composure had returned.

Vincent's voice over the PA drowned out the recorded warning. "Follow this hall to the end, take a left, and go down the stairs. The way looks clear."

The sudden loud noise blurred Kyle's vision. He stumbled back against the door.

Tim steadied him. "Jesus, man. You gonna make it?"

Kyle nodded, moving in the direction Vincent indicated. This couldn't be any stupider. They should be looking for ways out, not weapons to win an impossible fight. Those stupid kids in the army outfits hadn't done anything to save Memphis, and a couple pounds of powdered silver weren't going to do much here.

As they rounded the corner he saw the bullet holes in the walls, and he silently conceded the point. There was no out. More monsters covered the surface than he'd ever seen, even in the second trip to Memphis. They were fucked.

Something moved at the bottom of the stairs, but Vincent's voice blocked it out of hearing. "Take a left at the bottom of the stairs, and follow it all the way."

Kyle crept slowly, expecting something to charge around the corner at the bottom. Fucked they may be, but he wouldn't go down without a fight.

Five steps from the landing, a woman rushed around the bend. Her matted hair stuck to one side of her head, covered in sticky red. Her glasses were cracked. A bite on one arm poured blood. She held it out to Kyle, her eyes inhuman with fear.

"Please! Please, help me!"

"Incoming!" Vincent yelled over the PA.

A crawler hurtled into the woman and took her entire head in its mouth. With one stomach-turning crunch, it popped her skull, splashing brain and blood everywhere.

Kyle jumped the last five steps, machete raised, and landed it in the thing's neck. The steel dug into flesh, connecting with bone buried in the meat. Black tar flew everywhere, coating Kyle and the walls around him. It gurgled once as it fell on top of the woman it had killed.

Kyle pulled out the blade. The woman's corpse twitched, doing the death dance under the monster. All these little mice hiding in their hidey-hole, and now it was gone. No more safety. No more patiently waiting under the surface for the world's problems to blow over.

A roar echoed off the steel above them. "More coming!" Vincent yelled over the PA. "Run!"

They ran. Claws clinked on the metal stairs behind them. Lots of them. He could hear the snap of teeth over the warnings and the boots on metal. Kyle flinched at the roar that followed.

He looked over his shoulder. Six of them, maybe more, and coming fast.

"Shit!" Tim stopped in front of him.

"Wha—"

One of the hairless apes stood in the doorway at the end of the hall. It screamed, black teeth bared, bloody spittle flying from its mouth.

The crawlers closed from behind.

They came in the night—

"No!" Kyle grabbed Tim's arm as he raised the rifle, slamming his fist onto the button next to them. The door wasn't locked. He pulled Tim in and hit the button on the inside, his heart pounding out of his chest.

The door started to slide closed when the hairless ape's hand appeared under it, grabbing the bottom. For half a second it looked as if the door would seal.

The thing's impossible strength prevailed. Inch by inch, the steel lifted.

"Fuck!" Tim cradled the rifle in his arm and took aim.

"Don't waste the bullets." Kyle swung the machete on the thing's fingers, severing them in a shower of black gore. With a scream of rage, the creature pulled out what was left of its hand, letting the door fall closed.

"Oh fuck. Oh fucking shit, man." Tim gasped.

Kyle looked around the room. A goddamn storage closet. Rows of metal shelving, not unlike the ones at the entrance to the bunker, filled the room. Trapped in a storage closet in some shithouse basement for the second time in two days. His head pulsed with pain after the terror and exertion of the hall. Kyle punched a box, knocking it off the shelf. Glass beakers broke and flew out as it hit the floor.

"There's a second door at the back," Vincent said over the PA. "Go right when you go through it to get into the back halls behind the labs."

Tim, his face in his hands, still cursed under his breath. Outside the door, the ape-thing screamed and pounded, not denting the metal, but shaking it in the frame.

"Is it clear?" Kyle looked at the ceiling. He didn't see any cameras, and it occurred to him that Vincent couldn't hear them. "Vincent?"

Again, silence.

"Fuck. We have to move." Staying still was suicide. Every second more of those things poured in from the surface. He grabbed Tim's shoulder. "Tim." He wanted to say, *"Tim, we have to go,"* but black spots appeared out of nowhere, blurring his vision. He swatted at them for half a second then stared at Tim, confused.

"Kyle?"

Kyle heard him, but it wasn't the voice of someone standing at arm's length. It came from far away. Another hallway on another planet. He began to fall over.

"Shit." Tim held Kyle up as the world spun.

Panic hit him in the gut as hard as a fist. *Mother of god, don't let me die or lose it right now.*

Everything blurred. The storage closet became an MC Escher painting as Tim dragged him. They moved behind impossibly tall shelves, revealing a door in the back that looked infinitely far away.

The ape-thing pounded on steel behind them, creating a drumbeat in time with their steps.

"Just go on now. I'm okay. Leave me here."

Tim kept moving forward. "Fuck you, old man."

"I'm not kidding, you little shit. Go." He tried to grab a shelf but missed. He wouldn't be the reason their plan failed, though it certainly would. It was time to go out to pasture. He'd dodged it long enough.

"Let's go." Tim touched the button next to the back door, and it slid open.

Chapter 20

Sara

"They made it out!" Vincent yelled over his shoulder.

Sara barely heard him. She sat on the ground, legs crossed and sweat pouring down her brow. Kaylee held her hand. The girl had tried to talk to her over the last ten minutes, but Sara couldn't take her attention off what was happening in her head.

The Walking Cancer swirled around for another pass, trying to grab hold and devour her.

Gnashing teeth. Bloody, frothing drool. The warm, salty taste of a child's flesh.

She shook her head, screaming obscenities without saying a word. It vanished again, waiting in the wings for the lights to go up.

"They're going to make it to the… Holy shit! There are people in there!"

Sara looked at the monitor. An old man in a lab coat threw a handful of the silver powder at a claw reaching inside the half-open door. The flesh oozed and cracked, splitting apart. On the next monitor, a crawler rolled around on the floor outside the door.

"This might work. This might actually work!" Vincent laughed a manic, desperate laugh. A kid playing a video game, not grasping the seriousness of the situation.

Her attention momentarily divided, it closed in again.

It saw through her eyes. Looking at the monitor. The people. The silver. It heard the laughter as Vincent droned on, the voice far away.

"They're going to make it."

They wouldn't. It wouldn't allow it.

A whole world covered in black and red plants. The air burning with sulfur. A planet terraformed into Hell, no humans on its surface. Another world, another universe, conquered underfoot. A plague that spread out forever, beyond the reach of man or god.

Her mind opened to the infinity of worlds beyond her own. The endless stars in the sky of her universe multiplied by an untold number of universes, many already fallen to a legion not unlike that on Earth. An eternity of suffering from a thing of endless time.

She screamed in her real body. The Walking Cancer vanished from her, leaving her panting and reeling.

The vastness couldn't be seen. It couldn't be understood. It was like looking over a cliff only to see the top of your head a thousand upon a thousand miles below.

"Sara!" Kaylee shook her.

"I can't come over there." Vincent glanced over his shoulder then went back to the monitor where Tim half-carried Kyle down a hallway.

Vincent pressed something on the console. "Keep going that way; you're almost there. I'm watching your back." He flipped through a dozen feeds before looking at Sara again. Monsters filled the building. Entire hallways were crammed with them. Only half a dozen people showed on the feeds. Maybe some remained locked in their rooms. Maybe all of them were dead.

She couldn't see. Her eyes had become useless windows. An overlay of the unnumbered worlds had cast itself over her mind, drowning everything else out. Somewhere else, not so far away, black waves washed over the anthill, chasing all the critters out and eating them up one by one. The queen bee, the Walking Cancer, strode through the halls. Angry. Determined to stop this farce of resistance.

"Look out behind you!"

Sara's gaze drifted over. He wasn't talking to Kyle and Tim. The lab with the silver had exploded into violence. A tall, redheaded woman with a pistol mowed down two others. The man that had thrown the silver at the crawler put his hands up and said something, but the shooting woman didn't notice. Even through the feed, Sara could see the red from her bleeding eyes and the veins bulging from her neck. The Walking Cancer was inside of her.

"Sara." Kaylee threw her face into Sara's neck and put her arms around her. "Please do something. Please."

Please. That same word she'd said a million times as a girl. That useless word she'd cried out to make the hurting stop. It never had. She'd never gotten the luxury of reprieve by using something as simple as please.

It took her mind away from the edge. Away from the universe and its million secret siblings only one step away.

"It's okay."

It would be. They could do this.

On the camera feed, Tim ducked under the half-open door.

"Don't!" Vincent screamed, but too late. The woman with the bloody eyes and the bulging veins took aim.

The Walking Cancer had its hand inside her. A meat puppet. A child drawing a face on its hand and making it talk.

She traveled through the layers of steel as if they weren't there, grabbing its arm and stopping it with the woman's finger on the trigger.

Inside herself, the woman screamed. A prisoner of her own mind. The Walking Cancer had burrowed in, tearing out what made her human so it could have room to move inside. It gnawed and devoured, seeping in and ripping through her still living brain.

It would be a mercy to end this.

A ghost of a hand touched the screaming animal that had once been a woman. Sara's being was a gentle giant. She grabbed the light that made everything this person was in her palm and closed her fist, extinguishing the glow. The screaming stopped. Some small part of the woman vanished, the same way it had from her mother and sister. The soul fleeing the flesh.

Her body fell to the floor. The Walking Cancer looked on in awe. One of these meats shouldn't be able to do that. They didn't have the power. They were weak. Underdeveloped. They were an accident of nature. Evolutionary cannon fodder hardly fit to be food.

It screamed, a piercing cry that hurt her mind and made her nose bleed.

The sound cut through the building. Anyone near it would certainly be deaf.

"What was that?" Vincent rushed through all the feeds on the other screens. In the big one, Tim put two rounds into the screaming woman on the floor. Kyle swayed nearby, struggling to stand on shaking legs.

"Don't worry about it. Get them where they need to be. Fast." Sara wiped the blood from beneath her nose.

Downstairs, Kyle was dying. She could sense him slowly slipping away.

Mourning would come later. He couldn't die yet.

The Walking Cancer was in the building, and she didn't know if she could stop it again.

Chapter 21

Kyle

This was what it felt like to die. He always imagined it would be more dramatic. It wasn't a building on fire, everyone running in every direction to find an escape. It was a warehouse with the lights being turning off; one by one, row by row. Just the cold and the yawning dark before him.

He grabbed the edge of the counter to steady himself. He didn't have long. He probably should have been dead months ago. Vincent spoke over the PA. "On the counter next to you, Tim. The two big bags filled with the powder. Yes. That's it."

The bags were big, probably twenty pounds each. How they'd managed to make so much of it so fast, Kyle didn't know. A distant concern at this point. Something happening in a world he wasn't part of. He wanted to lie down and go to sleep.

A gentle whisper in the back of his mind, something sweet and sad, something familiar, told him no. He still had things to do. Elsewhere, further away, a woman's voice called out to him. She wanted him to come home. He wanted to go to that voice. He hadn't heard it in a long time.

Not yet though. Just a little longer. Help Tim get downstairs, and everything would be okay.

"Why won't you let me die?" he asked aloud. "I don't want to be here anymore."

No answer came. Just that sweet, familiar sadness.

"I can't get both of these and the gun." Tim didn't appear to have heard him.

Kyle dragged himself to the counter, his own steadiness surprising him. Apparently, someone was still in the building, and he couldn't turn the lights off yet.

He took the bags from Tim without a word. Their eyes met. Through the mountain of fear and anxiety, shock highlighted the young man's face. He must have looked bad for Tim's eyes to get that big.

"We're almost there, brother." He put a hand on Kyle's shoulder.

Brother. Kyle would have laughed if it didn't take so much energy. It had been a long time since anyone called him that, and it had never been a teenaged white kid.

"The hallway behind the lab has stairs at the end." A childlike tremor colored Vincent's voice. "I don't think any of them have gotten into that section of the building yet. Hurry!"

Tim set off at once, Kyle behind. They moved out of the lab. The sound of the beasts cut off completely, the sudden silence jarring in its pregnancy. Only the recorded warning filled the void.

"Follow this hallway to the end."

One step. One foot at a time.

"Take a left here."

Focus. Don't sleep.

"No, no. Go back and take a right. That room has bios in it."

Soon. Not time yet.

That feeling wasn't a feeling but a voice. Sara's voice.

"Sara?"

Tim looked back at him, but didn't speak. He knew what was happening. There would be no bright morning for Kyle.

The voice didn't respond, just kept him moving. He would have died minutes ago if not for that voice. Maybe he had. Maybe he was a moving corpse now, like one of the infected.

No. Those things didn't think or speak. He wasn't dead. But goddamn did everything hurt. His senses dulled in the wake of pain; so dull he almost ran into Tim as he stopped at the top of the stairs.

"Something's down there. The door on the far side of the sub-basement is open. I... I don't see anything on the camera, but be careful."

Careful, careful, careful. Everything he'd ever done had been careful. Careful to get good grades. Careful to meet the right people in college. Careful to say the right things to get tenure. Careful to keep himself alive after the world ended. If Heaven turned out to be a careful place, he'd ask nicely to go to Hell.

The lights downstairs flickered when they reached the bottom.

"I don't know what's going on. The ventilation room's at the end of the hall on the right. Just get in there and feed the silver in. There's a red button so you can manually purge—"

The lights turned off, and Vincent's voice cut. For a full three seconds there was nothing but blackness, then red emergency lights cast the hall in their bloody glow The recorded warning started again.

They stood still as stone.

"Vincent?" Tim called out.

Kyle tried to remind Tim that even if the cameras were working, Vincent couldn't hear them. The words didn't come. Instead, he walked past Tim, following the last directions received. They could still do this as long as the ventilation system worked. He had to put this stuff down. It was heavy, and he needed to sleep. Needed to be gone.

Tim cursed under his breath and followed.

Doors were open. In the dim light, claws reached for them from every shadow. They were in Hell now. Dante breaching the final layer to find the Devil frozen in ice. Here at the bottom were only the sinners and quiet spirts.

Maybe Beatrice would be at the end. Maybe Karen. Maybe nothing at all.

The silence wasn't total. Things moved in other rooms. Gruff noises and the ever-present clink of claws on metal grates.

The end of the hallway was in sight. A door on their right stood closed.

"I think we're here." Tim hit the button on the door. It didn't move. That would have been a great joke. Reach the end, prize in hand, only to be thwarted by a door. It finally slid open, revealing a room full of humming machinery.

A stack of huge filters sat against the wall to their left. On the right was a console like the one in the control room, covered in lights and buttons. In front of them stood a monstrosity of a machine. Valves and dials, a body the size of a garage. The air filtration system. Ducts led out of it into the ceiling and floor. On the far right side of it stood a large handle on a small hatch, *Emergency Filtration Chute* stenciled across it in big yellow letters. Kyle dropped the bags onto the floor and pointed.

"This thing?" Tim approached and pulled on the handle, opening the chute. "Do we just drop it in?" He placed his rifle against the wall and grabbed a bag off the floor. He ripped away the top and upended it, pouring it into the dark hole.

He opened the second one as something walked over Kyle's grave. "Tim."

A long, skinny claw wrapped around Kyle's neck and squeezed, pulling him off the ground.

"Kyle!" Tim dropped the bag into the chute, the weight of it slamming the portal closed. He reached for his gun, but his hand stopped inches away.

The thing lifted Kyle as easily as he would a child, throwing him against the console on the wall. He slammed headfirst into it, the color fleeing from his vision and his arm snapping. He fell to the ground in mute agony.

Its snout was long and thin, like a bird's beak but with rows of teeth. It had to stoop to fit its narrow body inside the door. The red light reflected off skin the same color as dead flesh. Two bright black eyes shone from over its mouth, and a long reptilian tail swung back and forth behind it. Fear shocked his system, but it was dull. Irrelevant. The voice that had kept him going stopped. Nothing held him here anymore.

"Tim."

Tim, the veins on his neck bulging, reached for the rifle. The creature screeched. The sound bounced off the walls and reflected back at them. The noise popped his ears, and he couldn't hear his own voice when he spoke again.

"Tim." He pawed at the machete on his belt, pulling it out. Tim pointed the rifle at him, taking sight right between his eyes.

Just one squeeze. One more bad moment, and it would be over. So be it.

Kyle closed his eyes. Time to go home.

NO!

Inside a white room with no doors and no windows, Sara stood across from him. Tim was there too, the giant black-eyed monster standing over him. It reached into his skull and controlled him, pointing the gun at Kyle even as Tim screamed in agony.

NO!

Sara screamed, and the creature retreated.

NO!

It covered its ears with its nightmarish claws, then it was gone. The nowhere room lasted a fraction of a second longer.

"I love you, Kyle."

That sweet, sad voice. Sara's voice. His best friend.

"I love you too, Songbird."

The monster stood in the doorway, its maw open. Shock. Surprise. Real emotion on an unreal thing.

The cock of the rifle drew its attention. It looked over as three rounds struck its face and chest. Black blood oozed from the wounds. The impact forced it back, and it grabbed the doorframe.

Kyle barely heard the click of the empty rifle before Tim appeared over him, grabbing the machete from his hand. With a scream of rage, the veins still bulging from his neck, Tim charged at the monster. It reached for him with a clawed hand and lost it to the blade. Black blood covered Tim as he raised the weapon over his head and brought it right in its skull.

Its protests died in its throat, and the light in its eyes faded.

Kyle pulled himself onto the console, his unbroken arm barely able to hold him. One more thing. One last service for the people he loved, and then he was free.

His vision was already fading when he saw the button marked *Interior Purge* in the center of the console. He slammed it before falling back to the ground.

Tim hacked wildly at the monster's corpse as the big machine whirred to life. The sound of claws on metal drew closer. They were coming, coming to see their leader's ruin.

"Tim."

Tim, chest heaving, stood over the thing. The machete fell at his feet. When he turned toward Kyle, there was still blood in his eyes. Red tears dripped down his face as he stumbled over and collapsed onto the ground.

The monsters and the hum of the machine grew louder.

The world became a gray picture, a still thing painted in muted colors. Kyle reached for Tim's hand, his movements taking the last of his energy.

"Listen to Sara, and look after Kaylee. Hear?"

The first sob escaped Tim's lips as more bloody tears left a trail across his cheeks.

"Remember your promise to me by that stream. Remember what I said."

Tim nodded.

"Be as good as your word. We define who we are, not circumstance."

Tim cried freely. "I promise." He threw his arms around Kyle and sobbed into his neck.

Something powdery fell on them from a vent, enough to bring a silver shimmer to the red lights. In the hall, the clicking of claws stopped, and screams of inhuman pain flooded the room.

"You'll be okay."

His last words were a whisper. With a final, quiet sigh, he found the rest he'd sought for so long.

Far away, a woman beckoned to him.

This time, he listened.

Epilogue

Tim

They watched the videos a hundred times. Ten thousand monsters melted like wet sand, dying even as silver blew out of the external vents and created a glimmering cloud on the surface. Weeks later and they were still cleaning blood, both human and otherwise, out of the compound.

The things hadn't come back. Maybe they couldn't come back. He'd always look over his shoulder out here though.

Sara, Kaylee, and Tim stood over Kyle's grave. It had become something of a daily ritual. A sobering way to unwind after a long day of cleaning and planning. Nearby were markers for the people of North Fifteen and Kaylee's mother. Chambers and the other people who'd died were buried only a little farther away.

His heart ached as he looked at the cross with Kyle's name carved into it. A good guy. A great guy. A second father.

Tim stroked Kyle's machete. He never took it off. He thought of that white room he'd seen in the final moments every time he touched. The mind room, as he'd come to think of it.

Tim was the first to break the silence today. "How'd you do it?" He didn't need to be specific, or suspected he didn't anyway. Sara had developed the uncanny knack for understanding things even when nobody spoke. It made his skin crawl, but he took comfort in knowing she wouldn't misuse it. He trusted her. He had to after everything they'd been through.

She shrugged the question off. "Everything's different now."

That was the fuckin'-a truth. Monsters controlling your body. Scanners that could fight them off. Silver clouds to kill armies. His eyes were still bloodshot all the time. He shuddered at the memory of that thing's fingers inside of him.

Vincent interrupted their vigil. He nodded at Chamber's grave as if Chambers would nod back. "We're going to have that meeting soon."

Sara had told Tim the old world had been like that. Endless talks. Constant ideas. One stalled start after another until things got done.

Tim didn't like it.

"What's left to talk about? Scrub the walls and make more silver."

"There's that. Some of us are talking about getting Miriam's Silver out there too. That's what tonight's roundtable is about."

Sara laughed. It had become cold and infrequent over the last few weeks, as chilly as the Tennessee winter. He wanted to ask her why, but she wasn't much for conversation anymore. "Are you going to run around throwing powder in their faces?"

If her harsh tone bothered him, Vincent didn't show it. He was no older than Tim, but he'd aged ten years in the last month. The surface did that to people.

"There was a facility in Florida we lost contact with when all of this started. An orbital launch station. Some of the brains downstairs think we could use it to get the silver into the upper atmosphere and make it rain down worldwide."

Tim didn't understand any of it until that last part. "Like a silver storm?"

Vincent waggled his head from side to side. The same maybe yes, maybe no gesture Kaylee made from time to time. "Something like that."

He sighed and turned away, back to their new home. He grabbed Kaylee's hand and started down the hill. "Well, I guess we better get to it."

It felt like something Kyle would say.

Authors make their living thanks to readers such as yourself. If you enjoyed Sara and Kyle's story, please take the time to leave a review on Amazon. Help someone else find this book.

If you'd like to read more of my work, be sure to look up Darker Shadows Lie Below, my first novel. It's a slower burn than this one, but a helluva lot scarier.

From The Author

Before I say anything else, let me say thank you to my readers. Writing is a solitary job, and it's easy to lose perspective on things when you spend so much time in your head. I'm happy to have you read my work. It means a lot to me, and I hope you enjoyed reading it as much as I did writing it.

While on the subject of thank you, I'll throw out a big one to Jenn Loring, my editor and writing Yoda. Because of her knowledge, diligence, and patience, you have this book. She is a wonderful person to work with, and I'm glad that she's the one I found when I was as new and fresh at all this as a naked baby in the woods. (I still am in a lot of ways, but don't tell anyone, Jenn)

Thanks to Jana Heidersdorf for making the amazing cover to this book, and thanks to Kristen Rogers for finding her for me. Both of these ladies are some of the most talented artists I have had the pleasure of meeting, and I count myself fortunate for having such dedicated people to back me up.

Thanks to Megan Nash, Brian Ditzek, Adam Rutherford, and all my other friends. I'm not always easy to be around, and these folks took it all in stride. Sorry about all the missed D&D sessions while I was being neurotic over comma placement.

Thanks to my Kung Fu classmates and teacher at Dojo Chattanooga. You folks are all champs, and if I didn't have a place to go and unwind, I'd probably have lost my mind a long time ago.

Thanks to my author buddies, S.A. Hunt and Ernest Dempsey. Both of them are great guys and talented writers. Having a few other people to lament my career choice with has been wonderful, and I enjoy all the talks we have. I'd be a much poorer writer without the company of such fine folks.

I learned a lot writing my first novel, Darker Shadows Lie Below, and I started writing this one before I'd finished editing that one. Since I started this, I've finished two other novels, edited one, and spent a lot more time learning the craft. As a result, this book required a massive amount of edits and re-writes to get up to the standards that I'd set since its inception. I'm glad I did all that. In the end Sara and Kyle's story is much richer for it. In fact, I was so pleased with the results of this novel that I went back and polished Darker Shadows Lie Below. Nothing huge, just cleaning up formatting and language to put it more in line with the later work.

As for Sara, Tim, Kaylee, and Vincent? Right now they're taking a much deserved rest. They're mourning the loss of people no longer with them, and planning their next move. I love where this story ended, and I very much look forward to seeing what they do with Miriam's Silver and Sara's newfound abilities. (Hint, hint)

-Al Barrera

August 2015

www.ingramcontent.com/pod-product-compliance
Lightning Source LLC
Chambersburg PA
CBHW072119250626
47159CB00007B/2504